I Love That Girl

by

Hannah R. Goodman

Copyright Notice
This is a work of fiction. Names, characters, places, and incidents are either the product of the author's imagination or are used fictitiously, and any resemblance to actual persons living or dead, business establishments, events, or locales, is entirely coincidental.

I Love That Girl

COPYRIGHT © 2024 by Hannah R. Goodman

All rights reserved. No part of this book may be used or reproduced in any manner whatsoever without written permission of the author or The Wild Rose Press, Inc. except in the case of brief quotations embodied in critical articles or reviews.
Contact Information: info@thewildrosepress.com

Cover Art by *The Wild Rose Press, Inc.*

The Wild Rose Press, Inc.
PO Box 708
Adams Basin, NY 14410-0708
Visit us at www.thewildrosepress.com

Publishing History
First Edition, 2025
Trade Paperback ISBN 978-1-5092-5716-4
Digital ISBN 978-1-5092-5717-1

Published in the United States of America

Dedication

To my family, whose unwavering support and belief in me as a writer has held me up when I wanted to collapse and never write again.

Chapter 1

NORI

At the first step up the shoveled walkway, a gust of freezing wind almost knocks me down.

I inhale through my nose. Close my eyes. *Be Zen*, I tell myself. The air is crisp and fresh, and the cold is delicious as it nips at my nose.

I brace myself against another gust of wind that practically blows my bags off my shoulders.

Fuck. This.

This is one of the cruelest winters that I can remember in all of my twenty-one and a half years—a winter that I'm mother-fucking psyched to be escaping in T-minus less than twenty-four hours.

I take more unbearable steps and blow out a long breath cloud, vowing, yet again, to stop using the word *fuck*. As in any form of the word *fuck*. Including *mother-fucking*.

Swami Nick says the words you put out are the words you become.

Not necessarily a bad thing to become the word *fuck*—the verb form, that is. The noun form too, isn't bad. But a *mother-fucker*…nope.

Note to self: Ask Swami Nick about the word *fuck*.

I push open the door with a giant exhale.

The house is cold and silent.

My parents and younger sister, Jeni, are celebrating

her early acceptance to Harvard by vacaying in the Caribbean, making me solo for the twenty-four-hour respite before heading out to Florida for a grand reunion with the best humans on Earth, one of which is my boyfriend, who I haven't seen since August.

This will be the most glorious college Christmas break ever. Not to mention the final college Christmas break. Ever.

Moments later, I'm upstairs in my room, incense burning and candle aflame, standing barefoot on my purple mat in mountain pose. I bow my head and begin to pray.

"Dear Universe," I whisper into the top of my hands. "Please stop my monkey mind."

Swami would say, "Do not beg when you pray. Thank the universe for giving you all you need." I take some deeper and longer belly breaths and try again.

"Thank you, dear Universe, for giving me all that I need, including stopping my monkey mind." I press my fingertips together so hard I yelp.

No, that isn't the right way either.

"Mother-fucking dammit," I grumble, shaking out my hands until the feeling returns. *You're fighting yourself*, Swami has said in class when he sees me struggling to stay in a pose or hears me fidgeting during meditation.

"Just be," he tells us all.

Just be, my ass. My thoughts are not letting me *just be*. They leap up and down, grunting and screeching. In particular, certain words, words of a certain letter I just received this week, a letter that lays still and silent on my bed. But those words from that letter, they are jumping and yelling: *Congratulations, Nori*

Mytowsky...one of five candidates to receive the Shanti Yoga Center fellowship...one year in India.

"My thoughts are leaves on a stream," I whisper hoarsely, hands clasped together again. Thoughts in the form of floating words and images: *Ethan...India...Airplanes...*Inhale...Exhale.   Inhale. *Ethan.*

I begin again, tightness forming in my chest. "Universe, please help me let go. Help me stay present to this moment." *Fuck.* I'm pleading again. See, this is why I need to go to India. I say *fuck* even during meditation, and I yell at myself for not praying right.

Exhale. Inhale. Breathe in, breathe out.

Eventually, as always, I slip into this warm, serene place where I'm filled with the moment. Awareness slides away, taking the screeching monkeys and the words.

I'm flooded with breath.

Inhale.

Exhale.

****

I practice for I don't know how long, then finish in mountain pose instead of savasana. Shoulders stacked over hips, hips over knees. Exhale. Pelvic floor neutral. Bare toes spread. The soles of my feet firmly implanted. Grounded. *I am grounded*, I repeat in my mind. I. Am. Grounded.

Does that sound desperate?

"FUUUCKKK!"

I open my eyes and grab my bag next to my mat. Rummaging through, I find my journal and a pen, then settle back on the mat, crossed-legged. The unlined paper frees me up to write a word here and there.

I scribble "freedom" and then "let go" and "dream" then—

I chew the end of the pen and wait for words to come.

Words don't come. Images. Me in an ashram in the mountains of India. My fingertips pressed together in prayer position.

I press the tip of the pen, thinking I will write those words. But. I don't.

I wait and wait.

Nothing.

Then one word comes to mind. I write it across the page in all caps:

F-U-C-K!

I put the pen in the journal and shut it with another loud sigh. My eyes close again, and I begin the alternate nostril breathing that Swami Nick taught me months ago. Breathing in and out and in and out. Index finger closing one nostril, alternating, breathing. Calm settles in. Peace. Breath. Calm.

Until—

"OoommmmOooommmm."

One eye flaps open. The flashing, moaning, and vibrating make my cell phone easily seen in the dimness of the room. The phone moans and moans; as I reach for it, I see that it says, "MOM," so I press Decline.

Mother-fucking dammit.

Mood broken, I flop on my bed, grabbing a soft blanket trimmed with satin that's folded at the foot. I close my eyes and rub the soft fabric with my thumb and forefinger, and think of Ethan, who is in Florida at his dad's condo, probably cleaning—his father insists on a pristine home and even more pristine if I'm coming to visit. I picture Ethan shirtless as he does his laundry or changes the sheets. Then I think of his chest, the muscles defined and hard. I rub the fabric again. We have the same habit of compulsively rubbing our fingers against soft things. Including each other's skin when we are watching TV on my couch in my apartment or on his bed. I sprawl out and pull the blanket to my chin, brushing the softness against my face and think more about Ethan.

The sound of a harp fills the room and I look to where I had tossed my phone to the floor right next to the bed and see "Ethan" flash, then more harp chimes with a text:

—*u home yet?*—

My stomach flutters, and I reach down and grab the phone. I type back.

—*yes was just thinking about you*—
Ethan—*Naked thoughts?*—
I smile.
Nori—*very naked thoughts*—
Ethan—*Take off your clothes*—
Nori—*k. u too.*—
Ethan—*k*—
Nori—*3 months is too long to go without you.*—

I'm a sucker for the written or texted word. But for the next ten minutes there are no words between us.

****

The boiler rumbles beneath me, and the wind howls a little outside as I stretch out under the covers. The phone is back in my hand. I tap the Favorites button and scroll to "Ethan" and tap again.

"Wish I could've seen that," he says when he

answers.

"Sorry, babe. You know I'm anti video-chat sex!" I close my eyes and picture his face, scruffy I bet. He won't shave until minutes before leaving to pick me up tomorrow so that he's extra smooth. I wish I could reach through the phone and rub his face with the palm of my hand.

"No one would see it but me, though," he says in a low voice.

"Doesn't matter, hon. There's a camera involved." My fingers play with the satin of the blanket.

"Damn, there goes my plan for a sex tape scandal."

"Oh, now that would go over really well, you know, with our parents and friends." The vision of their horrified faces at such news makes me grin.

"You think people at home would be surprised? East Bay High's class couple makes a sex tape. They would love that shit!"

"Class couple? That's what you think we were? Hardly. But the *East Bay Times* would be all over it. Sure beats all the stories about drunk high school students peeing in public places."

"Hey! I resent that remark!"

"Why? Be proud of your legacy."

"One time! *Once.* Come on. I was in a bad place, you know that."

"All I have to say is thank God you weren't eighteen yet because they would have totally published your name."

"This is why you should've come back to me then. I would've never stumbled out into the Shaw's parking lot totally drunk and pant-less if you had agreed to let me explain myself."

"Hey, I eventually did."

"Three years and a few more drunken confessions on your lawn later," he says softly.

"But when I finally let you talk to me, look where we wound up."

"Together."

The wind outside howls more and the boiler vibrates the house.

"Miss you so much, babe," he says.

I swallow the lump building in my throat and say lightly, "Again, never. We are NEVER recording anything."

"All I'm saying is it would have made the last three months go by faster."

Three months. My mind flashes to the letter for a moment. *One year.* I sit up and reach for the folded piece of paper. "The bra and underwear pictures I sent you didn't work?" I pull my hand back, changing my mind.

"Oh, they worked. Just now, in fact. Thank you, babe." We laugh together slow and sleepy, and in low and whispery voices we talk each other to sleep.

****

I float out of a semi-sleep by a chime and pick my phone up from beside my pillow. I blink and rub my eyes and read:

—Happy anniversary of our second first date.—

Technically, Ethan and I have two anniversaries. I don't like to celebrate the first one since we broke up in such a horrible way and that was back in high school. The second one is when we started dating again in college.

Nori—*Today?*—

I look up at the time at the top of the phone and see the date: December 13.

Nori—*12-13-2010—*

Ethan—*3 months after our first kiss at college.—*

Nori—*Took me a while to let you take me on a real date.—*

Ethan—*I know. I had a lot of proving myself to do.—*

Nori—*You hit the ball out of the park though.—*

Ice skating, dinner at Dino's, and then we went to see the Festival of Lights on the Commons downtown. Perfect. Romantic. I remember I didn't want the night to end.

Ethan—*We should recreate that before graduation.—*

A lump forms in my throat. I hesitate before replying. *It needs to be months before graduation. It needs to be now!* is what I want to say, but instead I type:

—Definitely—

Ethan—*Have I told you lately how glad I am that I followed you to college? You are my destiny, Nori.—*

I sink onto my bed and reread Ethan's last text and think of his thick wavy dark hair and green eyes that I never get tired of looking into. His pillow-soft lips. Sweet relief fills me.

Sweet, naked, partner-yoga relief that is.

Except.

The letter.

Inhale. Exhale. My heart begins to beat a little faster. I sink down onto my bed and wonder when the right time will be to tell him and my parents about the fellowship. To tell them I'm not walking at graduation, that school will be mailing me my diploma, because I won't be here.

Inhale.

I check my phone one more time:

Ethan—*luv u*—

I type back:

—*love you too*—

My mind starts again. The letter. Ethan. Parents. The letter. Ethan. The letter. If he thinks three months was too long, what will he say about an entire year?

Dear Universe, please stop my monkey mind.
FUCK! That's not the right way.
Whatever.

I do some alternate nostril breathing to calm down and soon I let myself surrender to sleep, wondering if India will cure me of my *fuck* problem.

****

ANDY

Inhale…Exhale…Inhale…Exhale…Exhale.

Wait.

Should I be inhaling?

Inhale…Inhale…

Ah, screw it!

I open my eyes and grab a pen from the bed stand.

Click. Click. Click.

Ugh!

Here it goes. I press the pen to the first page and then stop.

Click. Click. Click.

I stare at the small dot of ink on the paper until it gets fuzzy.

On my twenty-first birthday, Nori gave me a black leather-bound journal and then told me I should meditate for a few minutes each day, followed by a round of journaling. George, my therapist, concurred LOUDLY (and he is never loud) when I told him.

My birthday was back in May. The notebook is still empty.

I press the pen to the paper again and write. I write and write some more. The first word and then the second and then the third and then a lot of words, sentences, phrases. Things that I cross out. Things that don't make much sense. I stop. God, my handwriting is awful and my hand hurts. I shake my hand and then tap the pen to my chin. More thoughts. I press the pen again—

—and then my phone blasts this fanfare trumpet ringtone that Gwen programmed. I jump. The pen flies across the room, bounces off the wall, and slides under the bureau.

"Shit!" I roll to the side of the bed to go find the pen. The phone flashes MOM. *For the love of God, woman. STOP!* I finally give in to the inevitable and pick up the phone and tap the green answer button. "Hey, Mom." I keep my voice neutral and glance out the window. The sun hasn't come up yet and shadows cover the barren street below.

She launches right in: "I know it's early, but I can't seem to ever get you on the phone, Andrew Michael Kirschner! We have not spoken in five days. You didn't even come home on the last night of Hanukkah!"

I yawn and sit up. "Mom, we took you out to dinner a few days ago." I tap the pen to my thigh. She continues to rant. Something about *Hanukkah is a holiday of miracles, and as her first-born son, I am her miracle, and why didn't I want to join her in feeding the homeless?* Cutting her off is not even worth it, and it doesn't matter because she hasn't taken a breath yet, not an inhale or exhale.

"…I know that you have your thesis and your forty-two internships, but you do need to—for *Christ's sake*—call me once in a while."

"We talk every day." It's a waste of my breath to say this. I jam the button on the pen and click it up and down on my leg. "And I have *one*, one internship."

"It seems like you are always rushing off to all these different jobs and places. And, no, we don't talk every day." Huge sigh. A sigh cannot really be that loud. "Besides, I need to talk to you about one of the little boys in my class. You know, Oliver? I think I told you about him? He wears the red sparkle flats to school every day?"

Mom has been a Crusader of the Gay Cause since I came out in high school. Her specialty: telling those who are too young to even know what or who they like that it's okay to be gay.

"I've been reading *The Princess Boy* to the class and teaching them about tolerance."

And this is a subtle approach? I repress my own loud sigh because I know that will send her on another rant. "That's fantastic. Happy to hear you are helping the young come out and be proud."

"Andrew, don't make a joke out of this. Maybe if someone had helped you when you were that young…"

"Mom, I didn't think I was gay when I was eight. I didn't really think about much other than my Lego collection."

"But, honey—" She sounds like she's talking to one of her students. "—You know people are born gay.

While you were raised in a more tolerant time than I, and your high school was certainly more accepting—"

"Mom"—I tighten my jaw then try the breathing thing again—"listen, this is fun. But Gwen is grabbing us breakfast and will be back any minute. And I really need to start packing for the trip." I switch subjects so that I don't launch into my lecture about how Masters and Johnson say that sexuality is a spectrum or that psychologists now feel labeling a child pre-puberty as gay or straight can hinder their authentic growth as a sexual being and that actually wearing red sparkle shoes—especially at the age of eight—actually does not mean you are necessarily gay, although I will give her the benefit of the doubt because it certainly looks kind of gay.

Ah, screw it because she doesn't want to hear or know about the grayness of sexuality and gender. No one does.

Another noisy sigh. "Andrew Kirschner, we are having dinner as soon as you get back from Florida."

"Of course, Mom."

"And call your brother, please. It's the season of miracles."

I roll my eyes. "I know, Mom. But he could call me, you know."

Silence.

"Has he called *you*?" I ask, a little pinch in my heart when I think about what an asshole he's been to her.

"No, but I sent him a card with some gelt, and I called him. You know how he is." Her voice is high and tight.

I rub my head, thinking of Jake, silent and stoic,

like father, like son. Both, for some reason, find it a lot easier to ignore the family divide rather than deal with it. I guess I'm not that different either. I haven't called either one since…I can't even remember.

"Yeah," I say to her. "I know."

She coughs and says brightly, "Tell Nori and Ethan I say hello, and give my love to Gwen."

"I will. I love you. I'll call you when we get there."

I glance at my phone after we hang up. Seven thirty. Gwen will be back soon, and I have more words and sentences to write. First, I have to find that pen.

I live in a tiny studio apartment on the top floor of a house right off the hub of Providence, Thayer Street. Basically, I have enough room for a bureau, a queen-size bed, a kitchen table, and a couch. Gwen reads one of her Top Five Books Every Pre-med Student Should Read while I write papers for all my Poly-Sci and Gov. classes. We talk. We text friends and parents. We eat Chinese takeout on Fridays. She waits for her acceptance letters. I pretend to work on my thesis but spend more time playing Angry Birds and Temple Run and surfing YouTube for old episodes of Dr. Who. *That bed I mentioned. Yeah, that bed where we live and breathe. Our daily existence. That one. That's where it all happened. The unthinkable.*

****

The TV was blaring *Dr. Who*, and we were sitting up against a pile of pillows; Gwen sleeps with a lot of pillows, one under her head, one over her head, one to hug, and one in between her knees. When we make the bed in the morning (she's a little OCD), we pile them up and that's how the bed was last night—still made. We had come home from our respective days, and I had a whole bunch of finals and meetings with professors about my thesis—"Ding! Dong! The Warlock is Dead!"

Basically finishing a semester early from Columbia, Gwen had moved back to Rhode Island a few weeks ago after defending her thesis—The Argument for Making HPV Vaccine Mandatory—and was set to move back in with her parents in our hometown of Borington (a.k.a. Barrington, as we refer to it). But Gwen's parents, they love her a little too much, so she moved in with me, the idea that she would find her own place eventually.

Eventually, as they say, hasn't happened. She works three different jobs while she waits to get into med school and not because she needs the money. *I don't want to be bored*, is how she put it. Her jobs include being an assistant researcher at a cancer lab at the hospital, waitressing at a coffee shop on Thayer Street, and on-call as a paramedic. I'm not kidding. We come home most days exhausted, though I don't think I have a reason to be, not compared to her. The only things we want to do are order chicken kabob and grape leaves from East Side Pockets and stream our favorite shows.

We were in the middle of *Dr. Who* when the Doctor was about to use the Pandorica to reboot the universe to save his longtime companion Amy when the power went out.

"Oh damn!" Gwen sat straight up. This is a girl who isn't afraid to help deliver babies or pierce her belly button (that was high school) or climb Mount Washington in the rain (she has a bumper sticker on her bike that says it) but the dark, forget it. She isn't afraid when she's had to help stitch up a gunshot wound at the

ER (someone handed her a thread and needle, what's a girl to do?), and she doesn't hesitate to utilize her CPR training even when the guy is old and responds with a boner and wrapping his hands around her to press his tongue to her teeth. But the dark—forget it.

"Do you have any flashlights?" She was actually trembling.

I leaned over to the bed stand and opened the drawer; my hand rummaged around and grazed over a box of unopened condoms. Dusty, unopened condoms.

"Of course I do." I grabbed a small flashlight that was behind the condoms. "I was a Boy Scout for about a week in elementary school. Always be prepared."

She didn't even give me crap about that; I knew she was truly scared.

I turned to her and shined the light on my chin and mouth, grinning like a jack-o'-lantern. She let out a stiff, uncomfortable laugh.

"Where's my phone?" She jumped up and grabbed the flashlight from me. "I have a nightlight app on my phone." She shined the light over to the bureau where her phone usually was.

"You *what*?"

"It's part of the White Noise app." Ah, that is one of the many benefits of hanging with Gwen. Girl knows everything about apps and technology. Gwen hunted around the apartment while I sat back into the pillows and closed my eyes.

Suddenly a light shined in my face. I opened my eyes. "Hey!" I pushed the flashlight away.

Gwen was grinning, kneeling in front of me, and holding up her phone, which had this light bulb icon emanating a bright light. "I can put this in the base."

She leaned across me, popped her phone into the base, and suddenly the room had a candlelit glow. "I have about ten hours on the phone. The power will be back on by then, right?"

I nodded like I knew the electric company personally or the weatherman. Or God.

She handed me back the flashlight.

"Let's make shadow puppets." I shined it on the wall where hung the only picture in my room—a small black-and-white print of the four of us on spring break last year. All teeth and longish hair between us. Ethan and Nori looped around each other. Gwen's lips pressed into my cheek, a grin all over my face.

With my free hand I made a rabbit and started hopping it across the wall.

"Listen," she said, grabbing my hand, "we've got to find out what happened." She dropped my hand and peered out the window. Nothing was out there but our narrow street, all lit up with Christmas lights. She cupped her hands and tried to get a better look at the triple-deckers next to us. I joined her by the window and peered out. Blackness left and right. Dots of red, green, and white lights across the street.

"You know what," she said, her voice wavering. "I'll go out into the hallway and see."

"Gwen." I put my hand on her arm and pulled her back. "I'm sure the lights will come back."

"What if it's a blackout?" She shrugged off my hand and peeked over at the window.

I reached over to her and ruffled her hair. "It seems like it's just this side of the street. Someone must have hit a transformer or something." I stroke her soft hair again, feeling little stirrings inside my stomach—oh hell—lower than that. "We're safe inside here."

"But we're on the top floor. How will we get out without lights in the hallway?" She had panic all over her face.

"Listen, the lights will be back." Why would we be getting out anyway? But I didn't say that out loud.

She shivered. "And the heat! The heat is off! We're going to freeze to death!"

"Not right away, Gwen. Let's play twenty questions." I eyed the half-drunk bottle of wine we had shared for dinner. "We can have some more wine? Alcohol makes you warm."

"True." But her voice was faint and small, and she looked to the window again.

We locked eyes for a moment, the dim light and dark shadows between us. Her wavy sunset-blonde hair was in a messy bun, with tendrils falling around her face. I wanted to let her hair down, scoop it up with my fingers, inhale the flowery scent of her shampoo. I didn't move a single part of me except my eyes, which traced the dotting of piercings up her left ear and then roamed across to her smallish nose that had just a blush of light freckles that matched her hair and down to her button-shaped mouth.

"Okay," she said, her shoulder sliding out from the old sweatshirt that she cut the hood off of. I wanted to kiss her shoulder so badly, I had to put my hand over my mouth and pretend to cough.

The blackout made the moment dreamy. I reached over and pulled her shirt up to cover her shoulder, and when my fingers made contact with her soft skin, her expression changed, softened, and relaxed. She smiled. "I'll get the wine." She popped up, slid her feet into her fuzzy slippers, walked over to the kitchen area, and snatched the almost full bottle. Then she said, "Do you have a set of cards? We can play Bullshit. Remember how much we used to love that game?"

I laughed and said, "I think it was the only drinking game we knew in high school."

"I'm pretty sure we were the only people who actually found a way to make it a drinking game." In the darkness, her hair piled up, she looked like a princess but also like an angel, and while I couldn't find those words in the moment, that's what I saw. A princess-angel with a pretty but foul mouth. The combination was exhilarating.

We looked at each other in the darkness, and I knew we were remembering the same thing, how terrible we—Nori, Gwen, and I—were at partying in high school. Ethan didn't hang out with us during his douchebag years—post break up with Nori—and partying was his particular forte. He definitely played real drinking games, which he later taught us in college.

"Unless you found a pack when you cleaned out all the drawers in the kitchen, I don't think so," I said.

"Right!" She pivoted and went to, what used to be, my junk drawer and pulled it open. "Yay!"

She slid back onto the bed, kicked off her slippers, and handed me the bottle of wine.

There we were, she was dealing the cards, taking sips of wine from the bottle at each turn, and laughing. Her shoulder kept popping out of the shirt, and I could smell the lotion she wore. The wispy, clean scent wrapped around me, and we kept passing the bottle of wine between us. We snuggled into each other to stay warm.

And I was hard. Watching her swilling wine and laughing. At that shoulder popping out over and over.

If my most recent ex-boyfriend heard me say that I was getting hard over a woman, he would roll his eyes and accuse me of trying to un-gay myself. Like when I refused to go to the gay Pride parade with him, he told me I was a self-hating gay. I tried to explain my theory of The Downside of Gay, that it's the same as The Downside of Jew. Label. A stifling label. But he gave me his hand and said, "Talk to it" and flitted away. Yeah, he was really almost a girl. I mean he was smooth and hairless and pretty and pouty and had longish hair. Even the way he wanted me in the bedroom was over-the-top submissive—or I should say bottom, if you know what I mean. We didn't last more than a month. I wasn't gay enough was his problem with me, and my problem with him was that he had a terrible personality.

The wine was gone. Cards all over the bed. Her hair down and wild. Gwen was lying with her head in my lap which I carefully covered with one of her plush pillows due to the growing that was happening in my sweatpants. I was rubbing her scalp with one hand, my fingers threading through her soft hair, and she was holding my other hand over her chest. Not sexually, more like it was a small stuffed animal. She was cuddling it. I was very aware of her breast beneath the hand she held, more aware than I really wanted to be, and yet, I wasn't confused about the attraction I felt.

In the faux candlelight, Gwen twisted around, facing my stomach, and if she turned one more time, she would be facing something else. I was dying to stand up and adjust myself, splash some cold water on my face. Between my legs.

But I didn't have to because she slithered up from my lap over my stomach to my chest, pushing me down. I was now lying down with her mouth millimeters from mine. We were smiling drunkenly, not giggling, and then I pulled her to me with one hand and kissed her.

There was no hesitation.

In fact, we didn't break from that first kiss really until both of us were shirtless. Her breasts were perfect in the shadows, and we stared at each other, breathing—maybe panting. It had been a very, very long time since I had touched anyone. Guy or girl. But kissing a girl wasn't what I was thinking about. It was that I was kissing Gwen, this woman who I knew when she was a girl and I was a boy. Now I am a grown man.

I pulled at her jeans, the button popped, and then I pushed her down on her back and whispered, "Is this okay? Are you okay?"

She nodded, helping me to pull her pants off, and said back, "Get those condoms that are in the bed stand. We are going to need them. Don't want to add baby-daddy to this already confusing relationship."

I grinned at her and reached over to the bed stand and whispered, "I'm not confused, Gwen. Not at all."

Truth is, I know I should be confused, or that other people probably think I should be, but I'm not. I'm really not.

****

The pen lay on the journal, which is still on my bed. I stand by the window, staring out at the street, covered in pink streaks of sunlight. I search for her, bundled in her puffy winter jacket, her head covered in a ridiculous rainbow-colored snow hat. I spot her as she walks, holding a brown bag and the paper. I love this life we have together, and I love what happened last night. My phone fanfares. I'm lazy and have the same ringtone for everyone. I reach over and grab it to see who's calling.

Nori.

I press the decline button, and guilt hits me with a pang. She's probably about to leave. I should answer the call.

Shoving away the small flicker of guilt at avoiding Nori, I tuck the journal into the top drawer of my bureau and make my way to the kitchen to set the table for breakfast.

I don't think I want to write anymore today.

Chapter 2

GWEN

I slide the key in the lock and am about to turn it when my phone *cock-a-doodle-doos*. I reach into my pocket and press answer before tucking it between my ear and shoulder.

"Mom," I whisper. "I can't talk now."

"Why?" she whispers back.

"Because…" I had sex with my gay best guy friend who I've never stopped loving since high school, and I want to get back inside to do it again.

"I'm at the hospital. Working." Lies. Lies. Lies.

"All right." She's still whispering. "What time did you want Daddy and me to get you guys to the airport?"

Shit! Forgot about that. Forgot that we had even asked them. Jesus. Andy Kirschner, what have you done to me?

"Right." I'm no longer whispering. "Actually, don't worry about it."

"Oh." Silence.

Shit.

Then, "We were so looking forward to seeing you before you go. It's been two weeks. I know you're busy…but we're so proud of you."

I shut my eyes, trying to find a good reason. None. In a fog. In a post sex-after-almost-a-year-without-it fog. "Sorry. I'm a little tired. Yes, you can take us. We need to get to the airport by five thirty."

I could hear the smile in her voice. "Great! Be there at four thirty. Love you!"

I slide the phone back into my pocket and lean my forehead on the number eleven of Andy's apartment door. Mom has killed my mood and lifted the fog. Shit. Shit.

I've been in love with Andy since I met him in study hall on the first day of ninth grade when he told me that drinking soda at school was prohibited and I better dump it out before someone saw me. Turns out he was right. Soda was banned the year before we started East Bay High School, according to research I later did. I've loved Andy ever since that day and all the days after, through high school. Since he kissed me the first time the four of us got drunk in my basement the end of freshman year—maybe we all kissed each other that night. But later, at the beginning of sophomore year, right after Ethan dumped Nori, when, in our grief over losing both of our best friends in one swoop, we turned to each other and became make-out buddies for a few weeks. I thought Andy was falling for me then when it was just the two of us.

Then I found out he was gay…and not from him. My heart broke. By then, it was too late to tell him that I loved him. It didn't matter.

I thought I'd buried all that long ago.

His kisses stayed in my memory after he came out, through the rest of high school and into my relationship with Heyward, my ex-boyfriend I dated on and off through part of high school and college. Kisses I replayed in my head for years and then spent about the same amount of time erasing them all from memory.

And now.

I don't know what to think. What to do? Who to call? Not Nori. Definitely not Nori. How would I explain this to her? I bang my forehead lightly on the door.

****

Last night after we finished, Andy gazed at me in the glow of the faux nightlight that emanated from my phone.

"I haven't said this in six months. But I really want a cigarette right now," I said, leaning on my side.

"Wow," he said with a grin.

I couldn't stop my own grin. "I know."

"When was the last time you—?"

"A long time." I rolled over onto my stomach and put my chin in my hands. Andy. Shaggy golden brown locks falling in his eyes. "I want to know." I squinted at him. "When was the last time you had sex?"

"A while too."

Then I had to say what was pressing on my mind. Hard. "Obviously you've had sex with women."

He didn't say anything, just pushed the locks away, *adorable*.

"Because you seemed to know your way around the female parts pretty good," I said with a wink.

It was dark, so I don't know for sure, but my guess was that Andy was blushing. Always modest, that's Andy.

"I've hooked up with a few girls. Last year and the year before."

"And you never told me?"

"I didn't think you needed to know."

"Didn't need to know?" I clutched the sheets and

blankets around me and sat all the way up. "Andy, we're best friends. This is definitely something you should have told me. Did you tell Nori?" I try to keep any trace of jealousy out of my voice.

"No." He put his hands on mine and wrenched the covers away. He kissed my nose and then my neck. I closed my eyes and let the tingles shoot down. "You two are as into my gayness as my mom. Wouldn't want to disappoint you," he mumbled into my neck.

My eyes flew open, and I pushed him away.

He cupped my chin. "Do we really need to talk about all this right now?"

Yes. "No, I guess not." His breath was back on my neck. "But it's a legit question, Andy. And what do you mean? I'm *into your gayness*?" I was crumbling, my hands now raking through his hair.

"Doesn't matter," he mumbled and then traced my collarbone with his tongue. "You smell so good," he said into my skin.

"Jesus Christ," I whispered, gripping the back of his head, and then we went at it again.

****

After the second time, I scooted up to sit next to him, pulling the covers over myself, feeling his warm body next to me. "I'm confused."

We sat side by side, breathing in the dark. "You said you've hooked up with girls. You're not gay anymore?" I asked.

He pursed his lips. Blew some air out of his mouth. "I would say I fall in the middle of the sexuality spectrum. Bisexual. I've always been."

I let that sink in.

"You know how you always change in front of me

and walk around naked or in your bra in the morning to get dressed?" He stared straight ahead into the darkness.

I enjoyed that he was flustered. "Yeah…"

"And do you notice that I never get changed in front of you?"

"Yeah, but you don't even take your shirt off at the beach. I don't know why you're hiding, by the way." I rubbed his chest. He smiled.

I rubbed some more, my fingers lightly playing with his chest hairs.

He blurted out, "I've been getting hard."

"Getting hard?"

"A boner! All the time! Seeing you naked so much, here in the apartment. You know the long showers at night?" He turned to me. "Are you really going to make me say all this?"

I nodded, my heart beating fast and happy. "Yes! I am! I want to hear you say that you get a big, old—"

"Come on, Gwen. Haven't I already shown you that?" He stopped. "Is it? I mean, is it really big?"

"Huge!" I pushed him down and straddled him. "Say it or I will tickle you. Wait—oh, ah, ha! You're getting—"

"Stop it, Gwen!" But he was laughing.

I reached down and tickled him and then said into his ear, "Say it, Andy. Say the words. I'm hot for you. I've got a raging bon—"

"Stop tickling me!" He rolled me over until I was underneath him.

Nose-to-nose, he whispered, "I'm very hot for you, Gwen."

"Me too," I whispered back, even though inside, a

voice told me this might be a mistake.

****

I turn the key, letting the delicious memory of round three fade. But what lingers is the conversation we started but that he stopped. I'm *into his gayness*. What does that even mean? And always been bi? Meaning high school?

Facing the blaring light of daytime, I step into the apartment. The smells of our morning. He makes coffee for me every day before we leave for work and school. Today is no different. When we don't work, he makes pancakes or eggs or both. Today it smells like both.

I take a second soundless step. Today is different. That did happen last night. Right?

Hazelnut coffee. Freshly ground. A man who cooks. A man who makes me laugh. A man who makes me come. A triple threat.

A man who was gay. Is gay? Has been gay? The visual of that. Doesn't bother me. But then I picture him. Doing it with a guy. There is only some of that that I *can* do. Shit.

"Honey, I'm hoommee!" I call, making my footsteps loud and clumpy.

Andy appears in jeans and an apron that has a picture of Martha Stewart ironed onto it. "Hey, did you get the *Times*?" He leans over and kisses me the same way he would any other Saturday morning when I arrive after the gym with the paper to his scrumptious breakfast. Only he's shirtless and has an after-sex glow about him. Oh and wait. Was that his tongue sliding over my lips?

This is a little different.

"After breakfast, we need to pack." I hand him the

paper. He puts both on the table. The apartment feels warm compared to last night without heat, although we barely noticed. "And I need a shower."

"Right, I know. I actually already started to pack. I threw some stuff in a bag for both of us." His grin is silly and sexy.

"Which means I need to repack," I say.

"Hey, I did all right packing." He goes back to the stove, clicking the burner dial to off. "We should shower together. You know, to save time."

"My parents will be here at four thirty," I blurt, waiting for him to react and staring at the back of him, wanting to grab his soft, messy hair.

"Cool." He says it like it's any other day that we would meet them for dinner or go to a show.

"You don't think it's going to be weird to have them drive us?"

He turns around, not answering. "You cold?" he asks.

I realize I still have my coat on. "No." And I shrug it off and hang it over one of the chairs at the table, cross my arms and wait for him to reply.

"It's not like we're going to make out in front of them, because that would be weird." He laughs.

Hmmmmm. "Nori is on her way," I tell him, draping the coat over one of the kitchen table chairs and pull out my phone. "She sent me a text and left a voicemail from the airport. Weather is seventy-nine, cloudless skies." I read to him.

"Perfect." He turns to me and holds out a wooden spoon with scrambled eggs. Completely unfazed. Not worrying about what this all might mean to not just us, but the people around us.

"Try this. I used sweet cream instead of milk." He feeds me. I moan with how yummy it is.

He smiles. Hands me a glass of OJ. I sip. He takes it and then—we are making out again. He's pushing me up against the counter of the kitchen. He's getting hard. He's pushing up my sweaty tee shirt. I'm not caring. I'm not trying to stop him.

This is totally crazy.

"How about that shower?" he whispers.

I nod. Crazy. Crazy how much I love this boy.

In the background, as my shirt and workout pants fall to the floor, my phone calls out OMMMM OMMM. I shut my eyes and ignore it. The OM ringtone only means one person is calling me.

Nori.

Guilt hangs over me for a moment but then melts away as Andy slides my underwear off.

****

ETHAN

"Mmmmhmmm." Wet kisses—no—more like *licks*—tickle the shit out of my neck. But it feels fucking fantastic. "Mmmmhmm. God, that feels good—"

Jesusmotherfuckingchristwhatisthatsmell!

Nori, even in the morning, doesn't have breath this assy. And her tongue, no matter how turned on she gets, is *never* this wet or this—*JesusChrist*!—long.

Whatthefuck?

I snap open my eyes and see the friendliest grin followed by a rush of the rankest stench up my nose.

Delilah.

I grab her furry damp chin and stare into her golden eyes, then gently push her away from me. She whimpers. I say, "Sorry!" and pull her back, inviting more licks, this time to my mouth. Despite the ass stench, I submit and let her devour me. Without checking my phone, I know it's six o'clock. My dad takes her out every morning at "Oh-six-hundred. Sharp!" And even though he's been away for the last week, his dog sitter took over the same militant schedule for Delilah's walks, shits, and feedings. You can take a man out of the Navy, but you can't take the Navy out of old Captain Dad Ledger.

Satisfied with our love session, Delilah walks out of the room. I groan and roll out of bed. She returns with the leash in her mouth and her golden face grinning. Lady's gotta go. I throw on some shorts and flip-flops, yawning and scratching myself. We walk together to the kitchen and pause near the coffee pot. I rub my eyes and then press the On button. I preloaded the coffee last night after I got in, knowing Lady D would wake me at the ass-crack of morning. I yawn again, reaching down to rub her head. She sits next to me on her haunches, waiting. Pretty sure this is my dad's routine, too. The percolation bubbles begin. I turn to her and say, "Three minutes, Lady."

I swear she nods.

****

Coffee in one hand and leash in the other, we take a short walk around the street. It's quiet and the temperature begins to rise along with the sun. I yawn and slurp my coffee. I forgot the sugar. Gross. Whatever I need to wake the hell up.

When we get back inside, I rinse the cup and put it on the dish rack—my dad's rules: you drink or eat from it, you clean it. You shit or piss in it, you scrub it with bleach. That means after the dump I took last night when I finally arrived after what seemed like the longest flight in history thanks to the longest layover in Atlanta—was followed by rigorous toilet scrubbing. I kid you not, though, it was worth it since I want Nori to see the condo clean and sparkling and have it smell perfect for her.

I hang the leash back up and say to Delilah, "Come on, Lady!"

She follows me down the hallway, where I pause at the thermostat and see that it's up to seventy-five degrees inside. I adjust the AC.

We continue back into my room. I flop onto the bed and pat the space beside me. Delilah goes still, her eyes darting around as if she's looking for my dad, and then she sniffs the air a few times. Finally, not a whiff of Dad's middle-age-man-smell, she gallops over, jumps onto the bed, and curls up beside me.

I lay back and she inches closer, tucking right into me. Last night she stayed by my feet while I watched a *Kitchen Nightmares* marathon. Dad has Delilah trained to not jump on anything, and she even sleeps in her own dog bed every night. She's smart though. When I'm around, rules get broken here and there. Like how I shared my *moo shu* pork with her last night. She knows her daddy won't be back for a little while. She lets out a low sigh followed by a groan, and her big golden body pushes into me more. Then we drift off to sleep again.

****

Brrriing. Brrriing. Brrring.
Fuuuuuuuck.
Brrring. Brrring. Brrring.
I open my eyes and rub out the sleep crust.

Brrring. Brrring. Brrring.

Fuckingalarm...wherethefuckismyphone...wherethefuckisit?

I slide my hands around under the covers.

There. I grip the phone and pull it up through the thin blanket. I roll to my side and press the snooze button.

Delilah's gone. Probably out in the sunroom, sleeping in her bed until all the excitement arrives. She loves Nori almost as much as me.

I sit up like someone slingshot me.

Shit.

I need to get everything ready.

Still holding the phone, I squint at the bright screen—8:01 a.m.

Thank the fucking God. I've got two hours until I leave for the airport.

I roll back and stare up at the ceiling. Nori. My stomach knots with excitement and nerves. Nori says to use *positive imagery* if you need to calm down. I have some pretty positive imagery in my head right now about her. Pretty dirty, but positive, nonetheless.

Visions of Nori doing her morning practice, ass up in downward dog, lifting one endless, strong, perfect leg into the air...then doing a series of salutations, her body long...arching back and bending forward...her curves moving back and forth...her ass up...

I put the phone in front of my face, click on her name, and type.

—good morning. woke up from a dream where you were licking my face. turned out to be Delilah tongue-kissing me—

I wait, shaking my foot impatiently for her to reply,

and when it doesn't come, I type again:
—*god I miss you so much*—
I wait again.
Nothing.
Then I see bubbles and her text comes in.
—*Just finishing my practice. is Delilah a good kisser?*—
I laugh.
Ethan—*actually, despite the ass-breath, she's not bad.*—
I hit Send again, grinning just from word-to-wording with her.
Nori—*I'm kinda jealous of that golden-haired bitch.*—
I laugh again.
My fingers fly.
Ethan—*hey make sure you bring your yoga mat want to watch you practice…naked*—
Nori—*only if you join me. btw, right now I'm lying in goddess pose.*—

I have memorized her practice, literally. Before I left for South America, I made her go through it over and over, until I could see her with my eyes closed. I didn't want to rely on my phone or a video for it because I might have been off the grid where I was going. We once went two weeks without communicating after a relatively minor earthquake rendered me and the other volunteers in our apartment powerless. The worst part is an earthquake in Peru is just bizarre. I mean, I've never experienced a real earthquake, but in Peru there is this weird noise first, and while all the Peruvians know what's about to happen and begin moving to higher ground, us tourists have no clue—not the first time that is. All I will say is, I wound up skidding my way into an outdoor so-called toilet. It was a shitty—*literally*—shitty experience.

I thumb another text.

Ethan—*The one with your legs spread?—*

Nori—*Yes, dirty boy—*

Ethan—*Mmmmmmm now take off your clothes.—*

Nori—*They're off—*

Ethan—*Did u practice naked?—*

Nori—*Actually finished my practice. Had to do it early. Going to get ready to leave.—*

Ethan—*This early? Your flight isn't scheduled until noon.—*

Nori—*It's snowing. Want to make sure I don't miss the flight.—*

Ethan—*U better not. All this mindplay is killing me. Gonna explode if I don't get my hands on your body.—*

I hit the button to go back to the home screen and then press her phone number. She answers immediately.

"Hey," I say softly. "Miss you. Miss your skin. Your smell. All this mindplay is great. But I want real foreplay, not just the kind I see in my head. The texting last night before bed was hot, but I want your flesh."

"I miss you, too. And your flesh."

Comfortable silence. It's always comfortable with her.

"You're glad you went, though. Right, Ethan?"

"Yeah. But it also made me realize that—" Wait. Not over the phone. "—three months is a long time to be apart." The urge to confess what I bought her in Peru is mother-effing strong, but I shut my mouth and wait for it to pass, then I continue. "I missed talking to you about the day and sitting next to you and watching stupid reality TV and feeling your leg next to mine. Your body sleeping, all curled into me, on me."

I hear her sniffle.

"Don't make me cry, Ethan. I'm not losing it a few hours before I see you."

"Yes, you are, and so am I." Tears collect in my eyes too, but I don't care because it's Nori. The only girl I've ever loved.

"But—" She sniffles, and I hear her blow her nose. "You would have regretted not going, right? You would've been miserable and probably dropped out of school. I knew you had to do it. We're young, and we know we're going to be together."

"Forever!" I say this with too much enthusiasm in my voice. Does she know how forever I mean when I say that? She's kind of a mind ninja sometimes, knows what I'm thinking.

"Right, forever. We *know* that. But we also know that we're young and there's stuff we have to do—we *want* to do—and you did it, Ethan! I'm so proud of you. Watching you online in your videos and following your posts. I knew that this was the right thing for you to do. It made me happy, even though I missed you."

More water in the eyes. I rub at the tears. "See, this is why it's so good with us. Besides the fact that you're beautiful and perfect."

She breathes for a minute. I picture her hair, long and dark, smelling like flowers, me kissing her neck, and then sliding my hands down…

"Let me go so I can get on that plane, get to you, and have that naked yoga session."

****

An hour later, I'm on the deck in the humid sunshine, finishing the last set of push-ups from my morning workout—want to look as ripped for Nori as possible.

The house phone rings, and Delilah darts inside through the open screen door, tags and collar jingling. I finish push-up number twenty and jump up to follow her, throwing a hand towel around my neck to soak up some of the sweat.

The phone continues to ring as I step into the living room.

I grab it from the coffee table, and before I can say hello, a familiar baritone bellows, "Son! How's Delilah?" Who, panting beside me, barks a hello. I reach down and scratch her ears, and she settles down on the floor beside me.

"Hi, Dad. Missed you, too." I'm not surprised that despite not having spoken to him since before I left for Peru, his first words to me are about the dog.

Silence.

He clears his throat. "Listen, you make sure you don't destroy that place with those friends of yours."

"Scout's honor, Dad," I say, ignoring the daggers of disappointment in my heart.

"You were a Scout dropout, son."

"Still counts." Captain Dad, always reminding me of my many failings of him as a son.

Dad gives me some more orders about making sure Gwen doesn't blow up the microwave this time and instructions for the dog walker. He tells me he will be in Providence for a few weeks. No words are spoken about whether or not I will get to see him before he goes off to Europe with Ruby, his longtime girlfriend. At the end he adds, "If you can't handle watching Delilah, Ruby can take her."

I stifle a sigh of aggravation and channel some South American wisdom of patience, but all that I can think of is, *Gallinas encaramado en la parte superior, shit en los que se describen a continuación.* Translated: *Hens perched on top will shit on those below.* If nothing else, it makes me chuckle. I end the conversation with Dad and turn toward more important concerns: getting ready for Nori.

****

I'm in the kitchen now, Delilah waiting for me to give her a treat. First, I bend down and hug her with both arms and let her tongue kiss me. "That's the last one, Lady D. My girl will be here soon." She whimpers a little. Man, I love that dog. The only thing Dad and I have in common. I toss a dog bone onto the floor and grab a bottle of water, unscrew the cap, and take a long drink, thinking about picking Nori up, maybe a little something-something in the car. Then head back to the crib for a bigger something-something. Delilah happily settled with her bone; I decide to get to work on Nori's favorite dessert. Brownies slathered in marshmallow cream.

Everything ready to go, I head to the shower, stopping along the way to chuck the sweaty towel from my workout into a basket of dirty clothes waiting by the doorway to the laundry room. Out of the corner of my eye I notice that, poking out of the pocket of a pair of shorts in the basket, is the last half of a pack of cigarettes I smoked. I grab and toss them into a small closet outside the laundry room, pushing a thing of toilet paper in front of it.

Just in case. Nori thinks I quit months ago, which I did, technically.

I go into the bathroom and strip off my clothes, and catch myself in the mirror and flex, posing from side to side. Suck in my gut. Stick it out. Stare at myself for another minute and then turn on the shower, step in, and think about Nori. Nori in short shorts. Nori in a bikini. Nori naked. I'm more nervous than when, three years ago, Nori agreed to drive me back to our hometown the first week or so of school. The drive where I found out following her to college was the right thing to do. We rode in lots of silence, her driving and me watching her the whole time out of the corner of my eye. At the end, when we pulled up to my house, she turned to me and said, "I forgive you."

And then, she came inside, and everything changed.

****

In my room, I check myself in the mirror. Then hold Nori's favorite cologne an arm's length away and spray. Smelling good and hair shiny and waves under control. Keys in hand. Phone in back pocket. Time to go.

Wait.

Not yet.

I go to the closet in my room and dig into the inside pocket of my suitcase and feel for the velvet box. I take it out. It opens with a creak and a pop. *¿Por qué la amas con todo tu corazón? You love her with all of your heart? Si*, I told the old guy who was selling the diamonds at the market in Lima. *Si, mucho*, I added, showing off my Spanish. And then I said, pequeño...*poquito diamonte...no tengo mucho dinero. I want a small diamond...I don't have a lot of money.* The old guy held up a ring, the most *poquito diamonte* I'd ever seen. It almost wasn't there. The old guy grabbed my hand and opened the palm and then put the ring inside and closed it. He snatched the wad of cash I had in my other hand. Poof! I had the ring for the question that I've wanted to ask for a long time. *Poquito* but I had it.

I close the box and tuck it back inside the pocket of the suitcase.

Before I leave, I step into the kitchen and survey it all, gleaming and clean. Flowers, I need some flowers. I go outside to the bed of gaillardia Dad has in the back and clip a whole bunch. I go back inside and find a vase in the cabinet under the sink, stick them in, and place them in the center of the island. Next to it, a small plate of the brownies. I grab the jar of fluff I left out and poke my finger in it and then smear some of it on my mouth. With my other hand, I snap a picture of myself obscenely licking my lips. I punch in a silly caption and grin at my ridiculousness, then hit Send.

I love that girl. And I'm going to ask her to marry me.

Chapter 3

NORI

Sitting on my yoga mat, I peer at the screen of my phone.

What the hell is all over Ethan's mouth? I read the text below the photo:

—*Can't wait to taste your sweet cream.*—

I laugh. That boy. Ridiculousness.

I start to reply, thinking, *Can't wait to tell you about India.* Only I actually type:

—*Can't wait to taste yours.*—

I hit Send, thinking the letter will not be the first thing we talk about when I get there. Because we probably won't talk at all.

I practice a little more, extra child's pose and downward dog and Ethan's favorite, goddess, need to warm up for what I know will be a marathon of good, good lovin'. I finish my practice in lotus and chant quietly until my whole body hums.

Yoga is good, yet not as good as sex with Ethan, and that's what my body needs.

I sit in silence to try one more time to clear my brain from all the insanity flying around. But thoughts wiggle up from the darkness of my mind, more like a worm through the mud than a leaf riding the current of a stream. *Letter. One year. Ethan. Freak out.* I hold back another f-bomb and ask myself what would

Swami do? Make space, detach, he would say. I imagine space between me and the words, and somehow the wiggle-worm thoughts don't go away but they don't make me want to scream four-letter words. I just watch them and soon they dissolve.

****

In the airport, with too much time until the flight, I decide to tell my parents. Keeping this stuff inside is like a sneeze building up that you hold in because you're in yoga class and don't want to be *that* girl. Except, I am *that* girl. That girl who sneezes in yoga and even farts occasionally. What can you do? You are who you are. Right?

Anyway, I read somewhere that holding in a sneeze can make your brain explode. I have enough problems with my brain. Don't need to add explosions to the storm inside my mind.

Sitting in a black plastic chair, with the sounds of flights being announced surrounding me, I punch Mom's cell number into my phone, and she answers immediately.

I put a shaky hand over my other ear, trying to hear her better.

"Mom? I need to tell you and Dad something."

"Oh? What is it, dear?"

Deep breath. Hold and then, in a rush, say it on the exhale. "I'mgoingtoIndia."

"What, dear? I don't think I can hear you. Are you at the airport?"

Slow. Down. "I'm. Going. To. India."

Silence, save for her shallow breaths. "Right now, dear? I thought you were going to Florida." Then, in the background, my father. "Is everything okay?"

I sigh, my heart lurches. I rub my forehead. "Can you put me on speaker, Mom?"

"Sure, honey. Yes, now where is that button?"

"It's the audio one. Press that and then the one that says *speaker*." I mentally struggle to keep the frustration out of my voice and rub my forehead harder. Not at all Zen but fuck Zen right now. Again, another of the many reasons I need India. The only sounds in the background of the airport now are crying babies and people shifting and walking around.

"What's going on, Nori? Did you make it to the airport okay? Is the plane on time?" My father has snatched the phone from her, probably because she was stabbing at it to death trying to figure out the speaker button.

Normally, I would have already just told them— they never seem to doubt my choices, even if they didn't love them. I chose Clark University over Dad's alma mater, and yeah, he had to take off the Brandeis University sticker he had prematurely put on his car, but he got over it.

I draw upon all my mediation and yoga, my opened channels and chakras and shit and repeat it, slowly and loudly, but with *more* details: "I wanted to let you know that I'm going to India. In a month. I only have my thesis to finish, so as long as I finish it and send it to my advisor, I'm good. I don't need to defend it in person."

The background noises around me are deafening because…nothing. I hear nothing on the line. No one breathing, moving, shuffling the phone. Not-a-thing.

Then, loud and clear, Dad says, "What are you talking about? You're about to graduate…you *are* about to graduate, right?"

"Yes, of course. Dad." And I add because, again, I'm not as spiritually evolved as I should be, "Cum laude, actually."

This time the silence is filled with a lot of heavy huffing and breathing. Curiously, Mom is nowhere to be heard in the background. And I'm thinking her silence has something to do with her own *fuck it* moment as a young woman before she went to college: She took off to backpack through Europe for a year before she went to Brandeis where she met my father. I try to send a telepathic message to her. *Tell him, Mom, tell him this is a good idea. Tell him to trust me.*

Finally, I hear something in the background, and it sounds like she's saying, "Just talk to her, Roger. Talk to her." Then Dad clears his throat and says, "Nori, I've disagreed with some of your choices in these last few years and"—I hear a shuffle, my mom says something else in the background that sounds like a protest. Then he returns but I hear—"No, Kathryn, let me say this—I've kept quiet. But this, now this…you're my child, and I feel that I must tell you. This, this…woo-woo yoga trip is a very bad idea."

Reeling first from the "woo-woo" comment, I hesitate before saying, "I'm not a child." And it comes out louder and angrier because—sorry, Dad, I love you, but—FUCK YOU. WOO-WOO TRIP? And I'm anything BUT a CHILD!

Sorry, Swami.

Then I continue and say what I've wanted to say to him for years. "Dad, I'm officially off the hook from whatever it is that you think I should do with my life." And then, despite everything inside me screaming STOP THERE, I add, "Jeni is doing enough of what you want for the both of us."

And with that, I press End.

I sit, shaking, clutching my phone and looking around at all the crying children with their parents and think, I'm not a baby. I. Am. Not. A. Baby. I slide a finger under each eye and wipe away the tears that begin to collect.

****

I sleep the entire flight and wake up feeling guilty still about the Jeni part but not about anything else, and though I know I have to have another conversation with my parents—especially since Mom left five voicemails on my phone—the worst part is over.

I emerge from the jetway with anticipation and excitement fizzing through my body. Scanning the throng of people at the gate, I see Ethan before he sees me, and everything except *this* moment and *that* boy dissolves.

Sunglasses nestled into his thick black hair. A green tee shirt, the color of his eyes, clings to his chest. Arms tanned and more toned than I remember, muscles long and lean. He grips a bouquet of roses in one hand. His handsome profile familiar and strange as he searches for me. The voices and movement of the people in the crowd increase a little as I slow my stride and wait for him to see me.

A bent-over older woman with a cane crawls past me ever-so-slowly, blocking him from sight. I tie my sweater around my waist. I want him to see his favorite outfit: cream-colored lacy top, skinny jeans, and wedge shoes with my freshly painted Lacey Love Lilac-colored toes. I touch my hair, which is tousled and messy in a bun, then take a small tube of watermelon pink lip gloss out and smear a little across my mouth as the cane lady finishes her journey.

The rise and fall of more voices and the gliding sounds of rolling bags and the smell of coffee, fast food, and airplane fill the space between us while he scans and searches right over my head.

Then.

His eyes land on me. He erupts into a gorgeous grin.

"Nori!"

"Ethan!"

The wedge shoes make me wobble as I run, but I don't have to go far because Ethan's arms swoop me up, spin me around, and pull me against his body. His lips are all over mine. "Mmmmmm. Watermelon."

I giggle and then his mouth dips into my neck. I make a little noise. He kisses my hair then puts me down and it's like light is beaming from every part of my body to his.

"Hi."

"Hi."

We giggle. He takes my bags, and I grin at him, heating up inside and out. I hear someone whistle and another few people clap.

Hands entwined and lips aching from kissing and grinning so hard, we walk through the gate.

"Three months." He swings my hand.

"I know."

He pulls me against his side and winds an arm around my waist. I have to tilt my chin a little less than normal in these shoes, which makes my five foot five more like five foot seven to his six feet. We kiss again with our mouths open and tongues pressing. I curl my fingers in his hair, and he does the same around my waist. I almost lift a leg in the air.

Yes, it's that good with Ethan. Dreamy-romance-novel-that-I-love-but-hate-to-admit-I-read good.

"Is it bad that all I want to do is get you to the condo and take your clothes off?" he whispers in my ear, which makes everything on that side of my body tingle.

"No, it's all I thought about on the plane." I inch closer. "And I hope you want to do more than take off my clothes."

Clasping hands, we hurry to the parking lot. Ethan navigates through the endless walkway of gates and continually growing crowds of people. My feet don't touch the ground, floating and flying, a blur of noise around us. We don't say much, lots of squeezing hands and other parts. One-word answers and questions. Sidelong glances at each other. I don't ever remember feeling so high around him before. The last time we had a reunion of this sort it was nerve-racking, and this time it is the equal intensity but opposite circumstances.

We get to the parking lot, and he pulls me to him right in front of his car and kisses me, his hands cupping my butt, and I feel him through his shorts. I slide my hands under that tight tee shirt. His skin is warm, and we come up for air as I rub his chest.

"Get in the car," he whispers and then sticks his tongue in my ear.

I giggle as little electric currents shoot all over my ear and directly down. "We aren't going to make it home, are we, E?"

"Pray that there's no traffic."

We speed down the highway holding hands, the

humming of the highway noise whizzing by. More squeezing and smiling. Sliding hands onto each other's thighs and rubbing. It's all the foreplay I think I'm going to need tonight.

"I have this whole sushi thing I want us to make. Foreplay eating," he says, his hand up and down on my leg.

"Baby, food is going to have to wait." I run a hand over his hair.

"Fine with me," he whispers, kissing my neck. "Who needs food anyway?"

When we arrive at the condo, we are out of the car almost before the engine is off. He grabs my bags from the trunk, shoulders them, and takes my hand. We run to the condo, up the stairs, and he pushes the key into the lock in one swift and silky movement.

He nudges the door open with his foot, and there's the lady of the house, Lady D. She barks and wiggles and starts to jump on us, but Ethan puts a hand up and she sits immediately, her tail wagging. From I don't know where, he produces a bone and she runs off, ignoring us completely.

Finally, he drops everything in the foyer and takes me in his arms, pulling off my sweater and lifting my shirt, and he smells fantastic, and my lips are buzzing, and my tongue tastes his. He pulls me into the kitchen, and the smell of bleach makes me open my eyes.

"Did you clean the entire condo?" I say into his mouth.

"Mmmmmmhmmmm. I know how much a clean house makes you hot."

"Oh, it does. Bleach is an aphrodisiac."

"See how well I know you, baby? Did I tell you yet

how much whatever you're wearing is driving me crazy?"

"You mean my perfume or my outfit?"

"Both."

And somehow we're against the breakfast bar, and he releases one hand from me, and I smell something else too.

"Brownies," I say into his neck and draw a circle on his skin with my tongue.

I watch him reach around and slide a finger across one. "A snack." He smears the marshmallow cream onto my lips. It should be funny, like the picture he sent, but it isn't. It's really hot. I put the tip of his finger in my mouth and slowly work it up and down. He moans and bends over to lick the rest off my mouth.

"Bedroom," I say because I can't take it anymore.

****

Clothes litter the floor. Ethan interlaces his fingers with mine. My body vibrates with warmth and soft bubbly sensations. We move together over and over.

Sex has never felt like this. Multiple and orgasm are words I can now say accurately describe my sex life.

****

"This is definitely a record."

I prop my chin up in my hand, my arm on his chest. "In more ways than one."

It's the first full exchange of words spoken in hours.

"We are going to need more condoms."

"You grossly underestimated reunion sex, honey."

"Apparently. Speaking of condoms, you better—" He gently rolls me off him. I lie on my side, watching him from behind as he sits at the edge of the bed to remove the aforementioned.

"Oh. Shit."

Not what you want to hear after hours of amazing sex. Maybe we wore it down to a nub?

I slide over to him and put a hand on his back.

I peer over and see what's in his hands.

A condom. But it isn't filled with anything.

BECAUSE THERE IS A GIANT HOLE IN IT.

****

We're on his laptop in seconds.

I've leaped up and am jumping up and down, trying to shake whatever is in there out. I've peed three times, pushing and pushing until my already sore parts cry for me to stop.

Ethan is still naked, wrapped in sheets, in the center of the bed. He's been searching all kinds of things like: *If I come four times, am I shooting blanks on the fifth?* And *the condom broke, now what*?

He fingers the mouse pad until a medical website fills the browser. "This is what I thought."

I'm over his shoulder, reading the screen, a little out of breath from all the jumping.

"We go get this Plan B thing. Also, the condoms didn't break in the first few rounds, right? So by the time that last one broke, I was probably shooting blanks."

"Right. *Right*."

"How long do we have?"

"It says up to seventy-two hours. So no worries." He glances at his phone on the bed stand. "It's only six thirty."

I'm already completely dressed, with his car keys

in my hand. My heart pounds little fists in my chest.

As we walk into the pharmacy, the angry florescent lights shed total reality on the enchantment and dreaminess of the day. Our hands are mutually sweaty as we hold on to each other.

"I'm sorry."

I nod because I've lost the ability to put a coherent thought together.

"Me too."

I walk directly to the "Family Planning" aisle and pluck Plan B off the shelf as a Muzak version of some pop song rings through the store. When I place the box on the counter and the pimple-faced teenager rings us out, we don't say "Thank you," and he doesn't say "Have a good night."

****

I start to think about the whole afternoon. That we stripped off each other's clothes and lay naked against each other, moving and grinding for a while with N-O-T-H-I-N-G between us.

That when he pulled off the condoms all the previous times, he didn't check any of them. I know. Because I pulled them off, too. And threw them and laughed and rubbed against him right after. Bare skin. Fluid. Parts rubbing.

Ohholyshit.

When we get back into the car, we realize we didn't get a bottle of water and that I can't take the pill until we get home. I'm numb inside and out. Thoughts are firing off. Monkeys are leaping and jumping everywhere.

Ethan talks and rubs my knee. I nod. I follow him out of the car when we get back to the condo. I take the water from him in the kitchen. I watch him take Delilah outside as I rip open the package, which feels too easy to rip in my fingers. I put the pill on my tongue. I take the glass, cold in my hand, then I start to drink.

And this image wiggles through my thoughts. A small bundle. Then a feeling inside my stomach. Clenching. Icy.

I stop. The pill resting on my tongue. Panic seizes me. I spit it out into my hand, a sticky large pink oval. Putting the glass down, I tuck the pill into my pocket and exhale long and deep.

Chapter 4

ANDY

It's six thirty and the layover flight is already two hours late.

Time to call Nori. I press the numbers on my phone, which is hot from sitting in my pocket. Her phone is off and goes right to voicemail. I leave a message that we are running a few hours behind and that we'll take a cab there in case it's really late.

Gwen leans against me, her hand on my thigh, eyes closed. We've been entwined in each other the whole flight. In fact, I don't really want to get to Florida.

I stroke her hair. "Hungry?"

"Starved!" She presses her lips to my cheek. "I have a whole new feeling about turbulence."

I kiss the top of her head and grin. She turns and touches the spot she kissed on my face. "I really do love how easy it is to make you blush."

I blush more and say nothing. Then we sit, people-watching in silence. I glance around at all of the other people waiting. Some alone, on laptops or reading books or on the phone. Some eating or wiping their kids' faces. Sitting with Gwen among people who are living their lives as we are living ours, gives me a buzz, like a high. I pull her to me. She snuggles me back and breaks our silence with, "I don't think we should tell Nori about, you know, *us*, this."

Even though I agree with her logically, the high I have from being next to Gwen steals logic, and I say back, "But I like kissing you in public." I lean down and put my tongue into her mouth and kiss her. She kisses me back, right there, in front of the world.

When we come up for air, she stares into my eyes, not even blinking for a solid minute and then says, "Right here, sitting here among strangers, this is easy because to them, we are just another couple."

"Is that what we are? A couple?" I say, and I'm half serious. Maybe more than half.

There is a moment where I wonder if I've said the wrong thing, but then she bursts into a grin and punches me playfully in the arm. "I'd say we're a couple of insane people. You know what I mean, Andy. If you don't know us, you'd think this," she gestures between us, "was like any other two people dating or whatever."

"*Dating and whatever.* We actually need to go on a date. The *whatever* part is down." I kiss her neck, smelling her floral sweetness.

"Andy!"

Her neck actually tenses. Is that hesitation from her?

She pulls away and gives me her wrinkled nose, serious squint. "The last time you and I hooked up before yesterday, you were on your way out of the closet."

I hold my hand up. "That was high school. The idea that I could be bisexual freaked me out. You gotta give me a break."

Her eyes search mine, and I can see within hers that she's remembering something. Something maybe she would rather forget. Something long ago. Then she says, "Listen, I don't want to tell Nori and Ethan because we don't know what this is. Right?" She nudges me. "Right?"

"Right." I sigh. Except I do think I know what this is or at least beginning to be. But I say, "It's hard to keep things from that woman, you know. Nori's like a mind ninja."

Gwen laughs. "She is. But it might be easier to keep this from her than you think. I mean, how comfortable will we be making out in front of her anyway?"

I shrug. Then I say, "We've done it before. Jesus, we all made out with each other at one point or another."

"Yeah, Andy, in high school. We were drunk kids. Experimenting." Then she stops and shoots me an accusatory look.

"Gwen. Stop it. This is not an experiment."

"We *were* drunk last night."

"What about the three other times we did it, totally sober? What about on the plane? The turbulence?" I try not to sound mad. "Besides, I'm not fifteen. I was very confused back then."

"And you aren't now?" Her eyes search mine, and I get a little hypnotized by the flecks of green in her irises.

I put both hands around her face and get very close to her until I feel her breath on my mouth. "No." Then we kiss again, in front of the world.

****

Hours later, in the sticky humidity I was not prepared for, we stand in the doorway of Ethan's dad's condo.

"Hey!" Ethan holds the door open, letting cool air from inside rush out to us. I wipe my brow and welcome the change in temperature and smile at the two of them in the shadows of the darkness.

Nori and Gwen and I are instantly one big hug. Then Delilah is between us, nuzzling our hands and legs for love.

Finally, we break apart, and there's Ethan, just standing there. Not bad or anything but so not Group Hug Guy. He reaches down and pats Delilah.

"How was South America?" I ask him.

He laughs and waves us in. "Awesome, but not as awesome as home. Come all the way in, already." We do a weird fist bump, and it's awkward, awkward but fine. He's a good guy.

I swing my arm over Nori's shoulder as I walk in. So definitely not awkward. I catch Gwen watching us with the same tight smile that I saw when her parents dropped us off—like she's trying to hold back a burp or something.

Reunited and it feels so weird.

"You guys hungry?" Ethan asks. "We actually didn't even start eating—"

"—or cooking." Nori leans into Ethan, who puts his arm around her, but it looks like they're trying to prop each other up. They're more wooden as opposed to melting into each other like they usually are.

"Still catching up," Nori offers more to Ethan than to us.

More nodding.

Gwen starts to nod, then I nod too, and soon the four of us are bobbing our heads at each other.

Something's off.

And it's not only me and Gwen. I glance at Ethan to see if there's a hint about what might have happened, and even with his dark tan, his face does seem a little pale.

But I nod my head up and down, and we all walk like a four-bobble-headed monster into the kitchen where pizza dough sits unrolled out on a wooden board and bowls of cheese and other toppings are scattered over the island.

"Nori and I thought we'd each make a pizza." He pulls on the collar of his shirt. "But we also have some ingredients to make sushi."

"We didn't get to make it for lunch." Nori's smile is stiff at best. Doesn't match what the words hint at—they spent the afternoon in reunion sex. They do not look like two people who have been going at it all afternoon. What's up with them?

Nori puts her hands together and reminds me of her mother. When we would go to her house in high school, Mrs. Mytowsky would fix us snacks and serve them on a tray. It's kind of weird and comforting at the same time.

Gwen and I put our stuff into the spare room then get right to making the pizza, distracted by our hands in cheese and cutting up vegetables. I enjoy the brief moments of brushing up against her, her hand and fingers next to mine in the bowls. It gets especially intense when we roll out and knead the dough together. I linger a little when Ethan and Nori are both consumed in their own pizza making. Finally, we put both pizzas in the double oven and before anyone can say a word, Ethan bolts out of the room. We all freeze and then Nori follows him.

"Something's going on with them," Gwen says, and I nod.

"Kiss me," I say.

She swipes at me. "No! Our friends are in distress, and besides, I get really dizzy when you kiss me, Andy, and I can't stop."

My mouth is kissing hers and then—

"Sorry about that!" Nori calls from the hallway.

Gwen pushes me away, hard, and starts cleaning up the cheese that has sprayed across the counter.

"Is Ethan sick?" I ask when she steps into the kitchen.

"Just a headache. He's going to lie down for a few minutes. He took some medicine. He's been, you know, cleaning all week and working out really hard." She trails off and rubs her thumb over her forefinger. That's her tell. I've played poker with this girl. Nori plus finger-rubbing equals big fat lie. Finger-rubbing plus rambling means only one thing: she's not telling us the truth.

Gwen stops cleaning. "How about you and Andy monitor the pizzas in the oven, and I'll go take poor Delilah out? She's been staring at that leash on the wall. Then we can all sit down and eat."

Nori nods. Gwen is strategic. She knows something's up and thinks Nori might talk to me. But I'm not so sure.

After Gwen leaves, Nori grabs the spray bottle of cleaner and tears off a paper towel from the dispenser on the island. I watch her scrub the countertop like she's ironing out wrinkles from a skirt. Cleaning frantically confirms that something is wrong.

I take the spray bottle from her and grab a paper

towel and do the same on the other side of the counter, scrubbing until my arms burn, not to mention I'm not used to scrubbing anything. Gwen is the cleaner in the house.

"We need to catch up," I say. "What's going on?"

She sighs, stops cleaning, and smiles at me. "It's been a while, hasn't it?"

I walk over to her, tossing the soaked paper towel into the garbage.

"I miss you, Andy." We hug and I close my eyes, resisting the words that want to spill right out of my mouth. I slept with Gwen. I think I love her, but I think she's too scared to love me back.

When we pull apart, I open my mouth to spill it all, but instead, Nori's eyes fill with tears.

"Nori! What is it?"

"I-I-I…" Tears spill.

"Is it you and Ethan?"

She puts a hand over her mouth and shakes her head.

"Is it school?" I feel like a dad asking, but she doesn't look right.

She bursts out with actual crying. "No."

"Why are you upset? What is it?"

"Because-because…" Her eyes go back and forth. "I guess I miss you. We haven't spoken in a long time, and you and Gwen moving in together. I guess I feel kind of left out. It's pretty immature of me." She wipes her eyes with the back of her hand. "*So* high school."

"We love you," I say, rubbing her tears with my thumbs. "*I* love you."

I drop my hands, and we stand awkwardly, not saying anything. I know Nori. She doesn't do high anxiety unless it is serious, and something more than missing me is going on, which means that it's probably not a good time to tell her about Gwen and me.

And then if I do, and it doesn't go well, we're stuck in this house feeling more awkward.

I pull her into my chest and rub her back and whisper, "It's intense today, you know. You haven't seen Ethan in a while, and Gwen and I haven't seen you and the four of us haven't been together in a long time."

"Since your birthday," she says.

I smile. "The karaoke bar."

"All four of us, totally sober, belting out show tunes. That was a perfect night."

I hug her. "It's not like you to worry when everything's good."

She pulls away, tears falling. "I know."

I pull her back into me and wonder if maybe things really weren't all that good.

And when we break apart at the buzz of the oven, she asks, "By the way, have you started writing in that journal yet?"

"I have."

"And?"

"Very therapeutic."

****

Ethan returns with wet hair like he showered, and his color is back, so we sit down, eat, and joke like old times, even though something's in the air. The heaviness of the secret that Gwen and I carry doesn't help, but we seem to forget it for a few hours, and I resist all urges to touch Gwen, for the most part.

Under the table, I slide a hand over Gwen's knee, and she leans it into my thigh.

I rub her, and suddenly, she bursts out into a fake yawn, adding a little noise for emphasis.

So I yawn, because it is biologically contagious, and then add, "Man, I'm beat. Think I need to go to bed."

Ethan pushes his plate away and stretches back. "Better rest up, my brother. It's tee time tomorrow."

For a moment I actually believe that Ethan is taking me to tea, which actually sounds nice. Occasionally, Gwen and I go to Bristol back home and have high tea at Blithewold. She jabs me in the arm. "Not our kind of teatime, silly."

Nori nibbles on a piece of crust and says, "Maybe we should all go? Golf and yoga are very similar."

"Day one of our reunion trips always includes a guys' day and a girls' day. Don't mess with tradition."

Nori chucks the crust. "I love Ruby, you know that, Ethan. But I'm not exactly the mani-pedi-blow-my-hair-out kind of girl, you know?"

Gwen picks up Nori's discarded crust and says, "We are—" She points from her to me.

"I am not!" I protest.

"Seriously? Come on. I've taken you to Jazzy Nails many a time, and you've enjoyed getting your *man*icure, emphasis on the *man*, though to be fair—"

"It's actually called a sports pedicure, and Jazzy has a lot of male clients."

Ethan laughs. I turn to him. "And I have never had a pedicure. Just to be clear."

Ethan holds his hands up. "Hey, I manscape, dude. I get it. I trim stuff, and I've gotten a facial or two from Ruby's Salon. No judgment on my end."

I yawn again and Gwen follows. "Bedtime!" she

cheers, and we all say goodnight and head to our respective bedrooms.

****

After Gwen and I brush our teeth, I shoo her out of the bathroom so I can shower quickly. Then I slide into bed in only my boxers, turn to my side, open the covers, and strike a sexy pose. But Gwen is busy reading, playing with her hair, balancing her tablet on her knees.

She catches me ogling her. "We brought condoms, right?" she asks, pressing the shutdown button.

I lean down to my bag, produce one, and lift the covers of my bed. "Come on over."

She leans over and turns off the light by her bed, and then skips to mine, sliding in next to me, her body warm and her hair soft and smelling lemony. I start to kiss her, pulling her on top of me. My hands slide down to her butt—and God, she feels good—but then she stops kissing me. "We have to be really, really quiet, Andy."

"Yeah," I murmur, letting her hair fall between my fingers. "But I bet those two are doing the same thing we are."

Gwen stops moving against me, and I open my eyes again. "What's wrong?"

"This feels wrong…here…with them. Like my parents are in the next room."

"It's because we haven't told them."

She props herself up on one hand. "What do you mean?"

"I'm saying that if we told them, you wouldn't care about us, being noisy."

"We aren't telling them," she says quietly and starts moving against me. "And I don't want them to hear us because it's weird." Her tongue pushes against my neck, and she murmurs, "But I feel horny. Really, really horny."

I start to pull down her underwear and she leans over and grabs the condom. "So we still need to be quiet."

****

After Gwen is back in her bed, snoring softly, cuddling her pillows, I decide to pull out that journal and write some more. I can't talk to Nori about everything, so writing is the next best thing.

When I first started seeing George, I wanted to make a decision about my sexuality. It was right after my first hookup freshman year of college with this girl who I was hanging out with at a party. Somehow we started making out. I wasn't even drunk—not that I did that often. The kiss felt natural, but that in and of itself surprised me. The last girl before this one had been Gwen, my sophomore year of high school.

So I figured I needed to talk to someone.

****

I found George through the health center. He dressed like a lumberjack and had a healthy amount of graying scruff on his chin. The first thing I said to him was, "I'm not sure I'm gay."

George was very quiet and looked at me with absolutely no expression.

We stared at each other. Then I said, "And I'm not sure I'm straight."

He nodded again.

"Do you have any thoughts on that?" I really needed someone to say something.

"Yes, I do."

"Can you tell me them?"

"Well, I'm not sure that it matters if you are gay or straight."

I didn't go back to see him for another six months, after the semi-relationship ended with the girl from the party because she was too worried I would dump her some day for a guy.

The next session I spilled the entire story of my sexual history. Started with Gwen, our hook ups in high school, and then I went all the way to the girl I kissed at the party and dated for six months. In between, I mentioned Harry (my first kiss with a guy the summer before sophomore year) and our class president I had to hook up with on the down low in high school, my senior prom date, Jim (a kid who wasn't sure of his gender), and more recently Shane. Shane was, in a word, a douchebag. George nodded a lot and asked questions—not about the gay part but about why didn't those work out, normal questions you would ask someone about their past.

After I was done, George touched his burly scruff and said, "Hmmmm."

I almost stood up and slammed out of that office. But I was desperate to figure this out. "I don't know if I'm gay or straight."

"Yes, right, you told me this last time."

"And you told me that you didn't think it mattered."

He nodded and glanced at his notes about me. "Hmm."

I sighed. "Can you at least tell me if what I am feeling, what I am doing, what I have done is normal?"

"Sure." He shifted in his chair. "Yes."

"That's all you have to say?" I really wanted to punch this guy.

"For now, yes. Because our time is up."

And the last time I saw George, he said to me, "You know, Andrew, keeping your dating life a secret from your friends is more about not accepting yourself than the fear of them not accepting you."

I sank deeper into the chair. "It's hard to say, 'I'm bisexual' to people who have thought I was gay all these years."

He wrinkled his brow. "These are people who love you. Do you really think it will change that?"

I didn't say anything. I looked out of the window at the campus and the sky, which was gray. The word just sat there in the room like one of the heavy rain clouds I saw outside.

Chapter 5

GWEN

Andy has fallen asleep with his journal on his chest and his glasses at the end of his nose. My hand is tucked under my cheek, and I'm on my side watching him, the dim light from the reading lamp illuminating his pale face.

I stare at the journal, dying to grab it and read just a few pages. The sixth sense in me, the very same one that suspected Heyward of cheating when we were together, the very same one that was right about it, is flaring right now.

I lift the covers of my bed and roll out, my feet hitting the floor without a sound. I tiptoe over to him, hovering and watching his chest rise and fall. His lips are pink and turned down in a faint frown.

He's better than Heyward who gave me my first O. Andy is also the perfect friend and companion. Andy and I have a better thing going than any other relationship I have ever had.

Except.

He's gay.

He was gay?

Bi?

I lean over, gently pluck the glasses from his nose and when he doesn't move, I let one of my hands glide gently down onto the journal. My hand hovers. Heat emanates from what I might find in there.

Tonight, before we had sex, I wasn't reading a book. I was researching about bisexuality in men and came up with a lot of posts on forums that basically say bisexuality can't exist. Then I came up with a bunch of forums that said of course it exists. That everyone is bi, and sexuality is on a spectrum.

My hand grazes the journal. I let two fingers pinch the spine, and I close my eyes and take it. I open my eyes. It's in my hands.

Andy snores softly.

My heart is insane, pumping hard, making my whole body vibrate. I turn the leather-bound journal over and read what's on the pages fast, skimming it and not reading in full detail, scanning each page, reading snippets only: *is it normal for a gay man to masturbate to a Victoria's Secret catalog...I don't know if I'm gay or straight*...and then:

George, he said to me, "You know, Andrew, keeping your dating life a secret from your friends..."

Whatwhatwhatwhat?

Who is *George*? And why does he call Andy *Andrew*?

My heart doesn't slow. Like it's pumping the flood of blood rushing into it. I know how heart attacks happen. They can be stress induced.

I slap the journal shut and then freeze. I look over at Andy. Still on his back, snoring softly.

When was this conversation with George? And who the fuck is George? Were they dating?

Heart throbbing, I open the journal again, after all I didn't read it word for word. I must have missed the details of this George person. But then it occurs to me, I may not want to know the details. I close it and put it on the nightstand.

I want something. A cigarette.

I feel my way around the room for something to throw on. The anger that stirs in my stomach is familiar. Old, but familiar. High school. Heartbreak. Andy and me.

I have to get out of here.

In the darkness, I find my way to Andy's Brown University hoodie that he had tossed on the hook behind the door. With my feet, I feel for where I know I left my slippers and put them on blindly. My eyes have adjusted to the darkness, and I can make out where my suitcase is. I tiptoe over to it, lean down, and root for the sharp points of the soft pack of my favorite brand. I grasp it the same way I had silently plucked the journal from Andy's hands. I hear a loud snore and Andy rolling over. I freeze.

Stillness.

I tuck the pack into the pouch of the sweatshirt and inch back to the door. Silently, I open it and step soundlessly out of the room.

It's dark, but there's light coming in through the gauzy shades covering the large windows of the living room. I move quickly through the kitchen to the slider that leads out to the beach. I stop only when I hear a soft groan coming from where Delilah is sleeping in her dog bed. I wait to see if there's more from her then continue on, the hum of the refrigerator following me until I open the slider and the sound of cicadas and slight rustle of the palm trees overtakes the air.

It's calming as I step out. The night sky is inky and dark except for the golden orb of the moon high up and the glow shimmering off the water. Scents surround me. Salty, earthy smells of the beach mixed with the smell of the flowers that Dan's girlfriend, Ruby, must have planted in the large pots all over the deck. I walk across the wooden slats of the deck on tiptoe in case they squeak. The room that Nori and Ethan are in is to the left, off the deck and also connected by sliders. I creep down the stairs and when my feet hit the ground, cool sand oozes into my slippers, making me walk like I'm stepping through peanut butter until I reach a few feet from the low, flat tide.

I sit down heavily. Tears collect and fall as I remember way back when, before Andy came out, before we knew anything.

****

"So?"

"So, what I'm saying is I think we should stop hooking up."

Silence.

"I just don't want things to get weird."

"Things" had been going on between us, here and there, for over a year. "Weird" was already what they were! The word "weird" hung in the air like a mosquito I wanted to squash.

The couch felt prickly beneath my thighs. The skirt I had on was Andy's favorite. I hated it and only wore it for him.

I hated everything in that moment.

I hated Andy.

I folded my hands in my lap and stared at my ugly skirt. Short, flouncy, and maroon. Gross. "It's no big deal." I swallowed the huge lump of a lie and coaxed myself to a smile.

He brightened. "Oh, that's great, Gwen. Seriously, I'm so relieved." He even grabbed my hand and squeezed it. I remember feeling like my hand wasn't part of my body, watching him pump it up and down.

"We can go back to being friends. Maybe everything with Nori, you know, maybe we can all make up."

Nori. That's right. Andy and I weren't talking to her. Or maybe she wasn't talking to us. Seemed so stupid when I remember it all. She was heartbroken over the breakup with Ethan and "ignoring us" was how we felt. How stupid. How high school.

I nodded and even added for good measure, "Yeah, pretty sad about her and Ethan. She looks really depressed all the time."

Which I was happy about. I wanted her to hurt right now. I was jealous of her, of her name rolling out of Andy's mouth in such a caring way.

I wanted all of us to hurt.

****

Andy and I grew far apart after that conversation. I would see him in school, and we would wave and say hi. But he and Nori made up and then clung to each other, almost like a couple. I figured they might even be dating. I wondered if he actually dumped me for her.

The summer after sophomore year, I went off to Europe and returned for junior year with dreadlocks, piercings up the side of one ear and in my belly button and a new boyfriend too—Heyward. Big, beautiful, stupid Heyward.

We were at the bagel shop just a few months into the school year. Heyward was simultaneously whispering lines of poetry and tonguing between the studs in my ear when out of the corner of my eye—

"Andy," I whispered into Heyward's dreadlocks. Yes, we had matching hairdos. Heyward had been on the Europe trip with me, a kid I never noticed in school before. I had confessed on our trip, while traipsing through—ironically—gay Paris, that I harbored a deep love for Andy. Heyward, who had spent most of high school high, had no idea who Andy was and consoled me throughout the trip with lots of making out and fondling. But then—

"Where?" Heyward craned his neck. "Not that kid over there. *That* Andy? That's the one you've been talking about? That kid is gay. Totally and completely into dudes."

I punched his arm. "Don't be an asshole."

"Babe, that kid right there?" He pointed, but I grabbed his finger and bit it.

"Ow!" He yanked it out of my mouth and shook it and said, "You're talking about the one with long hair and the glasses, right? He's a gay dude."

"Shut the fuck up, Heyward."

"Babe, seriously, I've seen him before. At this under eighteen club that my buddy DJs at. That dude right there with the nerd glasses, I've seen him, like a few times. Dancing with this same guy and making out and all that shit."

I remember how out of my body I felt. Hovering over the two of us, over Andy.

"The guy he hooked up with, like every time, was there with my buddy. My buddy's sister's boyfriend—"

But I was still somewhere else. I pushed Heyward off me, and he called my name, but I stood up and walked over to Andy.

Everything around me, the sounds and the movements blurred and smeared all together.

Andy didn't stand up when I got to his table, but he glanced behind me, and I knew Heyward waved and grinned because Andy waved back.

I stood there, boiling, my eyes traveling over Andy's golden brown hair flying all over the place.

"So you know Heyward?" was all I could manage.

Andy nodded, as if nothing. As if knowing Heyward meant nothing.

But it meant everything.

"Were you ever going to tell me, Andy?"

"About what?"

"About-about..." My eyes searched his face for some flicker of recognition of the truth that he was gay, that he had kept this information from me, and that keeping it mattered.

And then it happened. A flicker, more like a grimace, and he dropped his head.

But he didn't say *anything*, and I needed him to give me *something*. I just shook my head and went back to Heyward and sat right in his lap and made out with him noisily. Andy got up and left shortly after.

****

I hate remembering.

The waves roll up on the shore in the moonlight, and the tears continue to fall. I don't make any kind of ugly crying face. Salty tears. I lick and rub at them and wonder if I'm going to wind up sucker punched again by Andy. I stand, and as I take a step toward the water, I hear a loud, sharp whisper.

"Gwen?" It's from behind me. I peer into the darkness, and I see—

Ethan.

****

ETHAN

"Gwen?" I step closer.

"Caught!" She holds up her hands. I notice something square and familiar peeking out of the pocket of the oversized hoodie she's wearing.

"Are those cigarettes in your pocket?"

"Or am I just glad to see you?" she offers, laughing and wiping at her eyes.

I take out my own contraband, snagged from my stash in the laundry room closet. A single cigarette and a lighter. "You might be glad to see me since I'm out here for the same reason as you."

She grins. "Awesome, 'cause I forgot a lighter, and there's no way I'm going back in there."

We huddle together. I flick the lighter and offer it to her first. "Ladies before gentlemen."

"By all means, Ethel."

I smirk at her, and she smirks back but leans in and puffs with her eyes closed. "God is that good," she says on the exhale.

I'm busy puffing and lighting the end of my own cigarette, so I nod.

We smoke side by side. She's shorter than Nori, and next to me, she could be my kid or something. This makes me want to pat her on her head, which I know will go over with an elbow in my ribs.

"Nori knows you still smoke?"

"Nah. And I really did quit before I left."

We smoke in silence. The water is shimmering and pretty and I think of telling Gwen why I'm out here, that I couldn't sleep, haven't been able to stop the whirling thoughts about the diamond, the proposal I'm now all confused about, and the words *family planning* that hung from the ceiling on the sign in the pharmacy. About almost throwing up when Nori went to take that pill and about me running out of the room like a giant pussy.

I puff and watch Gwen out of the corner of my eye. She's puffing as frantically as I am. Clearly, I'm not the only one with issues.

The ocean makes a gentle roar and rolls in a thin foamy line. I'm almost done with my cigarette. I pierce it hard between my fingers, sucking it like a joint.

"So you know how Andy is gay?" she begins.

I nod with my fingers practically all the way in my mouth, vaguely thinking this was an odd way to start a midnight conversation but far more focused on toking my stupid cancer stick and trying to get the words *family planning* out of my brain.

"He, kind of, may not be."

She's still, with the cigarette between her lips, the butt dangerously close to burning her mouth. Meanwhile, I've finished mine and after giving it a tamp, tuck it into my pocket 'cause I don't litter, and somehow, if I did, Dad would find out, even this far from his property.

"What do you mean?" I eye the unopened pack hanging out of Gwen's sweatshirt.

"We're sleeping together."

As the bright part of the cigarette is about to burn her skin, I reach over and yank it out. I tamp out the remains of the butt and tuck it into my pocket. Don't want Dad to find any evidence that I'm smoking or littering. Also, gotta throw these fuckers away in case my lady goes into the pockets.

"As in, you know, fucking."

Now that I can see her up close, I notice that her eyes are wet and puffy. And finally, because I have this great way with words, I say something:

"Oh."

"Ethel—" She sighs and fumbles around her sweatshirt pocket for the pack. "—You showed up out here, and I'm having a little mini breakdown, so I'm gonna have to talk to you."

She catches me staring at the opened pack of cigarettes. "See, now here's the difference between a straight guy and a not-straight guy: a not-straight guy can multitask in a conversation. If you were Andy, you would simultaneously be longing for the cigarette and hearing me, responding to me. Actually, Andy detests smoking, but whatever. This is why I fell in love with a not straight guy—because he has the soul of a woman. Maybe that makes me also not straight?"

I'm pretty sure my jaw is hanging. And it's mainly from desiring that fucking cigarette, but also from the mouthful she said. The thing about this chick is that she talks. A lot. And about every single thing that pops into that big brain of hers. I'm definitely neatly distracted from my own problems by her. It's like watching a one-woman show.

Then I remember something. "You did go to prom with a girl."

She sucks on the cigarette harder and squints at me. "Nori was the perfect date. Even if we went together by default. You know, neither one of us ever truly liked anyone after you two shitheads broke our respective hearts."

I ignore that last part and say, "I was jealous that whole night, especially when you two slow danced."

She laughs. "Your girl did look hot in that red slinky dress. Too bad we weren't a couple of lesbians." She tosses me another cigarette. "Here. But this one we share because I only have half a pack."

"Deal."

I light and suck it in silence.

Then I ask a question because I'm pretty sure that's what she wants, and I owe her for the cigarettes. "Were you and Andy drunk or something?"

"Not really. We had a little bit of wine."

I take another long pull on the cigarette. "Wine can make things very romantic. Or it can completely make you do stupid shit." I exhale the smoke with a whoosh.

She peers at me. "How many nights in high school did you spend drunk, clutching a bottle of wine, outside Nori's window?"

"Too many. I had a routine, you know. I would hear from someone that she was dating some guy and then *bam!*—right to my secret stash of vodka, stolen from Granny's freezer. I would get drunk and text Nori, call her, go to her house."

"Sans pants, right?"

"Yep. Romantic, huh?"

We both laugh, and I flick the orange orb of the end of the cigarette. Black ash falls to the sand, and I bury it quickly.

Gwen draws a circle in the sand and says, "I guess it all worked out okay with you two."

Silence and my puffing and her drawing in the sand. Rolling waves and ringlets of smoke and then—

"It's a miracle how"—she's drawn about four

circles now—"we all managed to get back together again, as friends. And as more."

"Agreed." I watch her pile sand over the circles until they disappear.

"You know—" She leans over and somehow I know she wants a puff, so I pop the cigarette in her mouth. She takes a pull and holds it before leaning back and exhaling. "In high school, after the four-headed monster blew up, I thought that Andy wanted Nori."

She coughs a little, and I take another drag and nod. "I knew that *you* wanted Andy." I exhale smoke out of my nose. "And I always thought that *Andy* wanted *Nori* until he came out," I say and hand her the rest of the cigarette. "But now, maybe I need to worry a little. That guy is a player!" I laugh but stop when I see that she isn't laughing with me.

She's holding the cigarette and not smoking, which makes me crazy for a minute. Instead, she sits very still, and a few tears come out. "This shit—this shit I keep feeling and thinking about is so old. Fucking high school. Do we ever get over it?"

"I obviously never did because I just kept going after my girl until she took me back." Then because I can't help it, I grab the cigarette back from her and puff a few times. My lungs start to tighten.

She wraps her arms around her knees.

"I obviously can't either because—" She stops and wipes her eyes. "I still replay our first kiss, and we were babies, really. All four of us were. Silly babies making out with each other, drunk off like, three sips of vodka—"

I laugh and exhale some smoke. "With orange juice, from my recollection. And since we couldn't taste the alcohol, we just kept drinking it all night. I'm pretty sure it was more than three sips."

"Right, but that was a tiny bottle of vodka. Remember? You found it in the freezer, naturally." She leans toward me again and nods toward the cigarette. I hold it to her mouth while she puffs a few times.

"Yes!" She blows smoke away from me and then says, "Then you replaced it with water or something and put it back."

"Right, and since they never drank, it stayed in the freezer until we graduated." I take a small puff because my chest hurts now, a stabbing pain. I cough to loosen it.

We laugh again. Then silence. She scratches her knee. "I couldn't stop thinking about my kiss with Andy. Eventually, after you completely dicked-over Nori—" There's the scowl heard round the world. The one she always throws at me on the rare occasions we all discuss my douchebagness in high school. "Andy and I started hooking up here and there."

"Did I know this?" I flick ashes and toke again on the cigarette, even though I shouldn't.

"Probably not. We don't really ever talk about it. I think Nori knows." She rocks a little, still holding her knees.

I finish the cigarette, tamp it out, and then tuck it into my pocket with the other butts. We stare up at the moon for a moment.

"And who knows, maybe it wasn't a big deal," she says over the ocean sounds. "We really only made out a bunch of times, and looking back, it makes sense that he freaked out. He was beginning to figure out he liked guys. I don't know. I'm over that, right? I should be.

Stupid. So long ago. We were kids."

The waves are loud, and the sky is dark blue ink with dots of faraway white light. We're both silent again.

"I'm assuming you guys are planning on telling Nori that you're together?" I say, stretching my legs out.

"We aren't together, Ethel." Her voice is sad.

"But—"

"We're fucking. Not together. I mean, we are fucking each other, but we are not *together*."

"You're fucking your not totally gay best friend who you once wanted as a boyfriend, and it seems like who you never really got over." I reach for my toes to relieve the cramp I feel in the back of my leg.

She watches me. "Ethel, when you put it like that, I certainly do feel a whole lot better. Thanks for the enlightenment."

"Can you stop calling me that?" I stop stretching.

"What? You insecure with your gender identity?" She stretches now, her arms overhead.

"No, are you?"

"Absolutely not." She drops her arms. "I'm insecure with the guy I'm sleeping with."

We stare at each other for a minute. Then she takes another cigarette out of her pocket.

"Sorry," I say. "That wasn't even funny, what I said."

"Nah. It's fine." She changes her mind and puts the cigarette back in. "Oh, fuck. I know we have to tell Nori."

"But you told *me*." I take a deep breath, which is hard since my lungs feel like they have a fist squeezing them.

"I know." She waves her hands in the air. "But you're Ethel, you know, we don't have any—" She gestures between us.

"I know what you mean." I lean back on my hands. "What does Andy think?"

"When my parents drove us to the airport, he kissed me on the mouth in the back seat. With tongue. I almost decked him." She looks off into the water and adds, "He even said he wanted to tell my parents. Can you imagine that one?"

"Yes, but no." I chuckle, thinking of her sweet and a little naïve, suburbanite parents. "So, he doesn't want to hide it. But you do?"

"No. Yes. I don't know. See, I read his journal tonight after he fell asleep—"

"That's kind of fucked up, Gwen."

"You've never read Nori's journal?"

"No way!"

"Ever gone through her phone?"

"Hell, no!"

"Maybe it's because you two are so perfect. But most of the world is not. Most of us are hiding shit."

"We definitely aren't perfect." I think of yesterday. "So, what did it say?"

"That he beats off to Victoria's Secret catalogs."

"Ha, my man is old school!" She glowers at me, and I add, "That's pretty classy, you know, as far as masturbation material."

"Great! That's fantastic to know, Ethel."

This shit is fucked up, and I do feel sorry for her and for Andy, poor confused guy.

She sighs, long and breathy. "I feel like he's hiding

something now."

We look at each other for a long beat.

I think for a moment. "Was the, uh, fucking just a onetime thing?"

"No. It's on, like, all the time."

I hold my hand up. "I got it. Are you sober while you are doing it?"

"Totally." Then she adds, "Just not the first time."

"That guy!" I slap my thigh. "That guy is a genuine stud."

Gwen punches me in the arm but laughs. "Come on, what am I going to do? This is totally and completely, all caps, fucked up."

"What's the problem if you like him and he likes you? People can be bisexual. People can be whatever."

"I know. But I read that studies have been done to so-called bi men, and it turns out that they aren't ready to accept that they are gay. I think Andy sort of fits that description with his daddy issues and how he never goes to gay Pride parades." She stops for a moment. "I guess I also worry that it could happen again. Like high school. Love me and leave me."

I put a hand on Gwen's shoulder and try to find something wise to say. Something Nori-like, but all I have is: "That sucks."

She smiles. "This is one fine, fine mess I have here."

We listen to waves roll. I stare out at the white foam that glows in the bright moonlight and wonder about the fine mess we all seem to be in.

"Ethel, should we go back?"

"Yeah." Then I add, "Tomorrow, you'll have all day to talk to Nori. You know it's hard to keep things from that woman." Believe me.

Gwen sighs. "Yes. I know."

"Gweny-poo, this was fun and informative." I reach down and rumple her hair, knowing now that she won't elbow me in the ribs. She reaches up and takes my hand.

"Thanks, Ethan. Seriously." She releases my hand.

"No problem. Are you coming back inside now?"

"No. In a few minutes."

"Are you sure? I mean it's pretty safe out here but—"

"Hey, I've handled myself alone in Europe. Twice!" She takes two fingers and pretends to jab her eyes. "Hit between the eyes and then the balls. I'm good."

"All right but come inside soon. And I don't mind it."

"Mind what?"

"You calling me Ethel."

She laughs. "Goodnight, Ethel."

"Goodnight, Glen."

****

I slide back inside the house and go into the guest shower right next to the laundry room. For a moment, I think about throwing away the remainder of that pack of cigarettes.

Either Nori told me this saying, or I read it somewhere: There are two days in every week which we have no control over—yesterday and tomorrow. I step into the shower to wash all traces of today.

Chapter 6

NORI

Sunlight slides through the bamboo shades that hang in Ethan's bedroom. I roll to my side. His eyes are closed, expression smooth and peaceful, long, thick lashes brushing his skin, and lips pink and puffed out a little. The tiny dots of black scruff from his beard and his hair tousled and sticking up everywhere. I could easily slide on top of him.

And then I remember.

I still haven't taken the pill.

And Ethan, last night, slipping outside to smoke. Obviously as fucked up as I am over all this.

I rub my belly. My throat tightens. The clock on my phone, which rests in the holder next to me, reads six forty-five a.m. I pick up the phone.

Two more messages from my mom.

Shit.

But my mind goes back to time. As in how much time has passed since The Incident.

The box said if taken up to seventy-two hours, it can still be effective.

My hand stays on my belly and tears gather as I close my eyes and breathe in and out, belly breaths, long and full.

It sounds silly, *Am I killing our baby*? For shit's sake, I'm pro-choice! What the hell?

This is ridiculous, but the tears are falling fully. I must be premenstrual, that has to be it. Nothing to worry about. Take the pill, because really, it's a precaution, I'm about to get my period anyway.

I rub my eyes hard and hoist myself up and out of the bed and walk to where I hung my jeans on the back of the door last night. My fingers rummage around the inside of the pocket for the pill. It sticks a little to the lining. I pull it out, don't bother to check for fuzz, stick it in my mouth, and go to the sink and slurp from it.

Done.

Belly breath in and out.

I go back to the bedroom, and Ethan is on his other side, curled up with the sheets over him. All I see is the top of his head. I ache to slide back into bed, spoon his warm, strong body, run my hands all over his chest. But I think of him sneaking out last night, just as scared as me about all this. Instead, I grab a pair of yoga shorts and sports bra from my suitcase. Sneakers and phone with my yoga tunes, and I leave the room. I walk through the living room and kitchen. The rolling sounds of the ocean outside get louder when I open the sliders.

I open and close the sliders as quietly as possible and see the beginnings of the sunrise, the sky blue, purple, and the traces of yellow and orange by the shoreline.

****

I pause before I walk down the steps and unclip my phone, slide it to unlock, tap the code in, and though it's the coward's way to apologize, I text my mom.

—sorry I was a brat on the phone to Dad. Will call you guys soon.—

I inhale the fresh air, clip the phone back, and hop

down the stairs. As soon as my feet hit the sand, I start jogging toward the shoreline where it's flatter and a little easier to move. It's a little cool but perfect. I run away from the beach house and pass only a few other joggers and older people walking dogs. The sun climbs until all traces of sunrise are gone, and it's another cloudless morning in sunny Florida. I stop and find a flat place. And while my Planet Yoga playlist plays, I bend and twist and stretch, and with each gliding movement, I let go more of the crap cluttering my brain. When the playlist ends, I lay in savasana. Then I run back.

When the beach house is in view up ahead, I notice someone sitting before the shore reaches the dry sand. Long strawberry-blonde hair and knees hugged to her chest.

Gwen.

"Hey!"

She tries to smile at me, but as I get closer, I can see that her face is covered in tears.

I sit down next to her. "Hey, what's going on?"

She wipes her eyes. "Nothing." She stops and rubs her nose with the corner of her tee shirt. "Allergies?"

"But you don't have allergies."

Before she can respond, I hear, "Good morning, ladies!" and turn to see Ethan and Andy traipsing through the sand.

Gwen forces her lips into a smile.

Ethan thumps down next to me and gives me a kiss. Behind us, Andy rubs my shoulders first and then Gwen's, who keeps pushing that smile bigger.

"Pretty pumped for guys' day," Ethan begins but glances over at Gwen.

Hmmmmm?

He continues, "Golf is the thinking man's game, bro!" He grips Andy's shoulder hard.

"Ow!" Andy says, rubbing the spot Ethan just practically crushed.

Ethan continues, "And you girls! You are in for a spa-cation day!"

Andy doesn't say anything, and Gwen wiggles her fingers and says, "Perfect!" But it's a little too loud and enthusiastic.

"Me and my guy get to hang on the green. Man, we're growing up!" Ethan throws an arm around Andy.

When Ethan lets Andy go, Andy cycles through bewildered to confused.

"Sounds fun," I offer, equally confused. Why is Ethan trying to sell this so hard?

Andy says, "Yeah. Guy time." He awkwardly slugs Ethan in the arm. Ethan slugs him back and sends him sprawling. I grab Andy but he laughs, and Ethan apologizes and tries to brush the sand off the front of Andy's pants and then stops.

We all talk about the weather and then nothing.

Ethan kisses me, and I see Andy eyeing Gwen, and he leans down to her like, I swear, he's going to kiss her on the mouth, but she grabs him into a bear hug and rumples his hair. More weirdness.

I hug Andy. Ethan and Gwen bump fists. I wait until the guys are climbing the stairs to the deck before turning to Gwen.

"Is it me, or is everyone off?"

"Jetlag?" she offers.

"From a three-hour plane ride that involves no time change?"

The wind blows gently, and the ocean rolls a little louder, and I watch Gwen's profile. Stray hairs blow around her.

"What's going on with you?" I ask her.

She doesn't turn to me but pushes the stray hairs away before saying, "I don't know."

"I know we really haven't seen each other in a while. Everyone is so busy."

"Yeah."

We sit in more silence, and then she takes a deep breath and holds it in.

"What is it?" I put my hand on her shoulder. She puts her hand over it.

"You don't want to know."

I put my arm around her. She leans in and starts to cry freely. I whisper, "It's okay." She cries for a bit, and I want to cry too, but I don't. Not about me.

I feel her nod, and she sits all the way up and takes a deep breath and this time lets it out before she speaks. "I'll tell you, but you can't interrupt me, okay?"

I nod.

"Andy and I—"

I nod again, encouraging her to continue.

"We've been—" She makes a noise like she's frustrated, like she can't figure out how to say whatever it is she needs to say.

"We've been…" She tries again and fails.

We've been *what*? What could they be doing together that is so awful? Binging on chocolate croissants from that bakery on Thayer Street? Arguing over which season of *Dr. Who* is the best?

"We slept together."

"You've been sleeping together. He only has one

bed. That apartment is so damn small. How do you live there?" I laugh.

"No. As in had *sex*."

She won't make eye contact with me.

"Many—*several*—times," she says, pulling her hair back like a ponytail, then releasing it and adding, "Don't worry, we're using condoms."

The irony of that statement.

I can't help but burst out in a laugh. "That's the first thing you think I would worry about upon hearing this news?"

We look at each other and crack up.

The cracking up turns into full-blown cackles and hee-haws and ha-has. Soon we're rolling on the sand and repeating, "Don't worry. We're using condoms."

Eventually, we quiet down.

The sun has climbed higher, and the clouds have all but disappeared. And the magnitude of what she has confessed hits me. "I don't really know what to say," I admit.

"I know you probably have more to say than that." There is an edge of defensiveness in her voice.

"You were pretty messed up about him in high school."

Gwen nods. "At first, I thought the obvious: I made him gay."

We both laugh.

"But then I felt mad." She slides her shoes on and stretches her legs out. "Like he used me to figure out if he was gay."

"Are you worried about that now?"

She looks down at the sand and whispers, "Yes."

I rub her arm. "You really think he's using you,

Gwen? Andy loves you, you know."

She sighs. "He's not *using me* using me. I mean not consciously. I don't know. What do you think, Nori? About this whole thing. Really, what do you think?"

I take a breath and then tell her, "I think that the only reason Andy hasn't told us about his dating girls over the last few years is because he's probably been trying to figure all this out himself. He's a thinker, a processor."

She doesn't look like she's buying what I'm trying to sell, though it's not really anything other than what I truly think about Andy. The other part of what I think, I keep to myself: What did they think was going to happen by moving in together and sharing a bed? Gay or not, boundaries were already crossed.

"Besides," I continue, "if you guys are happy, then what's the problem?" I see pain written all over her face.

"Andy is, um, GAY!"

"Obviously he's not totally gay."

She thinks for a moment and then says, "Have I converted him? Am I so amazing I can make men defy the confines of sexual preference?"

I have to laugh at that.

We both shake our heads.

"I'm afraid," she says. "I'm afraid of him changing his mind again. Of missing men, missing having sex with guys. And then what happens?" She stops and hugs her knees tighter and wipes her nose on one naked knee. "It's fucked up." She stops, tears forming again, and she holds her breath, trying to keep them in.

"I really don't think it's that simple as changing his mind, Gwen. Really, I don't."

We fall silent.

****

An hour later and we are on our way to Ruby's.

"Thank God it's not as humid as yesterday," I say to Gwen, who walks next to me, head down, waves of strawberry hair falling over her face.

She gives me an "mmmhhhmmm."

I try again. "Girls' day! Wha-what!" I put my hands up like I'm raising the roof.

She mumbles, "Wha-what." Without any inflection.

I try again: "Hoes before bros!" and put my fist out to bump with hers. She stares at it and shakes her head. But I do see the tiniest beginnings of a smile on her face. I want today to be a break for both of us—from everything.

Side by side we finish the twenty-five-minute walk to Ruby's Salon, staying on the sidewalk of Glades Boulevard, which is the main road that goes through Boca. Endless flatness stretches in front of us, all lined with palm trees and various businesses and apartment complexes tucked back from the street behind stonewalls. Lots of pastel or white stucco. I glance at Gwen again; I'm not worried about her because Ruby will give us the once-over and cut the bullshit, stick a sharp knife in said bullshit, to the point it will hurt. Last time we saw Ruby she told Gwen that all that was missing from her outfit was a Hello Kitty backpack; Gwen was in her pink, shorty overalls phase. Ruby volleyed one at me too, asking, straight-faced, "Where's your broom?" When I looked at her confused, she added, "Elphaba had better hair than you." This silent walk might as well be a last meditation before

Mother Ruby gets a hold of us.

As the black awning of the salon comes into view, I grab Gwen's hand and try one more time. "Fuck everything. Fuck relationships. Fuck all of it. For the next few hours. Fuck men."

She squeezes my hand before pulling open the glass door and replies, "Yeah, but isn't that really our problem. We fuck men?"

Naturally, this sends us into fits of laughter.

We step into freezing perfumed air, greeted by the sounds of blow-drying, the hum of female voices of various octaves. Then the highest pitched sound reverberates across the expanse of the spa: "Myyyyy girrrrrlllllssss!" I crane my neck to find the body behind the voice but only see magenta walls, ebony tiled floor, and the enormous front desk, sleek black with a matching Victorian lamp on the corner.

I must have missed her because she is so tiny, but there she is—Ruby in all her vampy glory, barely peeking up from the monstrous desk, her black hair cascading around her bare shoulders. She wears a white strapless something, but because I can't see her legs yet, I have no idea if it's a pantsuit or dress or a top. Her bronzed neck is decorated with an ornate plate-like silver and copper necklace.

"Oh girls, I have a fanfabulous day planned for you! While your men do their man thang, we—you two—will be maxing and relaxing. Facials, pedicures, body scrubs. All on the house, lady-friends!"

She steps out from behind the desk, arms extended, and hustles her tiny body perched on massively high black heels. Jeans. Dark, fitted jeans and a strapless silk top. She hugs us to her at the same time.

"Hello, ladies!" She eyes both of us up and down, reaches out with both hands and lifts up a strawberry lock from Gwen and a chestnut lock from me.

I brace myself for a caustic bomb, but instead, she just cocks her head and says, "Blow outs? Trims?"

Gwen and I look at each other.

Ruby's question is rhetorical. There's no reasoning with or talking to her when she gets you into her clutches, and Gwen knows that as much as I do. The last time we were with Ruby she insisted on going clothes shopping with us. She bought us each leopard print matching hot pants and made us wear them to dinner that night. Ethan gave her a high five, and despite my attempts to throw away the pants afterward, Ethan pleaded with me to keep them in my "special drawer" of kinky-ish lingerie. Most of which still has tags on it.

"Whatever you want for us, Rube!" Gwen answers, and I nod.

Moments later we've stripped off our clothes and are laying face up on massage tables. Chocolate sea-salt body scrub clings to our bodies, and oatmeal facial mask is slathered over our faces. Soon after, we are whisked away to a private room I have never seen in my four years of coming here on vacation. Two beautiful Spanish-speaking women sit us side by side and give us pedicures. Gwen and I are too relaxed to speak to each other.

Then we are ordered to get dressed, and Ruby meets us back at the enormous desk with keys in hand. "Taking you two to lunch." I open my mouth to protest that this has been more than generous, but Ruby holds up a long skinny red-nailed finger with a tiny diamond imbedded in it. "You know that this is as much for me as you. Come on."

We speed down Glades in her shiny, baby blue corvette, top down, blown-out hair blowing. She blasts Frank Sinatra and sings loudly along, off-key and high-pitched. She makes us join her; we know the lyrics, too.

She pulls the car up to a parking meter in front of a burnt orange awning that says Walla Cafe. "This is the best place. Dan and I come every Friday." I arch an eyebrow at Gwen. In our years of coming to Boca, I've never been here.

We all hoist ourselves out of the car, Ruby taking a little longer to get to her feet because of the stilts she's using for shoes. I glance down at my flip-flops and capris cargo pants. "Are we dressed okay?"

"Absolutely. You'll fit right in." She slides a credit card into the meter machine and waits for a piece of paper to come out. After tucking it into the front dash, she flashes us a pink-mouthed smile. "You two will love this place."

As soon as we walk in, a young woman in a hippy dress with gauzy fabric greets us with nods and hellos but then rushes to Ruby and embraces her in a hug. They exchange hushed words quickly, and then, once again, we're swept up and away by Ruby, along with her hippy friend, weaving through the sparsely filled café, which has music playing that reminds me of my yoga playlist. The aroma of curry and spices tickles my nose.

We're ushered farther back, and I swear that when we pass the bar, I see long tubes and vases that appear to be hookahs. Interesting. Not exactly what I would expect. Especially if this is a favorite spot of Dan's. The hippy girl weaves us through more tables that aren't filled until we go through a door to the outside and find ourselves in a private alcove surrounded by lush greenery and flowers, the air perfect with a gentle breeze. Hippy girl seats us, leaving in her wake the appropriate scent of patchouli.

Not more than two seconds pass, when another hippy girl breezes over, bringing with her the scent of patchouli. They look almost identical, and this hippy girl even reaches down to hug Ruby as well. Hippy girl number two smiles at us and says, "The lunch special today is spinach and feta *Borek*, and our special appetizer is *Ezme salatası* served with goat cheese butter and *pide*." Then she hands us each a single laminated page. "After your meal, please come to the hookah bar for some apple-spiced *shisha*. Ruby's favorite dessert." She winks at Ruby before leaving.

"Hookah!" Gwen exclaims, brightening fully for the first time all day.

Ruby nods like it's normal for a fifty-something woman to even want to do that. I picture my parents, who are a little younger than Ruby, sucking on a hookah pipe. My mom—definitely in her younger years. Dad—hell no. I picture Dan. Nope. Gwen's parents? NEVER. Can't see it.

Gwen, still happy like a little kid's first time at an amusement park, says, "What's *ezsme salatasi*?"

"Middle Eastern salsa, only a thousand times better," I tell her and scan the menu quickly.

Ruby adds, "*Pide* is what you eat with it. It's a puffy bread that is almost better than an orgasm."

I raise an eyebrow. "Maybe more like better than salsa and chips."

"I said *almost*, Nori." Another wink. "Don't forget, I've got myself a Ledger man too!"

I cough to avoid gagging at that statement.

"Delish!" Happy Gwen. "And that other thing? Borat?"

"*Borek*." I laugh. "How did I not know that you've never had Middle Eastern food?"

"Because living in NYC for four years means I should have. But Columbia was like a prison. All anyone ever did was study. Oh, and fuck. And drink. But rarely did we leave campus, unless to drink. Sometimes to fuck."

"It's yummy. Trust me."

The waitress returns with a tall bottle of clear liquid in one hand and a pitcher of iced water in the other. "*Arak*," I declare, thinking that I don't remember any of us ordering drinks.

"Now you want delish? This drink is delish." Ruby sits up a little taller—if that's possible.

The waitress sets the pitcher and the bottle down and then produces three glasses. She pours the *arak* in each, filling them halfway and then adds the iced water.

"That's kind of gross looking," no-filter-Gwen says.

"Watch." I stir mine up with a spoon, and Ruby does the same. The water and liquid cloud up. I take a delicate sip of the licorice sweetness, only good because it's ice cold. Gwen stirs hers and does the same.

"Wow. That is unpleasantly good!" she exclaims.

"Unpleasantly?"

"I hate licorice—black licorice. But this is weirdly good."

"Now, Nori, how do you know so much about Middle Eastern cuisine?"

"Ethan and I go to this place in Worcester all the time, and my guru Swami Nick is Lebanese. He has the teachers to his house every few months and serves a lot of Lebanese food. His mom cooks everything from scratch."

"Is this Swami hot?"

I laugh and blush.

"Oh, my!"

"I know our Ethan was gone a long time…"

"Ruby!"

She smiles and sips her drink. "Hey, what happens in yoga class stays in yoga class."

For some reason, I'm not amused by Ruby's *Rubyness.* She has no idea. None. The stirrings of my secrets form knots in my belly. I put my drink down.

"Hey, sweetie, I'm teasing you. Listen, I know how much you and Ethan love each other. Seriously, I know that. Drink some more. You're too tense. Even after all that relaxing." She furrows her brow at me. "Everything okay with you?"

I open my mouth to say—I don't know what—but the waitress arrives with a tray of food.

The aroma is intoxicating, and the *arak* melts away the beginnings of the anxiety that just formed. I grin big and say to Ruby, "Just PMS-ing. Sorry. Let's eat!"

Clinking and clanking of spoons and dishes and sounds of food being spooned out and passed take over. Mmmmmhmmmms and yummmmms fill the next godknowshowlong as we indulge in some of the best Lebanese food I've ever had. Swami's mother has nothing on this place.

We sit in silence when we're finished, a comfortable, satiated silence. The waitress clears everything out, and Ruby pats her flat belly and says, "Hookah time. Do you girls hookah?"

I burst out laughing.

Ruby looks at me with total seriousness.

"I just can't picture you doing this. And no. No, I don't hookah. Not good for the lungs." I thump my chest.

"Oh, if you do it right, it shouldn't bother your lungs at all."

"I love hookah!" Gwen says, that Cheshire grin still on her face.

"Really?" I say. There are more things I don't know about Gwen.

"Yes. Andy hates it. I go to this lounge near our apartment after my shifts on Tuesday and Thursday. When I come home, he lectures me about my lungs and shit."

The waitress returns before I can ask more, and we're whisked away yet again to the back, through the restaurant to the bar area we had passed on the way in. A few people are at the bar, pipes in their mouths, casually hookahing. For some reason it all feels illegal.

"Do they really just smoke tobacco here?" I ask.

"Only legal stuff." Ruby grins and adds, "Unfortunately."

We settle into three cushiony chairs surrounding a small round table that has a blown glass vase with black and white stripes decorating it. On top of it is some kind of chemistry-set-looking device. Three pipes are attached to the top of the vase where the mouth meets the contraption.

A handsome man with short dark hair, equally dark eyes, and very bronzed skin comes over, flashing white teeth at us as he sets up the hookah.

"Is this your first time?" he asks, his eyes drawing up and down my face in a way that feels dirty.

"Uh, yes." I blush yet again, more in this day than my entire life.

"You're going to enjoy this as much as the meal. I'll go over everything as I set you all up. This is the Delirium model, my personal favorite because of the black-and-white swirl design. Giving it a yin-yang quality."

I have to hold in a bubble of laughter. This is beginning to feel like an infomercial for hookah. Do they sell these things here? Is there a kickback on certain models from the hookah man?

Hot Hookah Man is still talking. "The part of the art of the hookah—aside from the aesthetics of the vase—is the lighting of it." He points to the top of the contraption where a bowl rests. "Hot coals are put in the top of the hookah, the shisha, or tobacco, goes over them. You'll be smoking apple-spiced shisha. Stand and gently inhale the scent." We all stand up and awkwardly lean over and sniff the bowl. It is a nice smell. We sit back down, and he continues, "As you draw on the hookah pipe, it both heats the coals to the point the shisha smokes and draws the smoke to you. That is basically how it works. This is not the same as smoking a cigarette or from a bong. This is an elegant and relaxing and, most of all, legal activity." Was that a script he was just reciting?

I watch as he puts some aluminum foil over the tobacco bowl and pokes holes into it with some long tool he produces, and then he puts another long pipe on top of the tobacco bowl. He uses tongs to place the coal inside. He lights it up and proclaims, "Take your pipes, ladies."

"It all sounds very wrong," I whisper to Gwen, but she is beaming, practically levitating.

I take my first drag and totally start to cough. Reminds me of all my failed attempts to smoke weed.

"Don't pull it into your lungs. It's not pot or cigarettes. Puff. Think of the Cheshire cat in *Alice in Wonderland*," Hookah Man instructs.

"Like a cigar," Gwen offers, and I wrinkle my nose at her.

"Because I smoke those all the time?"

I want to like it. I want to be chill. I try again, not really pulling on it or sucking, but God, this is really wrong. I just do as they said, puff lightly. Soon it's not bad, actually. The whole thing feels almost like savasana, and the scent is like burning incense.

We puff in silence and at some point Hookah Man leaves, and we all recline and puff. Eventually, I stop, drop the pipe, and feel myself close my eyes.

As I begin to melt totally into the soft chair, Ruby's voice, about three octaves lower purrs, "Fill me in, girly girls. The last few months. Life alone without Ethan—" I open my eyes and she points to me. "And your graduation—" She nods in Gwen's direction. "There's been separation. Reunion."

Gwen opens her mouth and spills, slowly, like syrup pouring from a pitcher, her story about Andy. Her voice is low and relaxed, and though just hours ago she was freaking out on the beach, the story, as she tells it, almost feels like it isn't hers.

Ruby, eyes half closed and nodding here and there, puffing away, actually listens to the entire thing without interrupting. A first, for sure.

I'm pretty sure they snuck some pot in that hookah. No apple-spiced shisha should relax us this much or keep Ruby's mouth shut for an entire story.

Ruby lets out a rush of ringlets, her lips no longer decorated in pink lipstick, her mouth opening and closing like a fish. She widens her eyes fully as she says, "Well, Gwen, you know, people aren't required to be gay forever." I watch the ringlets float up in the air and burst. "Just like you aren't required to wear underwear with tight dresses. Unless the dress is too short and your vajayjay is showing." She points to a woman, perched on a barstool by the bar, whose vajay is just about peeking out the bottom of her silver saran wrap dress and who has her hand curled around a beefy, tall guy with slicked back hair.

I glance at Gwen, wondering how that little gem of wisdom sits with her. She nods, that relaxed half smile on her face. Is that it? That's all it took to fix Gwen. Wow. Maybe I should share my shit with Mother Ruby.

But turns out I don't have to say a word because she's got something for me. By the way she is squinting at me, I can tell.

"As for you, Nori." Ruby takes a short puff and lets one ringlet out. "Three words: do not get tied down. Wait, that was—" She ticks off her fingers. "Five. Five words. I'll repeat, do not get tied down."

The room seems to go completely silent except for the sound of my heart beating.

Huh? This is my great advice?

I hear Gwen murmur, "Oh, snap." Then I feel her

leg shaking against mine because we somehow migrated into one single chair together.

"Date that hot Swami," Ruby says. "Date a girl. Live! *Then* you and Ethan can settle down and have your picket fence and babies." She sighs and puts the pipe down. "When I was in college, I got pregnant by my sweetheart." She smiles. "Nicky. Darling, darling Nicky."

Her smile dies. "I had the baby. I wanted an abortion, but I was a good, Catholic girl. Anyway, gave him away minutes after he was born."

FUUUCCKKKK. I do not need to hear this story. Since I haven't told Gwen a thing about what happened the other night, she can't rescue me, and naturally, she's going to ask Ruby—

"What happened to the baby?" Gwen sits up, her hipbone jabbing me. I scootch over a little, but we are sardined into the chair.

Trapped.

Ruby uses a finger to slide the tears out from under each eye. "His parents wrote me a letter once a year just to update me. When he turned eighteen, they asked him if he wanted to meet me, and he said no."

I don't move a face muscle, and I feel Gwen sag into me. "What happened to darling Nicky?" she asks.

"He married, had babies." She laughs. "We're actually Facebook friends."

"But your son, he's now…what thirty-five, right?" Gwen has her arm through mine now, holding on to me.

Ruby smiles. "Yes, yes, he is."

"And he still doesn't want to know you?"

Ruby puts her hands on her knees. "We're Facebook friends. He lives in California. I've visited him a few times. He's lovely."

Just because I need to do something, like chant *om* or do warrior pose, but it's not the right place to bust a yoga move, I grab the pipe and puff, and they follow suit.

All I can manage is, "Fucking Facebook." And we all laugh.

****

Sunshine fills the bright blue sky. Ruby drives us back home to wait for the boys to return from their man-day.

We hug her goodbye and thank her. She holds me a little tighter andwhispers, "Please don't be upset by what I said. I just think you are a spectacular, young woman, and I don't want you to regret these years. You remind me of myself. I know that's surprising. But you do." She kisses my cheek and reaches over to kiss Gwen's. "I love you both."

Chapter 7

GWEN

After Nori and I watch Ruby take off in her blue corvette, we go straight down to the beach. The sunshine is pouring over the sand and shimmering off the water.

We have a few hours until the boys are back. Nori has been eerily quiet since Ruby bestowed her words of wisdom upon us, and I'm not letting her go inside until she tells me what's going on. Ruby hit a nerve with her, but I'm not exactly sure how or where. That something weird in the air since Andy and I got here is crackling with intensity, and it's obviously about her and Ethan. I did have the opportunity to find out the other night on the beach with him, but I was busy working out my own shit.

Kind of getting *sick* of my own shit.

Nori and I chase each other down the beach and dip in and out of the warm water and then fall back onto dry sand. I nudge my Girlfriend Pink pretty toes against hers. Just like she got me to talk to her this morning, I want her to talk to me.

"Today was totally intense," I offer.

Nori nods. "The hookah—which I'm pretty sure I'm still buzzed from—all the scrubbing and"—she nudges me back—"this color!"

I laugh and lean into her completely. "I'm talking

about the advice from guru Ruby."

She makes an *hrrmmp* noise and says, "I would hardly call her a guru."

The words to live by didn't fly with Nori. "Maybe not, but she's lived. Man, has she lived."

Nori doesn't say anything, just digs her toes deeper into the sand.

I tilt my head and squint at her. "Something's up with you."

She lets out a giant exhale, as if she's been holding it in since the car ride. But doesn't say anything. I watch her swallow, take a deep breath, and let it out again.

The ocean rolls up and back, and I wait for her to talk, which is hard.

Finally, she says, "Yes. Something's up." The sand falls between her toes, and she watches the grains trickle through, avoiding my gaze. "Yesterday, the condom broke right after our reunion sex." She cringes and closes her eyes, adding, "On round three."

I whistle and say, "God bless!" Those two, I'm convinced, have the best sex life of any couple I know. Hell, any person I know. Not the point, though. "I mean, shit." Not exactly words of wisdom.

Her face crumbles and stops almost as soon as it begins, and she covers her mouth, holds whatever is about to come out in.

I crinkle my brow. It does suck, but it's not the end of the world. I mean, the likelihood of pregnancy, statistically speaking, is small.

Then it hits me.

"Oh my mother-effing God." I put my own hand over my own mouth and let it drop and say, "Ruby's story."

She drops her hand and nods, her face flickering I-don't-know-what exactly, but it's not happiness for sure.

"Fucking prophetic. Sort of." She leans back on her hands and says, "Except I took Plan B."

"So everything's fine!" I'm flooded with relief. "I've taken that before. Mother-fucking Heyward. Guy managed to put a condom on inside out, and it got stuck inside me," I babble. "That pill made me totally sick. You're probably feeling the hormones from the pill. You do not want to know what's in that shit. It's like a regular birth control pill times a million. I think I'd rather stick a coat hanger—" I stop myself. Too far, Gwen, too far. I put my hand on her shoulder. "Listen, this shit happens."

"I know."

"But it's taken care of. You don't have to worry. That pill has a really high efficacy rate." I rub her shoulder.

She nods, but tears leak out of the corner of her eyes. "For a moment, for several hours, I held this idea of possibly carrying his baby. Saying it out loud sounds so weird." She stops and looks out at the rolling water, calm now, almost no white crests. "But Ruby's fucking story. Completely screwed with what I was feeling."

"What were you feeling?"

"I guess it was a moment of the future. Not a future like what Ruby described. But of when Ethan and I *are* ready to have a family. This moment of knowing you are carrying inside of you the love, the actual product of the most awesome love. Gwen? I'm sorry."

I put a hand over my mouth for a second and then

drop it. "No, no. Keep going."

"Don't get me wrong. I'm on this very determined path. I agree with Ruby, you know. To a certain degree. I don't need to date other people, but I need to…live. Ethan has. And he's ready to move in together after graduation. But I have all these things I want to do before, on my own."

I wipe my eyes. God, what she and Ethan have is so beautiful. I flick that twinge of jealousy away in my mind. "Can't you do both? Be on that determined path of whatever and live with him?"

She doesn't answer me.

Then she says, "What did you think about Ruby's advice to you?"

"Smooth move, there, Mytowsky. Nice one. Back to me, right? I'll take it, but we will talk more about you and your man." I take a nice Nori inhale, and as I let it out say, "Let's put it this way, I'm not as evolved in my thinking as Ruby. I read Andy's journal last night."

"He's journaling?"

She seems pleased. That makes me laugh for a minute. "Yes. He finally listened to you."

"Not that I think it's the best idea to read someone's journal, but since you did, what did it say?"

"I mean, I didn't read it word for word. I scanned and flipped through pages, but he talked about crazy shit like masturbating to Victoria's Secret and not knowing if he's gay or straight. But the kicker was when he seemed to recall some conversation with a guy named George."

"Who's that? I've never heard him mention a George."

"Me neither. I have no idea, and I live with him. I know the names and the penis sizes of all his exes, but I don't know who the fuck is George."

We both giggle.

"I love you, Gwen!"

"If only that did it for me…"

We giggle for a minute. Then her face sets into serious, and she pushes a strand of hair out of my eyes and asks, "What were you looking for? In the journal."

"Answers." I straighten up and close my eyes, reciting the only line I remember: *"You know, Andrew, not telling your friends is more about not accepting yourself than the fear of them not accepting you."*

"Hmmm, calls him *Andrew*? That was from the George person?"

I nod. "Probably."

"Telling your friends what?" she asks.

"I think about the fact that he has been fucking women all throughout college!" I feel my anger sparking. It will definitely catch fire very soon. I just hope I don't ignite the whole damn house; Mr. Ledger will be pissed!

We don't say anything for a minute or two. I hug my knees like when Nori found me here this morning and rock back and forth. Together we listen to the ocean again and watch a smattering of people walk along the beach, bundled up in sweaters. One couple walks by us wearing matching Santa hats and Christmas vests. It's weird to see that when the temperature is in the seventies. I stop rocking.

"Really?" I say, staring at the couple.

"It's, at the very least, good comic relief."

"Can you even imagine dressing up like that? You

and Ethan? Matching fucking outfits? This is why being a couple is so fucked up. You do stupid shit like that."

"Not every couple does stuff like that. But that is stupid shit." She gestures with her chin at the next couple strolling by in a similar outfit.

I lean into Nori again. "Why is this happening to me, to us, to me and Andy?"

She puts her arm around me and hugs me close. "I don't know. Other than proximity. You live together. That is kind of a set up for something to happen, right?" She thinks for a minute and then says, "Swami Nick would say, 'Don't ask why. Ask how.' "

"What the motherfuck does that mean?"

"It means that instead of *Why me? Poor me*—sorry, Gwen, but that's what asking why is—instead of that, we ask ourselves—the universe—how? How can I increase compassion? How can I increase love? How can I give and receive more love?"

I cock my head and squint at her. "Seriously?"

She grabs my face and brings it close to hers. "It means, you silly bitch, that *why* doesn't do shit for us. It keeps us in self-fucking-pity. It keeps us stuck. Why did the condom break? Why did Ethan leave for three months? Why can't I—" She stops, like a self-correction, and I let that go by because she's about to tell me something I need to hear. "Why does Andy have sex with guys and girls? Why did Andy not want you in high school, and why does he want you now? Who the motherfuck cares? It's about what *is*. What's happening. So if it's happening, then fucking be in it and stop over-analyzing. Stop searching for an answer. Like with the journal."

I blink, and she blinks, then lets me go. I just got

owned. Though, she's right. To a certain extent. I hug my knees again. "But I'm scared."

"Of what?"

"Getting hurt."

She bursts out in a laugh. "Then go crawl in a hole."

"But he's lied to us! We're supposed to be his best friends, and he's kept a whole separate life from us."

She scoops a handful of sand and lets it fall through her fingers. "Technically not a lie. I would say he hasn't told us the whole truth."

"What the hell are you saying?"

"That people withhold the whole truth all the time. To each other. To themselves. It's not a mark against the person they aren't telling the truth to. People lie because of their own fears, because of what they aren't ready to face."

"Another Swami Nick-ism?"

She laughs. "Nope. My own. Listen, I don't think he wanted to be lying to us."

I extend my legs, stretch my arms up, and let them fall with a sigh. "He said something the other night, the first night we hooked up. He said to me that he didn't tell me or you about all this because we were 'into his gayness.' "

"What does that mean?"

"I don't know. I wanted to talk about it, and he was like, 'forget it' and then we went at it again."

She cringes.

"See, it's weird. Us, me and Andy. I see it on your face. You aren't okay with it."

"No, no. It's more that, you know, you're both my friends. And I didn't see this coming. At all."

"Neither did I."

We fall into another silence. More people walk by in ridiculous outfits. Reindeer ears and even a guy wearing his bathing suit and a Santa beard.

"This place is nuts," I finally say.

"And so are we."

****

ANDY

Endless manicured greens with perfect circles of water stretch out before us. The sky is cloudless, and sunshine radiates all around.

If only I felt as serene inside as the day appears.

Sweat—yes, actual beads of sweat have formed in my hair, making it appear like I put product in it, which I don't, didn't, and never will. My tee shirt has water spots underneath my pits, which I really wish I had some paper towels or tissues to mop up. Not to mention that—thank God!—we're on the eleventh hole (however, nine more to go, for God's sake!). I want to take a nap or have a sweet drink. The slowness of the game, the sunshine all over me, makes me want to sit by the pool with a mimosa.

Not exactly the proper vision of a guys' day. Actually, I could continue on if only I could sip a mimosa between holes. Oh, and be taxied via golf cart. But our golf pro, Bill, would have none of that. Believe me, I already tried and was met with what I want to not think of as sexist garbage: "If you want to be carted around, I'll go get you a golf skirt." Bill is older than our parents and is newly retired…and semi-angry.

I watch Big B—he insists on using these so-called manly nicknames all day—reach out to straighten Ethan's collared shirt and give yet another slap on the back; I swear I have a handprint already back there.

The two of them turn and grin at me.

Bill takes two long strides back to me and slaps my back.

I wince.

"My man. Your turn."

E-man walks over to the hole a few yards away from the tee.

Bill—*Big B*—stands behind me, instructing. "Remember, knees bent, butt out." He gives my ass a light slap.

I turn back and glare at him. He stands there like he did nothing, so I bend my knees and reluctantly stick my ass out. I would think with all this heterosexual sex, I wouldn't be emitting any signals of gayness.

Or maybe old golf pros are just naturally handsy?

"Lower your shoulders, A-game," Ethan calls from where he stands at the hole, which has a tiny orange flag next to it.

I feel hands on my shoulders. Seriously? This time I shrug them off. Big Bill gives a hearty laugh. "A-game, remember the idea is to imagine you're pinning a nail into a door frame."

My shoulders fly back up to my ears. I sense his hands coming and throw a don't-you-touch-me look. He nods. Sweat gathers on the back of my neck.

"Just pin the nail, A-game!" Ethan calls, grinning. "You got this, buddy! You've been doing great!"

My whole body hurts, my hands are sweating and sliding off the handle of the club. I adjust my grip. With a handicap we quickly determined as twenty-eight, the maximum allowed for men in golf, which I particularly find sexist, I take the longest at each hole, and the pressure to try and decrease my handicap so we can move the fuck on is getting to me.

"Nope, nope." Bill takes my hands and rearranges them. "My man, you're choking the hell out of the club." He pushes my shoulders back down. "Relax."

I nod again. Maybe he is just trying to help.

"Now let the hammer—that is the face of the club—just let the weight of it do the work. Got it?"

I don't nod. Instead I sigh, drop my posture, and say, "Bill—Big B—I've never picked up a hammer. I've never been on a golf course before today."

"Everything okay, A-game?" Ethan calls.

Bill holds up a hand, waves, then turns to me, his blue eyes crinkle. I brace myself for another slap on the back followed by old people wisdom. Even if this guy is an old queen, he's probably harmless.

Instead he places a hand on my shoulder. "You just have to relax."

"Go for it, A-game!" Ethan cups his hands over his mouth, and his words echo across the green.

I grit my teeth.

Bill leans in and whispers to me, "Try not to hit the ball. Just swing."

"Okay." I shut my eyes and rear the club back.

Whoosh. Thwack!

Plop!

"Dude!"

I open my eyes.

Ethan throws his baseball hat in the air and jumps up and down. "Dude!"

"Holy shit!"

"Well done, Andy! Well done!" I note the use of my proper name as Bill raises his hand. I brace myself again, but when it comes down, it just squeezes my shoulder. "See, like I told you before, golf is a game of the mind."

Ethan and I strut to the next hole. That hole in one, or whatever it's called in golf, is making me feel pretty darn good. Twenty-eight handicap—not anymore, suckers!

"Stay humble, boys," Bill tells us.

We slap hands. "Always, Big B. All. Ways!" Ethan does a full-on strut with his hands, diving them down one at a time.

Adrenaline I never knew I had pumps through me. A bead of sweat forms on my upper lip. I wipe it with the small towel that Big B made both of us carry. I whip out my phone, take a selfie, and hit Send to Nori and Gwen.

—*I'm totally sweating! It's a Christmas miracle!*—

Ethan and I stand to the side while Big B sets up for the next hole.

Ethan leans in and says, "I made reservations at a swanky restaurant tonight, A-man. Treat the ladies right!" He elbows me, and I practically fall down. The whole morning he's been A-game-ing me and slapping and fist bumping, treating me like…like a guy, guy. Not that he treats me like a gay guy normally, but he seems to be amping it up a little.

"Sounds good," I say.

We stop talking, watching Big B bend his knees and prepare to swing; he pulls back and pauses. Adjusts his blue baseball hat and kind of wiggles a little bit. A bird circles above us, making a chirping noise. It's gotten so quiet that I can hear the ducks in the pond behind us.

Thwack!

The ball drops onto the green, yards ahead of us. We walk, holding our clubs, and the caddy appears suddenly. He climbs into the golf cart and turns it on with a low rumble. It follows behind us.

We haven't really gotten a chance to talk this whole time, which I know is in line with Guy Day, but I need to talk. To a guy. Who's dating a girl. And I'm not really close with a lot of guys who date girls. So I try. "How are things, E-man?"

"Good, good, A-game."

I can feel Ethan's eyes on me. *Awkward.* I say, "South America was amazing?"

"Yeah, unbelievable."

We walk a few more steps and he says, "Lots of time without any distractions. Lots of time just doing real work, building sidewalks, a playground, fixing up a school. Those kids, some so little. It was intense." He pauses. "How are things, you know, with you and Glendolyn? She's a good roommate?"

"Yeah, yeah. It's been fun." It's right there. The opportunity to mention it, that Gwen and I are…we are…what are we? I wipe my face with the little towel again, stalling, trying to find the right way to say *it*, the right tone in my voice making it sound normal.

We both get quiet and watch another group of golfers ahead of us.

"She means a lot to you, doesn't she?" Ethan has this faraway look on his face.

The sweat forms again on my lip. I wipe at it again.

"We've loved those girls for a long time," he continues.

"What?"

"Nothing. Nothing." He sighs, takes his shades off and puts them back on.

From far away, someone calls, "*Fore!*"

"Listen, man. I gotta tell someone. I bought a ring for Nori."

"Oh! Like a ring, ring?"

"Yes, yes."

I digest this news and watch the caddy pull ahead of us.

"It was the orphans," Ethan tells me.

"The orphans?"

"Yeah, they came to see the school as we were renovating." He shakes his head. "This one kid, he carried a football, clutching it like a teddy bear. He came right up to me and asked me to play with him. He couldn't have been more than six. We played all afternoon. And when it was over, he hugged me really tight and said, I wish you were my papa. I wish I had a papa." He stops and his mouth kind of twitches. "Anyway, everything, and I mean, everything inside me changed like a kaleidoscope. You know and I saw my whole life, Dad, my dead mother, and everything with Nori. I got a second chance with her and with life. And there I was, standing there, giving this kid what I thought was just a fun afternoon, but it really was *important*. The next day, I saw this man at one of the open markets selling diamond rings, and it all came together for me."

I have to turn away for a minute; something tugs at my heart, maybe the little orphan, maybe how certain he is about Nori and how I know she is certain about him, makes me tear up. I cough and blink.

"That moment with that kid made me feel

significant. And Dad, as a father, he just wasn't around much. And all these years I've carried so much anger about that and about my mom, but that moment with that kid, it released the guilt. All because of that moment with that kid. Shit."

Now my lip is quivering a little. All these emotions, thoughts about my own father, Gwen, what will happen when we go back home, all of it explodes inside me.

"Oh, hey, man—"

I rub my eyes, swallow the explosion of emotion inside me, and clap a hand on his shoulder. "It's okay, Ethan. E-man. That's awesome about the ring. And don't worry, I won't say anything. Not even to Gwen."

"Thanks." We smile at each other.

"When are you going to do it?"

"You mean propose?"

"Yeah."

"I'm thinking the night before we leave to go back home. No offense, but I want us to be alone."

"None taken, E-man."

He laughs. "I guess we got our male bonding in today."

"Or female bonding. All this crying and emoting."

We both laugh.

"Hey, you two turkeys want to join me here? I just finished this hole. Anyone want to record the score?"

We hustle to catch up with Bill. Ethan scribbles the score on the clipboard hanging off the side of the golf cart. The caddy, a young kid, makes eye contact with me. He's got intense, blue eyes. He gives me a quick platonic nod. I nod back, going for a manly nod. I hurry away with the clipboard and hand it to Ethan.

We finish the rest of the holes in meditative silence. I even forget about mimosas and sweat. As we put the equipment away, Bill says, "Hey, Andy, give this to that young man there," and points his chin to our caddy. I feel the red crawl over my face. Cute guys and pretty girls sometimes make me blush. No. Big. Deal.

Ethan grabs the cash and says, "I've got it."

He thanks the caddy and turns to me. "I gotta hit the head."

Big B and I stand outside together.

"Not that it's any of my business, but you and Ethan…"

"What? God, no! I have a girlfriend. And so does he." Wait, is Gwen my girlfriend? Doesn't matter. Not the point.

Bill continues to look at me, and I shift a little. Sounds of the birds around us and the voices of other members getting into and out of golf carts float by.

"You and I both know that doesn't mean anything."

My fists clench and my inner manly man is ready to deck this asshole.

"Are you hitting on me?" I've been to enough gay clubs to know how to handle old queens. Direct and firm.

"No. Not at all. I thought maybe you and Ethan were together or on a date, and I was trying to show my support…I don't want to date you. I've got a partner. What I'm trying to do is give you some advice. You're lucky to be a young, gay man during this time period in history. It's 2013! You can be out and even get married—at least in some states—all because of people like me, so I feel it's my duty to step in and prevent you from doing what guys my age did. Get married. Have children. Then wreck lives because we cannot continue to deny who we are. We had an excuse. You don't."

My throat closes a bit. I swallow and manage to croak out, "You don't know a thing about me, Bill. A thing."

"I think I do, young man. I think I do." And he claps me on the back, which almost sends me sprawling on the floor.

Almost.

Moments later, Ethan returns. He thanks Bill, they shake hands, and I turn away.

"Ready to go home?"

You have no idea how ready!

****

After returning home to the girls and showering quickly, we go to the swanky restaurant that Ethan made reservations for. It's not too crowded, but the minute we get inside, Gwen darts off to the bathroom and then returns, commanding me to get us Mojitos. Ethan's driving, and Nori's staying sober by proxy.

I stand at the bar, waiting for the drinks for Gwen and me. The bartender who took my order seems to have disappeared, and another one comes back, drinks in hand. He flashes me a grin, and I smile back and go to pay. But he touches my hand and says, "Don't worry about it."

I mumble thanks and grab the drinks. He grabs my arm, almost making me spill the glasses, and says loud enough for people around us to hear, "I get off at midnight."

"I'm here with someone."

"So?" He flashes another smile.

"I'm with a *woman*."

"Whatever." He slides a card over to me. "Here's my number."

I push it back and slap down a pile of cash. "No, thanks."

Jesus Christ, what's the deal with people today? Am I emitting some sort of gay vibe? At school I don't think I was hit on this much. At least not in one day. Weaving through the crowd to our table, I catch Gwen's eye and smile, but she doesn't return it. I set the drinks down. Nori sips her diet soda. Ethan plays with her hair, and he puts his hand on the back of her chair. He points his chin at Gwen. I turn. Her mouth is set in a kind of frown with her arms crossed.

Luckily, the music and conversations around us fill the silence at our table. The waitress comes to take our order, and we try to talk about that, but it dies too.

Screw it. I lean down and kiss her neck. There. Screw you, gay vibe.

And see that bag? Cat is out.

"They already know, Andy," Gwen says.

Nori and Ethan point to each other.

"You knew?"

"You knew!"

"But how?"

"I told both of them, separately." Gwen is expressionless, and that's when I really notice how red her eyes are and how dead her voice is.

The noise of the restaurant is deafening, and my neck feels hot. I rub Gwen's shoulder, but she inches away. She stands up and wobbles a bit because she's wearing ridiculously high wedges. I reach out to steady her, and she swats me away. Pissed for sure.

"I gotta get out of here, guys," she blurts. "I'm sorry."

Ethan and Nori stand up as she leaves.

"I think I need to talk to her first," I say.

They nod and sit back down. I follow the back of Gwen's long hair, weaving and bobbing between all the people and tables.

"Gwen!"

But she walks right out of the restaurant, which is on the beach but still a good few miles from the condo.

"Gwen." She has her shoes in her hands and is running. I have to jog to catch up to her as she walks further away from the boardwalk area, and I have to dodge a few small children with their parents and someone walking two dogs. Confusion fills me. If she told Nori and Ethan, then what's the problem? Everything should be okay now.

Nothing is ever that simple or logical with my Gwen.

"Gwen! Come on!" I run faster.

When I'm inches from her, I reach out, but she stops and without turning around she says, "This is totally and completely fucked up. I don't know what kind of bullshit you are pulling with me or with yourself, but—" She wipes away her tears angrily. "—But I can't be your great experiment. Again."

Gwen is breathing hard when I walk right up to her and grab her by the shoulders. "What the hell are you talking about?"

"Why are you doing this to me?" She pushes my hands off her.

"Doing what?"

"Using me, ME of all people, to try out whatever

the hell is going on with you?"

I step back.

"I read your journal. I know all about how you are trying to 'decide.' " She puts air quotes around the word. "Oh, and that bartender. Come on!"

I take another step back.

"And, I want *that*." She turns and points to Nori and Ethan. "*That*'s what I want. Not this weird, confusing…I cannot compete with bartender guy. I do not have a dick."

Ah! That's what this is about. "I don't want his dick. I don't want you to have a dick. I want you. I love—"

"Do not say it, Andrew."

Andrew. Emphasis on my entire name. The fact that she has used my entire name makes the tiny hairs on my neck stand at attention. We're staring right into each other's pupils and hers are huge.

"I swear to God, you won't be able to take it back. Right now you can. We can go back. I'll move out; I'll move home until I go to med school. We can pretend none of this ever happened."

No. No. "Goddamn it! This is not about body parts!"

She pauses for a minute but then fires. "And what happens if we do this? What about when you stop liking vagina and breasts? What happens when I don't turn you on anymore? When a really hot guy catches your eye and your gay switch kicks in?"

"Gay switch?"

She turns and starts to march away, but she stops, turns back, and marches right back up to me. She puts her finger right under my nose. "What I really want to know from you is, why me? Me, of all the people in your life, why the hell would you pick the best friend who has always and forever loved you the most? Why?"

"Pick you for what?"

"To conduct this great experiment. To figure it all out. To decide what you like."

"Stop calling us an experiment!" I stop and step toward her.

But she holds her hands up. "Remember. I was your first great experiment and that went well, right? So, don't." Then she blows out a hard breath and announces, "Man, this is fucking déjà vu."

"You read my journal?" It finally fully hits me, but I'm more curious than angry.

"You were keeping things from me. That you were dating women. That you are still trying to figure out who you are."

I throw my hands up in the air. "What do you want from me, Gwen?"

A couple walks between us and for a moment Gwen is out of view. When they're gone, she glares at me and crosses her arms. "The truth, Andrew. I would love the truth."

"I've told you the truth!"

"Who's George, Andrew?"

"Stop calling me that!"

"Who the fuck is George, Andrew? Is he your boyfriend? I mean, if you are truly bisexual, it would make sense that you'd be double dipping."

The sounds of other people walking by and talking stop all at once. I feel the burning of other people staring at us.

I throw my hands up again. George. Really. She's worried about George. I thought she read my journal. Obviously not carefully. I almost laugh but instead turn and walk away.

She doesn't follow me.

People pass by me smiling, laughing, or holding the hands of children or leashes of dogs. I turn back down toward the small street where the restaurant is and notice the sun lowering in the pink sky.

A heavy pain settles in. *"You and I both know that doesn't mean anything."* Ah, but it does. I'm not that guy. I'm not Bill because I'm not confused nor am I denying who I am.

The bartender's smile. Gwen's crossed arms. Ethan and Nori, helpless. Mouths open. Heads shaking.

Once again, I've broken Gwen's heart.

But I don't entirely understand. I didn't want the bartender. Yes, I recognized he was hot—hot as all hell. But so what? Doesn't mean I want him.

I love her. But she doesn't trust me.

I see Nori outside the restaurant, her hand over her mouth as Ethan gets down on one knee.

Oh, man.

Chapter 8

ETHAN

I look up at Nori, her dark hair spilling over her bare shoulders and brushing across her face as she looks down at me, her hand touching her lips in surprise and pleasure that I'm at her feet, tying her shoe. I pause after I make a bow on her ridiculously intricate sandals that make her look like a Jesus follower, and I wish to God I had that ring because this is a pretty beautiful moment. Her face is relaxed and happy, far away from how stressed out we both were just last night. All is good—she took the pill. We can move on, and I can tell her my plans. God, do I want to tell her my plans. I rub her smooth leg and stand up and kiss her on the lips.

She kisses me back for a moment but then pulls away, knits her brow, and scans the scene around us. Lamppost lights give only a little light to the area and neither of us sees Gwen or Andy.

"They're gone." She plays with a strand of hair and then lets it drop. "So you knew, and I knew, but they didn't want to tell us."

We don't say anything for a moment.

Then I break the silence. "It's kind of weird."

"You mean that they are together?"

"She says they aren't together."

"She told you that?"

"Yeah."

She pauses. "When did all this come out?"

"Last night she told me." I stop and wait. *Don't ask me when.*

She looks distracted. "She told me this morning. But Andy hasn't talked to you or me about it. Why didn't they just walk in yesterday and say, 'Hey, by the way, we're dating'?"

I don't want to say too much else. She may figure out that I was out last night smoking. These little secrets creep up on you. Time to switch gears, switch to the *us* gear. Forget the drama of another couple—wait, are they a couple?

Right now, it doesn't matter. All that matters is us.

I take her hand. "Maybe we should just wait. I bet they caught up with each other and are talking it out."

We sit on a bench and watch couples stroll by. Old couples, young couples. Single people. Hipsters. People in Christmas sweaters that belong up north. I rub the top of her hand with my thumb. The skin is velvet. She leans into me and sighs. I shift and put my arm around her and continue to hold her hand.

"We haven't had a chance to really talk." I don't want to bring up the broken condom, the stupid pill, our friends. I've got an agenda. Something I need to talk about before I get back down on my knee and propose. "Graduation isn't that far away," I say softly.

In front of us more people stroll by, arm in arm. Smiling, talking. Nori watches them and stiffens up—except for her hand, which goes limp in mine. I get it. Who the hell isn't nervous about graduating? College is this safe bubble, an illusion of adulthood, but not the real thing. I know that.

"Are you nervous?" In all of our talking while I

was in Peru, she avoided any conversation about what her plans were after graduation. I don't really even know what she's thinking.

She doesn't reply, her body still rigid under my hands.

Fuck it. I'm launching in. I want her to know I'm thinking about our future. Maybe she's worried because she doesn't know I actually have a plan. "I'm applying for teaching jobs back in Rhode Island." Why won't she look at me? The dam I've built over the last few months bursts, all my plans fly out. "I mean, I *will be* applying. I have to student teach and then take the teacher test, but my advisor says I can start applying anyway, that most schools will accept a letter stating that my certification is pending."

Still nothing. Nervous energy forces a whole bunch of shit that I've been thinking out. "I'm thinking we should get an apartment in Newport. Right downtown. And you could teach yoga anywhere—get that five-hundred-hour training you want." I stop. Why the hell isn't she nodding, interrupting me with her plans, her thoughts? Before Peru, she'd talked about more yoga training and someday opening up her own yoga studio…but never mentioning where or how. I also saw a stack of grad school brochures last year at the end of the semester, and I asked her about it, and she said she wasn't sure.

Something isn't right.

Then, she tightens her hand around mine, opens her mouth to speak, and I see that her eyes are wide, the pupils large. My Nori is anxious. What? What is it?

And at that moment we hear, "Ethan! Nori!"

Andy emerges out of the dimly lit darkness. He's

out of breath.

We both stand up.

"What happened?" Nori asks.

"She took off, and I chased her. When I caught her, she told me off. Mumbled something about 'getting the hell out of here' and 'she doesn't need to be some great experiment.' " He throws his hands up, like he doesn't know what to do.

Nori says, "She's stuck on what happened in high school." We look at each other, knowing all too well how that can happen.

Andy rubs his head with his hand over and over. "I can't change what happened. I can't change the past."

"No," Nori says, "but could you explain to her what has happened over these past few years? The whole dating women again thing."

He's silent, just rubbing his hair over and over.

"Listen, not that I personally care one way or another, Andy, 'cause you're my boy no matter who you sleep with or date, but why haven't you at the very least told Nori or Gwen?"

He throws his hands up in the air. "Because I didn't know myself what I wanted, or, rather, I didn't know that what I wanted was different from what most people wanted."

"What does that even mean?" Nori asks.

"I think it means you're bi and that most people don't accept that. Probably harder to be bi than gay," I offer, surprised at my own wisdom but happy to offer it.

They both look at me in surprise. "Wow," they chorus.

"What? You're surprised that I'm so enlightened?"

We all laugh, and the tension deflates.

Our laughing quiets, and we hear only soft voices from passing people and cicadas buzzing. Nori grabs Andy's hand and says, "I just don't want our friendships to get ripped apart again. We need each other. I need all of you."

Suddenly, both Andy and I hug Nori. This all is far deeper than what's being said by any of us.

"Maybe we're all freaking out about graduation looming. About the fact that this is the last time we'll all be together while still in college," Andy says.

"Hey, we'll always have Florida. Right?" She looks from me to Andy. "We'll always come here for Christmas at least?" Why does she sound panicked? In theory, if Andy stays in the Northeast for law school and Gwen goes to med school anywhere in New England, and the two of us move in together, we will see each other more than once a year. My chest tightens. What is she not telling me?

Nori detangles herself from us and sinks back down onto the bench.

She looks up at Andy and says, "In high school, you broke Gwen's heart. You made her think something was growing between the two of you and then you told her you wanted to be friends…then she finds out you're gay. All of that felt like a betrayal—a lie. It crushed her."

"But by the time we were seniors, the three of us were all friends again. And she had Heyward—"

"Heyward!" Nori scoffs. Even I roll my eyes.

Andy keeps going. "But we doubled for prom. You and Gwen and me and that guy Jim."

"That was a double date by default because Heyward refused to go to prom." I remind him then add, "You honestly, this whole time, thought Gwen was over you?"

Andy is expressionless, silent, and his eyes are big. He sits next to Nori and then I follow.

"She feels betrayed." Nori touches his arm. "That the two of you rebuilt not only a friendship but you become the bestest of friends, closer in many ways than she and me or you and me. Then, you betray her again."

"How is my loving her a betrayal?"

I hold my hand up. "Andy, you gotta start looking at this from her point of view."

He folds his arms. "I would love for someone to look at this through my point of view."

More silence.

I try one more time because I actually think I understand this. "Apparently, you've been dating women throughout college—right?"

He nods.

"And apparently, you've decided to leave out that piece of information from any conversation you've had with her—actually with any of us."

Nori tugs at Andy's arm. "Listen to me. Personally, I don't care who you love or how you love but what I do feel is left out. You've been struggling, obviously, and I just wonder if we are all so close, why didn't you turn to me—to any of us?"

Andy's face is a red and sweat beads dot his forehead. "Coming out is hard. Coming out the first time, with the expectations of my father, of my friends…I know you all didn't care, but saying you like guys changes your friendships with guys—except you, Ethan."

"We made out before, so technically I'm a little bi,

too," I crack and then wait to see if my joke is totally inappropriate to the moment, but after a beat, the two of them laugh and punch me in the arm.

"Here's the deal. When you say you're bi, you're a circus freak, like you're the bearded lady or the two-headed man. In many ways, right now, Gwen is treating me that way because she's like, *How does that work*? Being bi is more of a *thing* than being gay because most people say, 'I don't get it. How can you like both?' And they're really talking about genitalia and not people."

I wish I had something wise and smart to say, but I don't because I think he's right.

Nori shakes her head. "I don't and never have defined you by your gay or non-gayness. I love you for you, and your sexuality has never been a factor. You, you make it a factor."

"That's like saying Black people make their blackness a factor when, in fact, white people do so by ignoring it and by the guilt they feel for what they feel about it."

"Huh?"

"And, in high school, hell, even throughout college, you guys are always pressuring me to go to Pride parades and events. Just like my mom."

"That's 'cause we wanted to support you!"

"Oh, come on, it's also because it's cool to have the 'gay friend.' "

I stand up. I have no idea what has just happened. All I wanted to do was have a mother-effing moment with my girlfriend, so I can lay out the cards and fucking propose to her, and now, this is going all Gender, Sexuality, and Race 101 on me. Which, by the way, was a pretty awesome class.

Nori takes Andy's hand and says, "I don't give a shit about your gayness but more about you. No matter what your sexual preference is, I love you and support you." She rubs her eyes and watching the two of them is making me a little teary too.

Andy sniffles and wipes his eyes with the back of his hand. "I love Gwen. I want Gwen. My past dating history is my past. I've liked people who happen to be men. But Gwen transcends gender for me. I didn't know this when I was in high school, and I didn't know myself. But now I do. I was so fucking depressed in high school and busy hating myself that I didn't know what I wanted at all."

I reach over and grip Andy's shoulder. "Dude, I get it. I get hating yourself and not knowing what you want. Gay, straight, or bi doesn't matter. That hating yourself shit is relatable."

We all sit silently, Nori between us, one of her hands in mine on my lap and the other in Andy's hand on his leg. The scene in front of us is the same—Christmas-sweatered Floridians, retirees out on the town, some with dogs on leashes, others young families with babies in baby carriers strapped to their bodies. We watch them all for a few minutes. I take Nori's hand and lean over to say to Andy, "A-game, it's time to go."

And just then Nori's phone *omms*. She takes it out of the tiny purse that's around her shoulders. She scans the screen silently, and I lean over and so does Andy. We read it out loud together. *"leaving don't worry call you when I land."*

"Fuck." We all say it at the same time.

****

GWEN

Tears blur my vision as I elbow my way through the crowds of people. I keep going until in front of me is the long stretch of beach that will eventually lead me back to the condo. The sun is almost completely swallowed by the horizon, and the ocean is flat. No foamy rolling waves, and the pinks are shimmering off the ocean. I hurry, like I'm back in Providence trying to get across town in time for dinner and *Dr. Who* with Andy.

Andrew.

I wipe all the tears out of my eyes as soon as the condo is in my view. After I find the spare key under the mat, I go inside, and start packing, only pausing to scratch Delilah's ears and then take her out for a pee. We hustle back inside, and I grab my tablet and within minutes I have a flight booked and a cab on the way. Delilah puts her head in my lap as if to say, *I know you have to go, but I wish you wouldn't.*

I've never been one to be persuaded by cuteness. Though Delilah is tempting me.

Instead I tap out a text to Nori:

—leaving don't worry call you when I land—

And then I hear a car pull up. Must be the cab. I kiss Delilah one more time before slinging my purse over my shoulder and grabbing my bag. I start to open the door but outside the window I see—

A baby blue corvette. Top down.

I put everything down and open the door. Delilah darts between my legs and runs outside. Up pops Ruby from the driver's seat, hair in a gauzy purple scarf, sunglasses covering her face. She waves and then reaches out to rub Delilah's head. I run down the steps, leaving my stuff in the doorway.

"Hey, girl!" Ruby says, cutting the engine and getting out of the car. "Where's the gang? I figured you guys would all be out getting loaded! Unless you're still recovering from today." She winks and then looks behind me and sees my stuff.

"Are you going somewhere?" she asks.

I busy myself with scratching Delilah's ears.

"Dan just asked me to stop by and check to make sure Delilah wasn't hanging from chandeliers or you hadn't blown up the place with the microwave. And to give you this." She waves a key in the air but then takes a step toward the condo, her eyes boring into me. "Everything okay?"

I avoid her gaze. "Everything's fine. No blown-up ovens or anything."

Delilah licks my fingers.

"I'm just going home." I keep my voice light.

Ruby takes off her enormous sunglasses. Then waves the key in front of my nose. "What about the trip tomorrow?"

I don't reply and continue to rub Delilah's head. She sits obediently.

"Why are you leaving?" She tucks the sunglasses into her cleavage. Eyeing me with total suspicion.

"Because…I. I need…to finish my applications." I meet her gaze this time. Hoping she doesn't know that med school applications are long, long done.

She shakes her head. "This is about you and Andy."

Delilah has walked over to a tree and is busy taking a pee against it.

"Sweetie, are you going to avoid everything in life

that could potentially break your heart?" Ruby strokes my head. "Sounds like you're already on that midnight train to get the fuck out of here before you've given Andy a chance."

"Didn't you tell Nori to sleep with her hot Swami? To live a little? Shouldn't I be doing that, too?" I feel her hand pause on my head.

"My advice is not prescriptive," Ruby says and lets her hand fall from my hair. "It's tailored to the situation. And I'm a firm believer in doing what scares you…especially when the fear is all inside your head."

I think of my last break up. Two years ago. Fucking cheating Heyward. I packed my shit in the middle of the night, and as I crawled out of the window of his living room, the house alarms went off. The cops arrived as I fell to the ground. Heyward, sleepy-eyed and tousled, was *très* confused. After a brief discussion with the cops, Heyward actually considered having them arrest me because he said it was a crime for me to steal his heart when he was sleeping in the middle of the night.

I find myself telling her the story.

"What happened with Heyward?" Ruby asks, unwrapping the scarf from her head and tying it around her neck.

Delilah is sitting under the tree, rubbing herself against the grass.

"Nothing. I left." I watch Delilah curl up under the tree. "In the middle of the night. That was it. *Fini*."

She looks very sorry for me right now and that only makes me feel more depressed and more wrong. Am I about to walk out on Andy before I even really give it a chance?

"Listen, I"—she touches her own heart—"took a risk. You have a wild girl like me who's never settled down, never been married, never raised kids, and Dan, don't mess with the military man. Has a kid. You know *we* took a chance. It's not always perfect, but we love each other, and you and Andy…you won't know for sure unless you take the risk."

Andy.

I cringe at those last words I said to Andy. *Double dipping. Andrew.*

"I'm an asshole," I tell her.

"No, honey. You aren't. I think you should go unpack your bags. Try to work this all out."

"It might be too late. I intentionally fucked with Andy." I swallow more tears and whisper, "I asked the bartender, before Ethan and Andy showed up, to hit on Andy when he came to buy our drinks." I drop my head in shame. "I wanted some kind of test that I could see right in front of me."

Ruby lifts my chin and looks me directly in the eye. "Everyone makes mistakes when they are afraid and in love."

"All you have to do is apologize and be honest," she adds. "Everyone appreciates honesty." She lets go of my chin.

I nod. "Give me that key. We're going to the park."

****

Ruby takes Delilah, so I sit down solo on the front steps after they leave. When the cab arrives, I pay him for his trouble and send him on his way. I call the airline and cancel my flight, rescheduling it for the day Andy and I are supposed to leave.

I feel lonely without Delilah. I check my phone and

then I hear Nori's footsteps, light and quick.

"Thank God you didn't leave!"

I don't stand up when they all come through the house to the front stoop. Silently, one by one, they sit down. Nori on one side, Andy on the other, and Ethan on the top step.

"I'm sorry," I say to Andy and put a hand on his knee.

"Don't go," Nori whispers to me.

"I'm not going anywhere," I whisper back.

We all sit silently, the four-headed monster. I tell them how Ruby stopped by. Remind them of the amusement park. Give Ethan the key to the townhouse Ruby's client said we could use. "What kind of monster would miss out on the greatest amusement park ever?"

They all laugh. I stand up first and reach for Andy's hand. He looks up at me with bloodshot eyes, and I stroke his face and whisper, "I'm sorry that I was kind of a monster before."

"Kind of?" Ethel says. I punch him in the arm, and then the four of us link arms and go inside.

Chapter 9

ETHAN

From the kitchen where Nori and I make coffee, I watch Andy and Gwen talk in low voices on the couch.

Nori leans into me and whispers, "Hey, thanks for tying my shoes before. That was the cutest thing. And kind of hot."

I laugh. "Taking care of my lady. Don't want you tripping all over yourself. Although, I know I have that kind of effect on you."

"All this mindplay, Ethan, you know what it does to me." With the distance between when I was gone, we would call our sexy phone calls "mindplay" as opposed to foreplay.

I think of the months of mindplay when I was in South America. What about when you've been mindfucked by a pregnancy scare? How do you get back to where you were before?

Fuck mindplay. I think I just want play. I put my hand around Nori's waist and pull her closer and let my lips barely touch hers. She breathes warm air into me. I make a growly noise, and she laughs and growls back. My tongue parts her lips and slides into her mouth, and she takes it all the way in. I grind my hips against hers, and she responds by opening her legs and grinding into me. The fabric of her dress is so thin, I can feel the heat between her thighs. This about does me in. My hands slide down to her ass and cup it. We kiss and move against each other until the beep from the coffee maker interrupts us. She doesn't pull away though. She moves back and slides her hands to the front of my shorts, skimming the waistband. "You can't do that," I whisper, feeling drunk in a totally sober way. "Not here. Not now." But she makes a *mmmmmhmmm* noise. Without breaking eye contact, she slides one hand all the way in and wraps her hand around me. Her tongue is in my ear, darting in and out.

Holy mother-fucking shit.

Then she releases me and pulls her hand out.

"What…?"

I automatically put my hand over my dick and shift it into place. But there is no hiding the boner I have.

Nori's devil smile makes me want to grab her, lift her dress right up, and stick it in bareback. Considering all we've been through, definitely not a good idea.

I lean back into the counter to catch my breath and calm down. I watch Nori pull out the coffee cups, search for a sugar holder and creamer. Her dress rides up a little as she reaches to the top shelf. Her thighs are golden from the sun and her hair is down and long, like waves of chocolate. This woman is gold and sunshine. She's my light. Corny shit comes to my mind when we are together.

She roots around the pantry, probably for something else to add to the tray. She finds a small vase and pops a single flower in it that she picked on the way back to the house. She tucks a strand of loose hair behind her ear, and all I can picture is her doing that for me in our own house, arranging snacks for us, for our kids, for a movie night.

The hot almost-hand job moment before and these little, normal things make me want to drop to my knees and propose to her. When we left the restaurant, she reminded me that we needed to get some soy milk for breakfast, and I nearly dropped right there. The sexiest thing to me is she and I playing house, except I don't want to play anymore. We've been playing for the past four years at school. I want our own. I want every day, with no breaks during vacations.

I would have proposed when I bent down to tie her shoe if I'd had the ring in my pocket.

She catches me watching her and smiles. I lean over and kiss her lips lightly. "I can't wait to watch you do this shit every day."

Her smile stiffens a little, but then she gives me a quick kiss before she says brightly, "Coffee, anyone?"

I follow her back out into the living room, where Andy and Gwen sit with both of his hands in her lap.

Nori sets the tray down, and I start pouring coffee into each mug, the smell strong. Nori sits across from Gwen and Andy and crosses her legs, revealing thigh and a little panty. She's been wearing her hair down a lot, which she knows I love, and she tosses it out of her face before taking a sip of coffee. Shit, I really want to rip the dress off her. Easy buddy, I adjust myself and sit down next to Nori on the loveseat with my coffee.

Andy holds Gwen's hand, and she says to Nori, "Turns out George is Andy's shrink."

Nori says, "Ah, that makes sense."

"George?" I ask.

"Don't ask. Doesn't matter." Gwen kisses the back of Andy's hand.

I slurp my coffee too loudly, and they all look at

mc and laugh, and I glance distractedly down at Nori's crossed, tan legs, smooth and silky.

Nori uncrosses her legs, flashing me a little of her upper thigh, making me squirm even more. "I love you both. I just want to say that."

Awkward vibes dance around us.

I take a stab and say, "And like I told you the other night, Gwen, 'people can be bi.' "

Andy shoots me a what-the-fuck look.

I stop talking. Gwen shakes her head.

"Was that the night you guys snuck out to smoke?" Nori asks and winks at me.

I've decided to sip my coffee and choke mid-sip.

"I have my ways." She winks again. "I woke up when you got out of bed. I saw you leave and watched you go outside. Saw the little orb of your cigarette butt."

Caught!

Andy glares at Gwen. "Are you smoking again?"

"Hey, not just me." She points to Nori. "She tried hookah today."

"No way!" Andy's expression is total shock. Eyebrows to his hairline.

"Gwen!"

"Now you're corrupting Nori?" he says.

"No! I'm not!" Gwen's exasperation is completely like a kid getting caught by Dad. She adds with a sly smile, "She's already corrupt."

"You smoked from a hookah?" I'm a little shocked at Nori smoking anything. "I thought you were getting manicures?"

"Apparently, this is a regular Friday night thing for Ruby and your dad."

Now I'm really shocked. Military Dad? I guess Ruby does get him to loosen up a little.

"So, Ruby brought us to their favorite place to hookah!" Nori continues and pushes a strand of hair out of her face. So pretty when she does that.

"Don't worry, Ethel. She coughed and hated it. It doesn't matter."

"You're right it doesn't. We were talking about you, Gwen. Jesus, you're trying to become a doctor." Andy turns to us. "When she first moved in with me, she was smoking a pack a day. Had to do that nebulizer thing practically every night. And you smelled like a friggin' ashtray. Do you want to wind up back on the nebulizer?"

"Yes, Andy, that's exactly what I want. In fact, I'd like to wind up in an iron lung." She crosses her arms and purses her lips.

"Do they even have those anymore?" he asks.

"Actually, they do. In rare cases of—"

"Guys!" Nori says.

Andy and Gwen stop.

"Look at the two of you." Nori leans forward. "You do love each other. Unconditionally. Beyond the label gay or straight." And then she adds, "Or bi."

They don't say anything. Just some blinking.

"Listen…" I try again, putting my mug on the coffee table. "We all know that people switch teams all the time." That's what I was going to say before.

"That's supposed to make me—us—feel better?" Andy asks.

"Uh." I look at Nori.

She puts her hand on my knee and says to Andy, "I think Ethan is saying that sexuality can be on a spectrum." She nods to me, and I nod back. "Right?"

No one says anything.

As we fall silent, Gwen nibbles on a nail.

"Gwen," Andy says, taking her hand from her mouth and putting it on his knee. "I'm sorry about high school. I know that's what you keep thinking about. But I didn't want to drag you into it all. And I needed you as a friend more than anything else at that time. I was a kid."

I think of our conversation last night and this; those words should finally break this wall that Gwen has up. I watch her face flush.

Nori and I exchange glances. "Gwen, we all have to let go of high school. Look at us. If I hadn't let go of all that shit, Ethan and I wouldn't be together."

Andy takes her hand again and holds it. "I'm not confused any more. All it means is that the pool of prospective applicants is wider for me than someone who identifies as straight."

She nods. Wall is crumbling.

"And I love you. I want you."

She stiffens and sighs. "I don't know why, but I can't get my head around the sex part of this."

"I wish you would understand that this is about so much more than sex and body parts." Andy sighs.

Another loud silence.

I launch in. "I'll admit, I don't understand how a dude can want to have sex with another dude but also want to have sex with a woman. Guys and girls are completely different. A girl is all soft and smooth and a guy is—you know—we're kind of rough and hairy."

Crickets. Eyes wide from the three of them. And then one giggle, and another, and another. Like we're freshmen in high school again, from all of them. At least that didn't offend Andy. I continue, "I don't completely understand being bi and maybe you don't either, Gwen. But what does any of that matter? I think you love who you love. You want who you want. A-game here wants Gwen. Gwen wants A-game. So?"

"Very profound, Ethel," Gwen says.

I stand up and curtsy, which makes everyone laugh again.

Andy nudges her and says quietly, "I don't think sexuality can be confined, at least for me."

Nori and I sit all the way back into the couch. I take her hand.

"When did you really know this, A-game?" I think I know the answer.

"That night, freshman year. In the hot tub." He closes his eyes. "Does that freak you out, Ethan?"

I consider this, rub my chin, and wait a minute before saying, "Nope. I told you if we kissed, then in my memory, you have really soft lips."

This lets the air out of the tension in the room again as we laugh.

"But it's taken years for me to really accept it and really know it," Andy says quietly.

We're all silent for a few moments.

I watch Andy watching Gwen as he says, "That guy at the restaurant who hit on me, did I find him attractive? Yes. Did I want to run off with him? Did I think to myself, 'Right! Dudes! This is what I like, not girls. The jig is up!' No. Absolutely not."

She pauses, sips more coffee, and says, "I get it. I get it. But I still think that us being together…" She blows air out and thinks for a minute. "I can't help but wonder if any of this would have happened if I wasn't living with you, sleeping in your bed, being with you all the time."

Nori bites her lip. Apparently, she thought of this, too.

And based on the look that has flashed across Andy's face, Gwen just struck a nerve.

This is one of those moments where as much as I want to rush in with some kind of joke or more of my cents, I think silence is better. Silence and then getting the hell out of the room to let them talk this one out alone.

Too late. Gwen and Andy are looking at Nori.

"Is that what you think, too?" Gwen asks, putting her coffee down.

"I don't know." Nori takes her hand from mine.

Gwen leans forward. "No, tell me, you obviously think something."

"This isn't about me." Lame, lame cop out. Something is going on in her pretty head. Then she says, "This is about you two."

"Bullshit," Gwen spits out.

"Gwen, I don't want to get in between you two—" Nori starts.

But Gwen has that scowl. "I knew you were being way too careful today."

"No. I wasn't." Nori is wringing her hands. I know she feels helpless.

"Be a friend now and be honest and answer my questions."

"I—"

"Say it."

Nori sighs loudly and closes her eyes and blurts, "I

think it's possible you guys are hooking up because it's convenient."

Andy wrinkles his brow.

I rub my head. *Oh, no. Nori, what are you doing?*

She looks like she knows she has said too much but that it's too late.

"You both have been alone for a while." She looks at Andy. "You haven't had a relationship since the breakup with whatshisname."

"Shane," Andy and Gwen say at the same time.

I remember him vaguely. Kind of a douchebag.

"Right, Shane." Nori stops. "And then Gwen moves in, and you know how much she adores you, Andy. And you, Gwen, haven't been with anyone really significant since Heyward."

"Are you saying I'm using Gwen?"

"No! No."

Everyone is on edge, literarily; we moved to sitting at the edge of our seats. Even me. I turn to face Nori. Waiting for the rest.

Nori's eyes are wide and looking right at me. "You know what? I'm sorry, Gwen, Andy. I might be just projecting my own shit onto you two."

Wait, she's talking to me now?

"Like how you want us to move in together," she says, and I notice that she's rubbing her forefinger over her thumb. Nervous. Trying to calm herself. "I just worry that maybe we need to explore the world as individuals. You have, but I haven't."

"Huh?" This comes from me.

"And I guess, with all four of us about to enter this huge transition period of graduating, I do wonder if we cling to each other because we are afraid to get out there." Nori takes a deep breath, looking around at each of us. "Maybe we all need to get out and see the world a little."

We all fall still and silent. What the fuck is she saying? "Is this coming from that fucking Swami Nick? Who calls themselves Swami fucking Nick? That fucking guy."

"That's not Swami. It's me!" Nori says.

Andy pipes in. "I think the reality is that it's scarier to stay with the people who have known you for a long time. Most of the people we know from high school have not stayed together like we did. Everyone bails when things get difficult or when things change, and we've never abandoned each other. If anything, that proves how courageous we really are."

Nori stays silent.

The sound of the ocean is all we hear for a minute and then Nori says, "I'm going to India. To study yoga."

"What?" This is from all of us.

"I've been wanting to deepen my practice. And seeing how much Peru helped you grow…" She has stopped rubbing her thumb.

I'm standing up now, and my entire body feels covered in a prickly sweat.

"I was going to tell you." She stands too and reaches for me, but I step back.

Andy stands up and grabs Gwen's hand. "Let's go for a walk, Gwen." Then he turns to Nori. "Funny how you said you didn't want to say how you felt about us because you didn't want to make it about you, but actually, you just did."

Gwen gives Nori a long look before she and Andy

leave. He doesn't even look back at Nori.

I throw my hands in the air. "What are you talking about?"

"I leave in a month." Her voice is too calm.

"To India?"

"Yes, to India."

"Like across the globe?"

She nods. "I'm finished with everything but my thesis, so I got special permission to work via email with my advisor. I'm going to complete my yoga teacher training. It's for a year." No emotion in her voice, but her eyes tell me she's nervous. I tear mine away and sit back down and notice my hands are shaking, but she sits next to me and grabs them. "This is all going to work out great, and don't worry, we'll be together. I finish in April. It's not quite a full year." She squeezes my hands, but I don't feel it.

I can't compute this all.

****

NORI

My heart is thudding, and my hands are clammy. Part of me wants to stop this conversation and run after Gwen and Andy.

Guilt.

I'm an asshole to them, to Ethan.

But first, I have to fix this, with Ethan, right now. "I wanted to wait until Andy and Gwen left, but I couldn't hold it in anymore."

"I just got back from being gone for a whole semester, Nori."

We're sitting with our knees touching. He moves back slightly but enough for me to no longer feel the pressure of his knee against mine.

"Don't be mad." I'm pleading. "I applied to this program and talked it over with my advisor back in the early part of the semester, but the yoga center didn't let me know until two weeks ago." I grab his hands, but they hang limp in my own. "Honey, they only accept twenty-five people into the program and five get full scholarships. I got a scholarship. It's an incredible honor and opportunity."

He pulls his hands away, and I see they're shaking.

"Listen"—I plow ahead, a surge of energy darts through me—"I did this so that I wouldn't regret not doing it. Like you said about going to Peru. And then once I come back, we can move in together like we've planned to."

"But we haven't planned anything." His voice is small. "Every time I've brought it up you say nothing."

"It was because I was trying to figure this all out."

"Or is it what you said before to Gwen and Andy? You think us being together is some kind of default." He finally makes eye contact with me.

"What?"

"You said it." He raises his voice now. "Basically, that we are together because it's comfortable."

"No, no. That's not what I meant. I meant…" I sigh. "I meant that I want to be able to explore and take a risk and do the thing I love. The thing that's my passion."

He stands up. "I get that you are afraid of the next step with us." He talks like he didn't hear what I just said. "It's not like I'm not, but to run off to India to avoid the next step."

Now I stand up. "What are you talking about?"

"I know you're afraid to move in with me. But

what I can't figure out is why. We've been rock solid over the past three years. Things couldn't be better. We love each other. We have fun." He stops, and I swear those are tears in his beautiful blue eyes. "Why do you want to leave me?"

"How can you even say that to me when you are the one who left me to go to Peru! And it's not like we had a discussion about *that*."

Ethan becomes Buddha still.

Uh, oh. Did I mean that?

I kind of did.

"When you got into the program you just said that you were going. Period, end of story. No discussion. You know what I did? I said that is awesome, and I shut my mouth about myself even though I was dying *dying* inside about losing you again, Ethan. I worried that you going away would mean you might, I don't know, meet someone else. I had no idea, but I dealt with it. I shut up and never ever told you how scared I was. I trusted you, Ethan. I trusted you, and you sound like you don't trust me."

I'm out of breath. Like I finished the hardest run. Up a hill. Up a mountain. Adrenaline pulses through me.

Ethan hasn't moved. Not even to blink, and he's not shaking any more. He is grave, the weight of everything I've said has fallen right on top of him.

Finally, he rubs his face with his hands and when he stops, we lock eyes.

And I step a centimeter toward him. We're almost lip-to-lip. I curl my fingers around the front of his shirt and whisper, "I love you." And then I kiss him softly, but he doesn't kiss me back. I kiss him again and again until he pushes his tongue all the way into my mouth. It's so forceful, but I get it. I suck on his lips. He pulls back and glides his tongue along the bottom of my mouth. I kiss him back deeply. He grabs my ass and breaks the kiss and whispers, "I love you, too," and pulls my dress up. His fingers slip into my underwear and press into my butt. I open my legs.

"Bedroom," I say into his mouth.

"Not yet," he says and slides his fingers toward the front of me.

"We can't stay here—"

"Shhh." His finger goes inside me. I buckle, and he pulls me back up. Can't take it anymore. Pushing him backward, we fall—me on top—onto the couch, and I reach behind and put my hand over his and guide him in the right rhythm. He lets me, and then stops, pulls his hand away and rolls me onto my back. Shoving my dress up, he slides down between my legs and moves my underwear to the side.

"Ethan, we have to go to the bedroom—"

He runs one hand up under my dress that's hiked up to my chest. He cups one boob and mumbles something. I have stopped thinking coherent thoughts.

He stops. Fixes my dress and rolls up to stand, tottering a little. I see his enthusiasm poking out of his shorts.

I grab at it. He pushes my hand against it.

"Bedroom," he says and then lifts me up.

We stumble into the bedroom, and I go straight to the condom stash, knowing if we don't get that thing on now, we may have another problem on our hands, and I will be facing the family planning aisle again, and I'm not sure I can handle that.

He takes it from me and walks me backward onto the bed and in a fluid motion, his shorts are down, and the condom is rolling over him. I grab his butt and pull him toward me, and he reaches down and lifts my hips, sliding a pillow underneath. Even in these throes of the most intense passion we have ever had, he always thinks of me. I adjust the pillow.

"Ready?" he whispers.

"Yes, yes. Hurry."

He reaches down before sliding inside. I pull him down and kiss him, and as we kiss, he moves slowly until he is inside, and we begin to move together in that perfect rhythm.

****

I pull my dress down as Ethan sits at the edge of the bed.

"Are we good?" I ask, fluffing my hair.

"Yes." He glances back at me. "All contained."

I watch him stand up; his body ripples with the perfect amount of muscles. He goes into the bathroom. I lay back in the bed and close my eyes, letting the hum fill me up. I hear the water running and the toilet flush. He comes back out and joins me in bed, pulling the covers up and over us. His shoulders droop.

I cup his face and say, "I'm not scared of moving in with you. In fact, now that I know what I'm doing, I feel even better about coming back and taking the next step."

His eyes are red and glisten with tears. "I really didn't see this one coming."

I kiss him. Rub away one escaped teardrop. "Listen, we have another month together before I leave. Let's really enjoy it."

"It's a long time to be gone. To not be able to do this with you." He kisses me again. Slides a hand up under my dress and under the bra that we never took off. Tingles dart down my body.

"We can do it every single day over the next month," I whisper.

"Oh, it will be more than once a day," he says, pushing against me. Then he pulls back. "If going to India will make you happy, then we do it. But after this, we're never going to be separated for months at a time. Not even for days."

"Never," I promise him.

Chapter 10

ANDY

We walk along the sidewalk of the condo complex. The sun is almost completely down, but there's enough light in the sky. Gwen doesn't hold my hand and walks far from me.

Finally, I say, "Should we talk more?"

"No," she says. "Walk with me around the block." She talks to the sky, the back of her to me, when she says this.

Far away, birds chirp, and someone roars by on a motorcycle. I wish we were at a jazz bar downtown or listening to some obscure band at a club, leaning into each other and sharing a dirty margarita or a shot of whiskey and a cigar at one of those basement cigar bars. I wish we were running all over Providence, and I wish she would let me hold her hand.

We walk and walk, with her eventually right next to me. We pass houses with small picket fences, and continue past beds of brightly colored flowers, past palm trees and doors painted different pastel versions of the rainbow. Past cars and trucks and bikes left outside and a family getting out of their car. Her hand wraps around mine by the time we circle back to the condo. The whole time, all I want to do is stop Gwen and tell her I know she's afraid, but if we stop now, we will never know what we might be.

"Ruby says that no one says you have to be gay forever."

I don't say anything. Cicadas buzz around us.

"I just don't see myself as a category to check off," I say quietly. I'm trying to see this from her perspective, to be patient. My phone vibrates, and I check it. "Nori wants to know if we flew back home, or are we coming back to the condo."

"Why do I want to tell her to fuck off right now?"

I stop walking. "That was kind of a selfish move there, but maybe she just had to get it out."

She stops. "I didn't mean that about Nori. I'm pissed and jealous that she and Ethan's biggest problem is they barely have any friends because they're so into each other. And—*oooh*—big revelation, she's going off to study yoga in India."

"That's kind of a big deal," I say.

"Yeah, I know." She comes to me finally and lets me hold her.

Then she whispers into my chest, "I have to tell you something."

No more secrets today. Please.

"What is it?" I say, trying to keep my voice normal.

"I set you up. I paid that bartender to hit on you. It was a test."

I let it sink in, way deep past my heart and down into my gut and when it does, I push her away. I rub my forehead, see her out of the corner of my eye just standing, wide-eyed, shifting back and forth on her feet.

"I can't even." I try to calm my heart, but it's racing, so I burst out, "Seriously, Gwen! Seriously! What the fuck?" There goes all patience.

"I'm sorry!"

We stare at each other. The only thing between us now that all secrets are out is the darkness of the night.

"I want to let go of the past. But I'm finding things out just now. It's hard." She bites her lip, and her mouth quivers. My heart aches a little. I want to reach out to her, but I'm also pissed. Set me up? Who does that? She continues, with her voice shaking, "I completely gave up on you after you came out in high school, and it was so hard, so, so hard." She puts her hands over her face. The darkness and hum of nighttime noises surround us, and then I see her body shake. She's crying.

My anger melts. I watch her cry, and as I do, I finally understand what I did to her back then. Not that I meant to. Not that I was capable of anything else. Not even that I have regrets. But that it happened. I really broke that girl's heart.

I can't think of anything to say, so I walk to her and put my arms around her, and we just hold each other.

****

We don't talk about anything else as we walk back to the house. Ethan and Nori are canoodling on the couch in the living room. They both stand up. They have rumpled post-sex hair and bleary eyes. Nothing a little roll in the bed can't cure. I can't really smile or chuckle at my own thought. My whole body is sad and heavy.

"Hey." Ethan reaches out and does some awkward fist bump with me and then goes to do it with Gwen, who rolls her eyes at him—even after sobbing uncontrollably she's still got her spunk. She sits down. I follow.

Nori starts, "I'm sorry, guys. I have no idea why I said all that stuff except that I guess I have my own shit I'm dealing with."

"I know," I tell her.

Gwen is set in this pensive stare at the floor.

I don't have any idea what should come next.

Nori mouths, "Everything okay?"

I shrug.

Gwen, still staring at the floor, says, "I know I need to let go of the past."

Nori and Ethan look at each other, and Ethan asks, "Are you sure you guys don't want some privacy?"

"No, no," Gwen says.

"I guess we'll stay," Nori says, loaded with hesitation.

"I want to ask you some questions," Gwen says to me.

I nod but am definitely scared what she's going to ask.

"The bartender guy—I know I shouldn't have set it up—"

"You did what?" Nori says.

"I set it up." She drops her head again. "I know it was wrong."

Ethan opens his mouth to say something, but then Nori shakes her head.

"I know it was wrong. And I really am ashamed and sorry that I sunk to that level, but I can't help but wonder." She lifts her chin and turns to me. "Were you tempted?"

"Tempted?"

"To take his number? To hook up with him?"

"No!" My face is aflame now.

"So is your gay part in remission?"

"Remission?" The anger boils. I turn my head back up to her. "Being attracted to men is not a disease."

Ethan and Nori shift on the couch.

"That's not what I mean!" she says, her face red.

"What the hell *do* you mean?" The anger is about to shoot out of my eyes and ears.

Gwen blows air out and says, "I don't really understand how you can truly be attracted sexually to both men and women."

Nori leans forward like she is going to say something, but she doesn't.

I take some cleansing breaths, as Nori calls them. Then I make my voice really calm and say, "I have answered that question, it feels like, a million times. You just don't want to hear that, yes, it is possible to be attracted to both men and women." *Uh oh, I need some cleansing breaths again.*

Actually, forget it.

"But who the fuck cares, Gwen, if all I want is you!" Anger erupting all over.

No one responds.

I'm breathing hard. Actually we all are.

Then, Gwen says, "You had the hots for Ethel in high school, right?"

I can't stop the eye roll that I do. It's either that or punch something.

"Me?" Ethan sits up and points to himself.

"Yes, you, green eyes." Gwen has a kind of wild-eyed look when she says, "Tell me, check out Ethan, right now. Is he hot?"

This is ridiculous. *Fucking.* Ridiculous.

"Are you kidding me?" I say, red creeping up my cheeks.

No one says a thing.

"It's a valid question," Gwen says, folding her arms.

"Couldn't I ask you the same thing?" I snap back at her.

"Go ahead," she challenges me.

I roll my eyes again. "Do you think Ethan is hot?"

"Yes," Gwen says. I watch Nori and Ethan out of the corner of my eye, but they don't move. Gwen continues, "He's dreamy and cute but not my type. End of story."

"I feel the same way."

"Really?" Ethan sits up straight. "Thanks, man. Listen, if I were into guys, I'd say—back at you." He winks again and points his finger.

I have lost all words…but at least my anger recedes. Ethan is one good dude.

Gwen closes her eyes and sighs.

Nori starts to say something, but Ethan puts his hand over her mouth and says, "This is where we leave."

He stands up and reaches for Nori's hand. She pauses for a moment, shoots me a long and sympathetic look, and then they walk out.

Once they're gone, I sit back and close my eyes.

Gwen flops back and sighs again. "I have a question."

"Go ahead." I keep my eyes closed. This is exhausting.

"Butt sex." Now I open my eyes. Her hands are over her face.

This makes me laugh, even though I'm still pissed at her.

"What about it?" I ask her.

"Is that something you like?" She peers at me between her fingers.

I open her hands up and put them on her lap. "I've done it, but it isn't something I particularly like." I want to tell her that some heterosexual men also like butt play, but this isn't the time to get into all of that.

"Hmmmm."

"There's more than one way for two guys to have sex. Gwen, come on, you don't know this?"

"You mean blow jobs?" She stares at me with her mouth almost to the floor.

"Why is this a surprise to you?" I ask her.

Her pupils fill up the blue of her eyes, and she says, "I guess it's not."

I am unable to find words.

Finally she says, "Will you miss that?"

I know I shouldn't lose my patience. I get that this might be confusing to understand. But still. Enough is enough. I feel like a freak for the first time with someone who usually makes me feel the opposite.

"Gwen, here it is. Yes, I've been with guys, which means I have touched and kissed them, and they have touched and kissed me. You already know this. Why does it matter?" I shift on the couch and take her hand. "I like you. I like touching you. Kissing you. Being inside of you. You make me feel good, and I make you feel good. In all kinds of ways."

She's listening to me. I can see it by the way she sits still, not even twirling her hair or biting her nails.

"Can you, for sure, tell me that you will not miss

having sex with guys?" She doesn't move her hand, and her blue eyes have a softness to them.

"No more than you would miss Heyward, let's say." I move closer to her, still holding her hand.

"What does that mean?" Her hand tenses.

"The answer to your question is that I won't miss sex with guys because I had sex with those people when I did because of who they were, and the fact that they were guys wasn't the reason I was with them. Those relationships ended because it didn't work." I feel frustration begin to simmer again.

"You're saying that the fact that I'm a girl doesn't matter? You don't care that I'm a girl."

I think about this, and somewhere in the back of my mind I know that there's a right answer. "No."

She doesn't move for a moment, and then she bites her nail.

That, obviously, was the *wrong* answer.

****

GWEN

Andy tries to grab my hand when I stand up. He says something to me, but I'm so fucking pissed again that I jerk it away and glare at him through tears, which I rub away.

Fuck. This. Shit. Not caring that I'm a girl? But that's what I am!

I back out of the room calling for Nori.

"What? What? Are you okay?" Nori bursts out of the bedroom she and Ethan are in. She's flushed and in only a bra and underwear. I scan her up and down. Ethan comes out in only his underwear.

Andy is behind me. "Oh, uh."

I clench my jaw. Some feeling is brewing, strong,

inside me. I don't know what it is, but it's now moving beyond percolating.

"Go ahead, Andy. Check Ethel out," I say. "I mean the fact that he's a *guy* is irrelevant, right?" I turn to Nori, the wild is brewing in me, spinning out of control now. I grab her bra strap. "Let's test this theory out for real. Nori, show *Andrew* your tits, like that night in high school. I'm pretty sure we got down to our bras that night. Hell—" I stop and reach for the bottom of my shirt. "How about we all get naked and see what happens. This isn't high school anymore." *Whoosh*. Off my shirt goes, and I'm wearing nada. My tatas swing in the wind.

They all blink and blink. Nori clutches her bra strap, terror rolling over her face.

I step forward. My eyes dart from Andy to Nori and then over to Ethan, who is searching for something to cover himself up with. "Who does Andy really want? Chocolate or vanilla. Both? Right? You want us all swirled up together." And with that, I jump on Ethan, who doesn't see it coming. I land on his back.

Nori gasps, Andy mutters fuck, and I press my naked boobs into Ethan. Poor guy doesn't know what to do with his hand, so they flail around, and Nori grabs my back and starts to pull down, but I lock in with my legs. We are screaming at each other and then—

Andy yells out, "You're out of your fucking mind!" And then he backs out of the room.

The three of us are frozen in this weird configuration of bodies.

Ethan pries my hands off his shoulders and puts me down gently and grabs a pillow and thrusts it at me. "No offense, but cover your shit up, please." He adds,

"That was kind of fucked up."

He turns to Nori, who is unmoving. Shit.

Finally, she grabs a throw from the couch and wraps it around herself, not even throwing a glance in my direction. "I'm going to get dressed," she says and then adds before leaving, "Ethan, go talk to Andy."

"I'm gonna grab some pants first." Disgust boils from him.

I clutch the pillow to my parts.

"Good job, Glen," Ethan says before following Nori back into the bedroom.

I stand by myself, and before the tears start, I just shake and shake. If I was drunk, I could blame my behavior on the alcohol. I wish to God I had more than two drinks tonight. I wish I could blame what just happened on booze, but that behavior, that shit was me, all me. All fucked up Glen. Tears stream down and I just let them fall while I pull my clothes back on. Each movement is heavy and painful. I love that girl, Nori, and those boys, Ethan and Andy. Why can't I just let that be enough? Why do I have to screw everything up? My shaking is now more shivers, and I turn and flail for a moment. Hushed voices come from Nori and Ethan's room. Silence from the kitchen where Andy went. Where do I go?

I walk back to our room and pause at the threshold, looking at my stuff, still packed and piled up. The urge to flee is strong as hell, but I'm not following it. I fucked everything up in just a few moments and somehow I have to find a way to fix it. I step into the room and turn and shut the door. Sadness overtakes me, and I go to bed, curl up on my side, and cry some more. I want to be the calm Andy, the evolved Ethan, the enlightened Nori. But I'm not. I'm the toxic Gwen. I'm the can't-get-over-the-past Gwen.

Do I really care that he's had sex with men? Does it matter if he finds both men and women hot?

Do I care that he doesn't care that I'm a girl?

I know beneath all my insecurities is the simple fact that I don't want to hurt any more over him. But all I keep doing since we slept together the first time is try to hurt him and, in turn, hurt myself.

I look over at Andy's side of the bed and see his journal. What was I looking for? I went in there looking for evidence that this was a sham so I could have an out. Because I'm scared.

I stand up and wipe my eyes. Maybe I can be the evolved Gwen.

Maybe.

Chapter 11

ETHAN

After I grab a pair of pants, I walk back out, pausing at Gwen and Andy's door. It's shut. I stand there for a minute, not sure what to do.

From the kitchen, a glass clinks around and someone turns on the water. I walk down the hall. Andy stands at the counter, his hand around a glass.

"Listen, man," I begin and put my hand on Andy's shoulder. Poor guy is shaking. When he turns, I can see that he's crying. He wipes his eyes. I see a thing of paper towels and grab one. "Here." He takes it and blows his nose.

"Fuck," he says quietly. A-game is not having a good day.

"Yeah." I have no idea what to do. I continue to pat his shoulder and stand there.

He smiles. "Thanks."

I stop patting and lean against the counter. He takes a long gulp of water and wipes his mouth with the back of his hand. "You know, I love that girl. I do, and I have no idea why that's not enough for her."

"Listen, uh, personally, I think it is, but girls, they're complicated."

He drinks the rest of the water. "You're right. Guys. Pretty simple."

"Right. We get hungry, we eat. When we're bored,

we play video games or whatever. When we're horny, we, you know." Where am I going with this? "We don't have all these complications."

"Exactly, I like Gwen. I *love* her. I want her. Period. Why does that have to be analyzed?"

I nod, grab the fridge door, and open it. I take a can of soda and crack it open. "Hey, I hear you, man."

He drinks more water, and I drink half the can of soda and then burp. Andy laughs.

"What do I do now?"

"Your situation is kind of out of my league." I sip the soda.

"Right." Andy holds the glass and stares at the tiles on the floor.

"But we have something in common. We've loved those girls for a long, long time, and we've got this history with them. When Nori finally agreed to talk to me after a year and a half of me begging her for another chance, I made myself a promise that I wouldn't ever let her go." Jesus Christ. I put the can down and wipe at my eyes.

Andy nods.

"I know I hurt her, and I knew that she might not trust me, and I had to show her that I'd grown up and changed. I knew if I wanted her to believe me, I'd have to follow her so I could show her. I guess that's what I'm thinking you have to do. It's different from Nori and me, but the similarity is a bottom line—trust. Girls, even the strong ones like our girls, they need the guy to show it to them."

"I thought that's what I was doing." He puts the glass on the counter.

"It takes time, A-game. Time." I grab the can and

drain it dry.

"Yeah." He finishes the water and puts it back down. "You don't know what I told her, though."

"You mean why she went ape shit out there and started humping my back?"

"Yeah, I was answering all her questions, even though it was a humiliating interrogation of what sex acts I've done with guys."

"What did she ask you?"

"She asked me if I cared that she was a girl."

"What did you say?"

"No."

I tap my chin with a finger. "*Hmmmmm*. I'm not sure what I would think about that, like if Nori said she didn't care if I was a guy." We both look at each other and then I say, "You know what, whatever. Gwen didn't like the answer. Is that what you're saying?"

"Right, and before that, she asked me if I would miss being with guys."

I know I shouldn't do it, but I do step back, cover my bare chest with my arms. Andy ignores me. I force myself to drop my arms.

"And you said?"

"No more than she would miss having sex with one of her exes."

"Mmmmmm…"

"What?"

"I think the right answer was a simple no…unless that's not true." I eye him.

He stays quiet a minute, then says, "I'm not thinking about other people right now. I'm thinking about Gwen." He stops. "I should have listened to George."

"The shrink?"

Andy nods. "He said that despite my claiming to accept my sexuality, the real acceptance is telling people who you love the total truth. And he wanted me to do this way back when I first started seeing him two years ago, and I was going to do it. Eventually." He sighs.

I pat his shoulder and say, "A-game, bottom line is she's worried that this is a phase and that you're eventually going to want to date and hook up with guys again."

"But I don't want that, again, any more than she would want to hook up with an old flame. Mine happen to include guys." He walks to the fridge and opens it.

"Are you sure, A-game? Are you sure you don't want a dude?" I say to the back of his head.

He pulls out a gallon of water and shuts the fridge. "Yes. I want *that* girl out there." He plunks the water onto the counter. "I want Gwen. This is pretty frustrating that the people who probably know me the best and for the longest don't get it."

"I think you are expecting too much." I reach over and unscrew the cap to the water and refill his glass.

"Thanks," he says but leaves the glass on the counter. He thinks for a minute and then says, "I was hiding it for this very reason. A few years ago, I thought I had to choose a side. I wasn't sure if I was gay or straight, and I, like a lot of people I'm finding out, didn't think being bisexual was a real thing."

He takes the water but doesn't drink.

"Andy?"

I turn, and there are Gwen and Nori.

"I'm sorry. Again." Gwen's eyes are red, and she's

gripping Nori's hand in hers.

"Tomorrow is the amusement park. Where dreams come true." Gwen wipes her nose with the back of her free hand. "And my dream is to stop obsessing over this."

I kind of want to both laugh and hug Glen at the same time.

Andy doesn't say anything. I put my empty soda can down with a small thud.

Everything kind of freezes. We're waiting for Andy.

"You really are the monster, Gwen," he says.

"I guess that makes you the princess?" It's out of my mouth before I can stop it, but luckily, I see the corner of his mouth twitch.

He laughs.

Another moment of ruination saved by the magical amusement park.

****

NORI

After last night, I'm not surprised that the ride to Orlando this even-too-early-in-the-morning-for-me is so quiet that I can hear the different rhythms of breathing from all three of my passengers. In the backseat, Gwen and Andy, propped up against each other, alternate making little hissing sounds through their noses. Do they ever wake each other up with that noise? And Ethan, whose hand is, even in his sleep, clutching mine, his head tilted to the side, the just emerging sunlight illuminating his peaceful, chiseled face. He makes quiet sigh noises every few minutes. I call it his happy sound because over the years we've been together, I've witnessed E sleeping through everything from his freshman year roommate doing the nasty with his girlfriend in the bed across from us to turbulent flights to Florida. Unlike me, E can sleep through everything and when he does sleep, it's always with a slight smile crossing his lips and the happy sound coming out.

Last night though, neither one of us slept well, and I know Gwen and Andy didn't either, with all the turning and tossing and murmuring through the walls. The entire condo was restless. Ethan and I didn't talk about India or the almost-wanna-be orgy that almost-but-definitely wouldn't have happened. We only said things to each other like "Are you cold?" and "Should I turn down the AC?" and "It's gonna suck getting up tomorrow." But beneath all that was all these hazy thoughts and words and feelings I couldn't really hold on to.

And worse was, when I finally fell asleep, I think it was four in the morning, and we had to get up at six. My original plan was to get up at five to do a half hour of *asanas*, but that didn't happen, and I feel myself paying for it now. My mind is monkeying all over the place. I am doubting my decisions now about everything about India, about going or staying, about Ethan, about Andy and Gwen, about the four of us. Are we all clinging to each other because that's kind of what we've done since high school? Swami told me that if people really love each other they don't have to cling because the bond is unbreakable.

And now we have to go hang out with cheery families and kids, little babies, and happy couples. There we are, the motley crew of confused, sort-of adults frolicking around. Are we even up for this? The thought of long lines for roller coasters that used to be fun when I was a kid but now just make me want to throw up…And after last night, I'm not sure how much we even want to be around each other. I love each and every one of them, but last night? It was weird.

Every trip to Florida we all say we're going to make it to the park because of the free townhouse from Ruby's crazy client—a film actress obsessed with all things related to that famous mouse's girlfriend—but instead we go to South Beach because it's a shorter drive and involves less walking around and more drinking.

We make it in just over two hours because everyone stays asleep, and after checking in at the main building—with all bodies still noisily asleep—I pull around to where our townhouse is at the end of a winding road lined with perfectly groomed palm trees and bright green lawns of other duplicate townhomes.

I cut the engine and stretch my arms. None of them move. I sigh, loud and long. Nothing. I dig into the pocket of my sundress for the itinerary that Ruby's travel agent set up for us. Not sure if the travel agent understands what a bunch of almost-college-graduates considers fun. But it's all paid for, so we can't complain.

I fold the paper back up and lean over to Ethan. "Baby," I whisper into his ear, catching that slightly sour unshowered man-smell I love. "We're here." He makes a soft moaning noise, and I lean down and kiss his earlobe.

"Man, my mouth tastes like ass!"

Apparently, Gwen is awake.

"Morning," I say and give a little wave through the

rearview mirror. She growls and nudges Andy in the shoulder, but he is still out cold. I have a feeling those two were up all night talking. And maybe more than talking because they seemed awfully friendly this morning when we were getting ready. Quiet but very kissy and huggy.

Speaking of…

Ethan is kissing my cheek and nuzzling my neck now. "Baby," he whispers, "did I sleep through the whole ride?"

"I have to pee!" from Gwen in the back.

"Me too," Andy chimes in.

Ethan kisses my cheek and then says, "The kids need to pee. We better get them inside."

I laugh.

"We hear that, *Dad*." Gwen says, poking her head between the seats and glaring at me.

Ethan palms her face lightly and nudges her back.

We spend the next few minutes gathering our duffle bags and getting inside the townhouse, which is a lot nicer than we expected. Ruby warned us, "Listen, she's an out-of-work former soap actress, so don't set your expectations too high."

We wander through the three bedrooms, all pastel colors and double beds except one, which is the master bedroom. "Ours!" Ethan declares and throws our bags on the king-size bed of the very pink room.

"Come here," he says and grabs me by the waist.

We kiss long and dreamy and then he's pushing me back onto the bed. Suddenly, the fatigue of not only not sleeping well last night but also driving over two hours hits me, and I yawn right into his mouth.

He stops kissing me. "Do I bore you?"

"No, no—"

"Good." He grinds into my pelvis a little, and I wince.

He stops.

"I'm kind of, you know, sore from last night."

He pushes himself up and looks down at me. "Really?" His smile is pure I-am-the-man.

"Yeah, you big stud."

He frowns. "You're just sweet-talking me. Besides, you promised at least twice a day."

"Did I promise twice a day?"

"Hey, cats and kittens!" Gwen barges into the room with Andy behind her, yawning loudly.

"Can we just take a little nap?" Andy yawns again.

"You guys got to sleep the whole ride. I need the nap." The contagious yawn strikes me once, twice, and three times.

"Poor Nori!" They all pile onto the bed.

"Please do not all start making out with me," I joke.

Everyone freezes, and I open my eyes and see lots of blushing and moving away from each other.

"So…we just need to catch one of the buses that will bring us into the park." Ethan has produced a copy of the itinerary that I had in my dress pocket.

"Right. Should we change?" Gwen is all business now, but her tinged cheeks give away that she is probably embarrassed about last night.

"Can I shower?" Andy asks. None of us showered this morning because we all woke up long after the alarm rang, not once or twice but three times.

"Nope," Ethan says. "Come on, kids, we gotta go."

****

Many hours and several laps around the park later, we are on a boat that will take us from the park to a tiny island that has a world-renown fireworks show. Ethan is behind me with his hands on my hips. We look out onto the water at the setting sun shimmering pink off the rolling waves. The giant roller coaster we all braved (and promptly got a little nauseous from) is slowly getting smaller as we glide farther away.

We made it the entire day without talking about India or last night. I feel the heat of Ethan behind me as I keep staring at the increasingly pink sky and let the thoughts in about everything.

I break the silence. "Do you remember the first yoga class I ever took, that we all ever took?"

Ethan laughs, dipping his head into my neck so that I can feel the whisper of his breath on my skin. "In gym class. You were so adorable and so mad at us."

I turn and punch him lightly in the arm, but he hugs me close, and I let him. "I was so serious about it, and you all acted like a bunch of asshats while poor Ms. Whatshername tried so hard to teach us the sun salutation."

"Come on. It was pretty funny. She was this very large, very old lady trying to fold herself up into all these poses, and then she let out a fart." Ethan laughs.

"Yeah, but remember, I didn't even notice. She had a video on for us to follow, and I just kept going the rest of the class."

"Right, and we were all clapping at the end. Like I said, adorable."

I inhale the salty air and rub the tops of Ethan's hands that have wound themselves tightly around my waist. "That day I found my thing. You know everyone around me had a thing. Andy and Gwen were perfect students. You played football. Me…I just floated from thing to thing and never felt passionate about anything."

Ethan doesn't say anything.

So I continue. "I've devoted so much time to studying yoga, and it's not just a hobby. It's what I want to do with the rest of my life. I need to go to the best place to really hone my craft."

For several very long moments nothing is said. Then, he releases his grip on me and leans against the railing of the boat, his eyes boring into me. "When were you going to tell me? The last I knew, you were thinking about business school."

I turn to him, my hands gripping the railing. "Business school? Me? That was my dad. Business school and move home to take over the business."

Ethan knows this. I'm choking the railing at this point. I continue on, "In fact, I never want to step inside a classroom again unless it's to take another yoga certification exam or to teach children in school how to use yoga to de-stress."

Ethan makes his aggravated sigh noise. "But a year is a long time. It's longer than I was away." Why does he sound so whiny right now?

I look out onto the water because I don't have any reply to that.

Then he says, "Take me with you."

I let out a laugh because now he's talking total silliness. "You really want to go to India? Doesn't that pose a little wrinkle in your own plans to get a teaching job?"

He darts his eyes away, making me think he doesn't buy it either.

"Hey, you two!" Gwen wobbles across the boat to us with a bottle of prosecco in one hand and two plastic wineglasses in another.

"Drinking before noon?" I quip, grateful for the momentary distraction.

"Free alcohol means drinking any time of the day," she says and hands us each a wineglass and pours the wine until the glasses are filled to the brim.

"Go back to your hanky-panky." She winks at us.

We watch her wobble away, swigging from the bottle. Fuck this all. "To drinking before noon," I say to Ethan, whose face relaxes with relief. We clink glasses and then drink in silence.

When we've drained our cups, Ethan steps farther away from me, the wind lifting the hair off his forehead. "I did a lot of thinking while I was in South America, and I guess I had it in my head I was coming home to you, to us, to our future."

Now I make my aggravated noise. Can't we just get drunk and forget this conversation? Sometimes talking it out isn't the thing to do. Especially on a boat to see fireworks on an island.

"I'm sorry. I can't just drop this now." He taps the empty glass against the railing.

"Fine." I toss my cup into the garbage nearby. "Let's not drop it. Here's the thing, Ethan. We can't just make decisions based on the us-factor."

"Why not?"

I cross my arms and feel the frustration building. "Because we aren't even out of college. Because we don't want to regret not doing things. This is what you said to me. This is what you taught me by going to South America."

"So you going to India is *my* fault?"

Now I explode. "This isn't a fault! India isn't a punishment!" I feel the eyes of other passengers looking at us. Not caring about that right now, though.

We stare at each other. I've never felt this far away from Ethan. Wait. Only one other time long, long ago.

Sadness seeps in. How do I make him understand how I feel? He thinks this is about him, or us, but it's not, and having this time apart made me realize that I need to not only be an us, I need to be a me or an I.

Ethan holds the empty glass up and then says, "Going to get more. Want some?"

I nod, then realize I don't even have a glass. I wonder if Swami ever just gets drunk. Ever just says, "Fuck it all." I mean, I want to be a true yogi, but I hope I can still drink my prosecco once in a while.

I feel a hand on my shoulder and turn. Andy.

Chapter 12

ANDY

"A-game." Ethan claps a hand to my shoulder, then, grinning a little like he's tipsy, walks over to Gwen who's at the bar getting more prosecco. Not that she needs it.

Scratch that, we all need it. I tip my glass back and drink the remains of my bubbly. I look down at Nori who's staring at my empty glass.

"You want some?" I ask.

"Yes, please!" She grabs my glass.

Nori and I wander back over to Gwen and Ethan who are doing a shot together. *Uh oh.* I check to see if any of Gwen's clothes have come off, but she's still wearing her adorable white shorts and purple tank top. Her hair is all over the place and her make-up a little smeared.

I take the shot out of her hand and finish it. She lightly punches me in the arm, and I pretend to cry, but she hugs me. Meanwhile, Nori and Ethan stand next to each other like strangers, looking away and nursing respective glasses of wine. I can only hope that whatever is going on between them will melt away with some alcohol.

"Give me a shot!" Nori says suddenly and pushes between Gwen and Ethan at the bar.

"Bar's closed," the bartender says and gives her a

nod. "Boat's docking."

"Just one." She pouts, but it's not as flirty looking as I think she's going for. Ethan puts his hand on hers.

"Nori, honey, you've never done a shot in your life."

"Yes, she has…a shot of wheatgrass!" Gwen says and then cracks herself up.

None of us laugh, though. Nori wanting a shot means…I don't even know because it's never happened. When we drink, she's always after the prosecco or the super sweet, fruity drinks, heavy on the fruity and light on the alcohol.

I think I hear Nori say *fuck* something…maybe *you* or *me* or *this*, and then she's behind the bar and has a bottle of whiskey in her hands. What happened to the bartender?

"Nori!" Ethan is up and behind the bar with her. He's wrestling the bottle away from her, and she's f-bombing all over the place, but no one else besides us notices because everyone is swarming over to the exit out to the set of stairs that will lead us to getting off the boat.

"Hey, I'm not drinking wheatgrass now!" she shouts and wrangles the bottle from Ethan and takes a really long pull. Both Gwen and I gasp, and I put my hand over my mouth, just thinking about how gross that's going to feel in her chest and stomach in about five seconds. It makes me want to puke.

But she shakes her head and lets out a whoop. "I'm ready to go, biatches!"

She puts her hands in the air and wiggles her hips like she's starting a conga line and shimmies her way out from behind the bar. Ethan looks miserable and sad.

I grab Gwen's hand, and we look at each other like *I guess we have to be the parents now*.

We manage to get off the boat, but Nori cannot be stopped. She dances, almost tumbling into the water and continues to shimmy her way down the dock. We make it to dry land, and she stops, stands in the middle of this path that will probably lead us out to the main island, which is all lit up and sparkly in the distance. I want to go watch the fireworks and then go home and make some sweet love to my lady. But that doesn't look like it's going to happen because now Nori is staring at Ethan and he is staring back at her, showdown-style.

Nori taps her foot to the music that's suddenly playing, electronic dance music, vibrating under our feet, and people have gathered, dancing with each other and not noticing the standoff happening in the middle of everything.

Nori sees this and starts to dance this messy, sloppy, hip-swishing and hand-waving dance. I can't help but laugh and then Gwen shrugs and joins her. Ethan and I stand next to each other, watching them. It's like we're watching a time warp. Us, in Ethan's basement, dancing. The fearsome foursome, stolen bottles of beer and wine coolers in our hands. The girls dancing together like video vixens, grinding and rubbing on each other. Right now, they're dancing far more innocently, more like two little girls dancing in the backyard, making up a dance to a pop song. God, they are beautiful.

Ethan slaps me on the back. "I'm going in," he says and steps in between the girls. They dance with him, Gwen from behind and Nori in the front. It's sexy and lovely. I watch.

Then Gwen points to me and wiggles her finger. So I join too, behind Gwen, holding her hips, feeling her ass against me. I don't know how long we are all there dancing, but more and more people join, and it's like this outdoor club happening.

But suddenly Nori is out of the group, to the side, her arms crossed over her chest and Ethan by her side saying something.

"Don't be mad!" Nori throws her hands in the air. "It's not fair!" She wobbles. "I was fucking happy for you!" She points at his chest, wobbles again. "You be happy for me!"

"Let's go back to the townhouse." Ethan puts his hand on her arm, but she takes both of her small but strong hands and pushes him away, hard. He reels back and steps toward her again. But she steps back and then he stops.

We've stopped dancing, watching this. Doing nothing. Gwen clutches my hand, and I clutch hers back. I don't know what to do.

Nori looks over at us, and I realize she's crying. "Ima sorry," she slurs, then runs over, tripping on her own feet. We all rush to her, but she puts her hands up. "Ima fiiiiine! Fine. Lemme say this godamnit! Gwennie. Andy Pandy. Love you twos. Love that you twos love each other. I love that you make love…" She stops and shakes her head and then plops right down on the ground.

We rush to Nori, all of us, murmuring things like *it's okay*, but she's crying and not letting us touch her. She pushes us away and stands up, wiping her eyes. People around us are staring. Ethan sees it too, so he takes her by the elbow and whispers something in her ear, and she nods. He waves us over.

"Let's go find a place to sit for a minute," he says. Just as we are about to walk toward a bench in the grass nearby, sharp shooting noises fire off.

The fireworks. We all look up, and bursts of color shoot out. A small shot of white and then red and then blue and then a huge burst of green. We gasp along with the crowd of people that are around us. I'm holding Gwen's hand, and with my free one, I reach for Nori's, and she puts it, sweaty and small, in mine, and then I see her and Ethan clasp hands. We stand there with the sparks and lights flashing over and over. We don't move. Just watch all the colors and listen to all the booms and pops. Together.

****

GWEN

Somehow we make it back to the townhouse that night, drunk, happy, sad, silly. No one showers. Again. We tumble into our respective beds and fall asleep immediately, or at least that's what I can remember when I wake up the next morning, my eyes opening and closing about five times. Andy is solidly asleep next to me. I nudge him. He only moves in response to my nudge. I roll to my side to look at his sleeping face, but the movement is exhausting. My God what did we do last night? I don't think I've gotten that drunk in months. I watch him sleep, my eyes trace the soft pout of his lips and his hand tucked underneath his cheek. His lashes thick and eyebrows thicker.

I think I love him.

I think I never stopped.

This scares the mother-fucking shit out of me.

I reach over to stroke his thick, messy, dark hair

and let it sift through my fingers. It's crazy, bed-head, indie-rockstar hair. The gay thing I realize now after everything these past two days is not the scary part of us. It's being this close, and this loved. I don't know how to do it, to be vulnerable because it seems like when I do, I can get hurt.

I roll to my back and stare at the white ceiling and watch a tiny spider walk by one of the recessed light canisters. It's time for us to go. Me and Andy. Go back home. And when we do, we need to go on proper dates and be "out." My mind races though with the possibilities of what our families will say, his mother especially. His father will be thrilled. *Asshat.*

"Gwen." Andy puts a warm palm on my naked shoulder. "I think I have a hangover."

I laugh. "Probably. We all are going to hurt today."

He smiles, but his eyes are still closed. I turn and put a finger on one of his lids and gently pry it open.

"No!" he protests, grabbing my hand and pushing it away.

"Wakey, wakey!"

I roll on top of him, noticing that all he has on are his boxer briefs and all I have on is my thong. I feel him hard against me while he digs his fingers into my sides. I laugh, but then I feel dizzy. "Ugh. We have to stop. I kind of want to throw up."

"My mouth tastes like throw up. Did I throw up last night?" He puts a hand over his forehead.

"Who knows? I don't really remember anything after the dancing in the street."

He slides me off him, and we lay side by side, his hand curling around mine. "I want this to work," he says quietly.

"Me too."

We lay silently, listening to the sounds outside of people slamming car doors, a kid laughing, people talking. No sounds of Nori and Ethan.

"Wanna shower?" He slides closer to me, propping his chin on my shoulder.

"Whew! You do stink." I plug my nose.

"You love my stink." He nuzzles my neck.

"No, I do not. Let's go hose you down."

****

When we manage to get our bodies upright, my head feels, literally, like it's filled with lead. Luckily, there is a bathroom in our bedroom. We stumble in and—

"Jacuzzi!"

I fill the tub and Andy finds our toothbrushes. We stand side by side, brushing and foaming at the mouth together. God, my body is heavy, and my stomach is murky but to be standing here doing this mundane task with him is home.

I watch him spit and rinse. "I'll hold your hair for you," he says.

Tingles go up and down my arms. *I'll hold your hair*. Who thinks of that? He scoops my hair up while I spit into the sink and then rinse my mouth with water. Although I'm still a little dizzy just standing, I'm getting melty all over, so I turn and wrap my arms around his waist and kiss his minty mouth. His tongue is cold against mine as he reaches behind me and pushes the lock into the door and whispers, "Just in case. I think we've all seen enough of each other naked."

We kiss again, and he walks me backward toward

the tub. Without releasing me, he bends down and shuts off the water. I step away from him and start to pull down my thong, but he grabs the tiny string that covers the front of me and pulls me back toward him, his eyes heavy-lidded like he's about to fall asleep, but I know that's not what's about to happen. He pushes the piece of fabric aside and rubs me with his hand.

"You should probably let me get a little cleaner before—" Too late. He's on his knees, and the swatch of fabric is around my ankles. I grip the top of his head and part my legs a little. He slides both hands to my butt and grips tightly. The sensations shoot all over me, and I almost fall back. But he slides back up my body and kisses my neck and whispers, "Delicious."

"Are you still drunk?" I ask him. "'Cause I'm pretty sure that wasn't exactly delicious."

He nods lazily. "Yum."

"Dirty boy!" I kick my thong off my ankles. We kiss, and I mumble against his lips, "Condom."

He nods and reaches over to where the toiletry bag is with our stuff and produces one. I grab it and rip it open and then roll it over him. How can I doubt that this man likes vagina? He grabs one of my legs, and then the other, and lifts me onto the sink counter and even though the cold marble makes me yelp, he's inside of me so quickly that I don't feel anything else but him for the next ten minutes or whatever it is. I can't kiss him anymore, so I just bite his shoulder while he does most of the work, whispering all kinds of filthy things in my ear. I can't believe that in this position I feel things building up and up inside, and then, *bam*! "Holy shit!" I scream, and when I come back to earth, I feel instantly embarrassed.

But he just laughs softly into my shoulder.

****

In the tub, we are warm and lazy, our legs tangled up in each other. My whole body is in this cocoon of ease and relaxation. We haven't said much since my *holy shit*.

"Let's go home," I say, running my fingers up and down his leg.

"You mean back to the condo?"

"No, let's go back to," I pause and almost say "our home" but instead say, "You know home *home*. Rhode Island. I think I've had enough of the sunshine."

"I think you just want me all to yourself." He grins.

"Maybe." I push some warm bubbles up my arm and watch them pop.

He wrinkles his brow. "What about Nori and Ethan?"

We sit in the silence of worry and concern, which we haven't had for those two in years.

"They always rally," I offer.

"True." He takes my soapy hand and kisses the back of it. "How about round two? On the bed this time."

Chapter 13

ETHAN

Nori and I lay in bed holding hands and not talking, mainly because we have twin headaches. Mine feels like someone is taking a drill to my left ear and then pounding on the side of my head with a cleaver. Nori's is more of a "being stun-gunned in between my eyes" as she described it when she woke up, which only happened because some people in this house fuck each other really loudly. Let me say that waking up to the sound of A-game working his game on Glendolyn—maybe I shouldn't refer to her in the masculine any more considering—is more jarring than an alarm clock, more terrifying, too. Those two make noises like my old college roommate who would bang his girl in the bed across from where I slept. Low moans like someone is in pain. Though if they have a hangover like I do, maybe that is pain I'm hearing and not lots of sex.

I glance over at Nori and see her eyes closed and her brow furrowed. I reach over, my whole arm heavier than an arm should feel, and take my thumb and press it in the crease above her forehead. She makes a not-sexy-at-all moan of true pain. But then adds, "Don't stop." Normally, I would find a little dirty humor in this, but I'm in too much of my own pain.

We lay for a little while more, and as the time passes, we hear the sounds of Andy and Gwen's weird-sounding love stop, and then footsteps down the hallway and to the kitchen, where the sound of banging pans and pots makes both of us jump a little. Nori is alternate nostril breathing, which is exactly what it sounds like. It's the "calming breath," and I'm tempted to join, but lifting my arm hurts too much.

Last night comes to me in a rolling fog. "I carried you all the way from the dance club to the boat."

"There was a dance club?" She stops mid left side nostril breathing and looks sideways at me.

"Oh yes, there was." I rub some sleep from my eyes. "And some twerking on the bar."

"Promise me no one took any video of that." She starts breathing again.

"I can promise. But I can't promise what Gwen might have done."

"I'll just threaten her with the drunken karaoke of some old disco song. You know how she hates to hear her own singing voice."

I roll to the side of my body that hurts less and happens to face her. "I've never seen you that hammered."

She grins and then cringes. I rub her forehead again. "Poor baby."

"Would you be upset if we just went back today instead of tomorrow? I feel bad because Ruby had all these plans for us, but—"

"You mean the adventure safari at the zoo followed by the lunch with cartoon characters?" I shake my head. "She means well, but I don't think any of us really want to hang out with a bunch of screaming children. I think we had enough yesterday."

She nods slowly with her eyes closed, and I push

myself up and lean over to kiss the top of her very sour-smelling head. "I'm okay leaving, as long as we can take showers first. There's some kind of funk happening here."

She leans into me, and I hug her. And when she pulls back I see her eyes are wet.

"I'm sorry," she whispers, the tears spilling down to her lip, which I rub away with my index finger.

I tilt her chin up, but she won't look at me, and she cries harder. "No," I soothe. "No, your head is going to explode if you cry, honey."

She shakes her head and pushes herself so she is sitting all the way up.

"I should have told you about India as soon as I found out, and I only didn't because I was afraid if I told you, I wouldn't go."

I continue to brush away her tears, and then I pull her to my chest and let her cry. I murmur that I love her, that we will work this all out, and that I want her to be happy.

We fall back in bed and hold each other for a while.

****

Later, we get out of bed, down a handful of ibuprofen, and join the late breakfast in progress that Gwen and Andy have prepared—oatmeal with syrup, which they got from I have no idea where. We all agree that it's time to go home.

As Nori and I roll our bags into the hallway, she looks over at Gwen and Andy who are sitting in each other's laps playing kissy face.

"I hope this turns out okay," Nori says, and for a second I think she means us, but then I realize she means the two rabbits practically boning in the corner. "If this doesn't work, it could be the end of the fearsome foursome."

"We all need a shift in thinking," I say, sounding far wiser than I feel.

Nori grins. "Look at you. My yoga charms have rubbed off. I can see the future now, Ethan. Maybe we can own a yoga studio together."

"I like hearing you talk about our future together." I lean forward and kiss her.

We gaze at each other for a minute, and then I say, "I'm thinking that tonight I cash in on my twice a day."

I slide my tongue into her ear, and she laughs and says, "I never break promises."

****

After we get home, Nori and I go out to the beach for a run, and then she starts her yoga routine. I watch her. The setting sun, the waves rolling gently, her eyes closed and hands together in what I know is called prayer position. I know way more about yoga than I probably want to, but, on the other hand, I get to watch my very hot girlfriend bend and twist and stretch in barely any clothes, so it all works out.

Soon I'm following her lead and let myself get into the breathing, twisting, and stretching, and when we finish, laying side by side on the beach, my body feels almost as good as it does after sex. Almost.

We touch fingers as we lay there, the sun warm all over my chest and legs. The waves make a lapping noise, and the sand is soft and cool underneath me. As always when I lay like this with her, I think the same thoughts: I want to do this every day, I want to wake up every single day and watch her do yoga and then watch her make us coffee and then sit and read the paper together and make plans for the day. I want to cook her dinner and clean the house together. And then the images of us coming home from work: I'm a teacher, and she might own a yoga studio. It's all normal and calm; it's exactly how I want my life to be.

Nori stares at me. "Let's go back inside."

We run back up to the deck, and before we go inside, I grab her around the waist and brush sand off her, lingering over her boobs and butt. She laughs and swats at me but then brushes sand off my man parts. We lean against the railing of the deck, and I kiss her neck, brushing more imaginary sand from her ass.

The slider door opens, and we stop like we've been caught.

"Hey—oh, should I come back later?" Andy says, hiding his eyes.

"Nah, I think we're all cleaned up now," I say and step back to let Andy step out. Behind him is Gwen, and they're both dressed in jeans and tee shirts with wet hair. Andy has a mug of coffee in his hand.

Gwen eyes Andy, but she's talking to us. "We're going to fly back a few days early."

I stifle the urge to high-five the air.

"Don't cry or anything, Ethel," Gwen smirks.

"I'll try to control myself," I say, pouting.

Nori punches me lightly but turns to them. "Things good?"

"Yeah," Andy says, sipping his coffee. "I made an appointment with George."

"Our first official date will be dinner and a shrink appointment."

It's hard to read Gwen, but she smiles and drinks

Andy's coffee.

We stand together on the deck and gaze out on the beach.

"What time do you guys leave?" I ask.

"We called a cab." Andy checks his phone. "The flight is in three hours."

I grab Andy and give him a hug with a slap on the back, and then I hug Gwen, careful not to make her spill the mug of coffee she's still holding. Nori hugs both of them.

"Nori, you're really going to India?" Andy says, taking the mug from Gwen and sipping.

"I am." She glances at me.

"When do you leave?" Gwen asks.

"A few days after break ends." She grabs my hands, and I know she is trying to soften the whole thing. "Then when I get back, I'm moving in with Ethan."

And maybe getting married to him? Wish I could say that out loud.

Gwen grabs Nori again. "Call me when you guys get back to RI. We can do one more dinner before you leave?"

She nods.

We follow them back inside. Their bags are packed and by the door. We make small talk, but it seems like all of us are distracted, probably thinking about what's next. The cab arrives, I take the mug from A-game, and we say goodbye.

And when I close the door, Nori puts her arms around my waist. "Let's shower."

****

I turn the dial of the shower, and water rains out. I

step back and open the glass door wide. Nori wraps her arms around me from behind, her soft skin and breasts smashing against my back. I take her hands in mine, rub them against my chest and turn around, pulling her after me into the shower. The water is hot, and steam floats between us.

I grab a bottle of lavender body soap and squirt some into my palms and then rub the soap all over her breasts and down each arm, around her wrists, and turn her palms over, rubbing with my thumbs. She makes a *hmmmm* noise. I glide my hands to her stomach and then her hips. She moves into my hands, and I make circles over her hips and then grip them gently. I smooth my hands down her long, strong legs. I look up at her, and she has her eyes closed. I slide up, rubbing her whole body against mine. I have to stop for a minute and breathe; I don't want to lose it before we even start. I reach up behind her and take the showerhead down and start to rinse her body from top to bottom, lingering in between her legs. Her noises get a little louder, and then she opens her eyes and giggles, which makes me giggle. She takes the showerhead from me and rinses my chest. She points between my legs. "Poor baby, that looks like it hurts." And puts the water shower on me. Torture if we don't speed this along. I take the showerhead and slide it back into the holder.

The droplets fall onto her skin, and I watch her nipples harden. I rub my fingers over them, and she leans into my hand. I push her against the tile wall while the water falls on one side of both of us. I put my mouth over one nipple then the other, and she rakes her fingers into my hair and takes one of my hands, putting it between her legs. I rub her with my fingers, and she opens her thighs to me. I move a little faster, and she grips the top of my hand with hers and dips her mouth into my neck, biting my skin.

When she slows her breath and moves my hand away, I put her hand on me, and she strokes until I whisper, "Bed." And she whispers, "Not yet" and slides all the way down my body. I start to protest, which sounds insane, but one suck and lick down there, I will be done.

"Don't worry," she reminds me. "We have all night."

Can't argue with that.

By the time we get to the bed, the edge of explosion has been taken off for us both. We crawl under the covers and kiss and hold each other for a while until things get heated again, her body tensing and my body pushing into hers and her hands gripping me. But I make her wait a little and begin to slide down under the covers.

"No, no." She pulls on my shoulders. "Now. Please."

"But we have all night," I say innocently and slide all the way between her legs.

She grips the back of my head.

She moves against my mouth, and I press into her soft, smooth skin until she practically yanks out my hair. I crawl up to her, and we are both ready, and she is gripping my ass so hard that I slip into her just for a second, but I pull out just as fast. Her nails dig into me. She already has the condom in her free hand and hands it to me. I rip it open with my teeth because everything is wet and slippery. I slide it on and melt into her.

****

Who knows how long we go for or when we finish and fall asleep, but when I open my eyes, I reach for my phone on the side of the bed and see that it's eight p.m. After I put it down again, I look over at Nori, her head buried into the pillow, hair splayed out, and lips puffed out from sleeping.

My eyes linger over the curve of her mouth and the smoothness of her cheeks, and something, maybe sadness, pulls at my heart. I don't want her to go, and it's a deep down, never-felt-before feeling. A year is a long time.

Brushing away the hair from her cheeks, a chill runs through me; I'm running out of time.

I roll out of bed soundlessly so she won't wake up, and I pull on my shorts. I don't know anyone personally who has proposed to his girlfriend. Most of my friends at school are more interested in seeing how many girls they can bang, and when I tell them my goal is to be married to Nori, and the sooner the better, they shake their heads and say, that's what you get for never partying. And I tell them, imagine the quality of girls you guys could get if you stayed sober once in a while, and then they grab me into a headlock and force me to smell their ass-smelling armpits.

I go into the kitchen and realize I need to do something significant for this moment, and I probably don't have a lot of time before she wakes up.

That's when it all becomes crystal to me.

First, I go get that little black box out of my drawer.

****

NORI

My eyes open, and I stare at the ceiling then look

over and see darkness through the blinds on the window. I roll to my side and burrow deep into Ethan's favorite squishy pillow, inhaling his body scent.

My body hums inside from all the love.

I sit up on the edge of the bed and stretch a little. The clock on my side of the bed says eight thirty p.m. My stomach growls, so I slide into Ethan's fleecy, gray robe and pad out to the kitchen, half expecting Ethan to be here, maybe making dinner. But the house is silent, and I don't see him anywhere. I peer outside and see the car. I'm starving but figure maybe he walked to get dinner. I go to the fridge and pull out stuff for eggs, which is the only thing I know how to cook.

I check my phone first to make sure I didn't miss a message from him but also because Andy and Gwen said they would text when their flight left. Two messages, one from each of them, but nothing from Ethan.

In the kitchen I crack eggs into a stainless steel bowl and mix. I grab a saucepan and pour a little milk and butter; I'm making it the way Ethan taught me, where you put the eggs all in a saucepan on a high heat and stir and stir until they are fluffy and light and perfect. I turn the oven on low so I can put them in there when I'm done, in case Ethan isn't back.

I hear the door open. "I'm making breakfast for dinner, babe," I call to him. "I'm starving."

I hear his footsteps but don't turn around right away because I'm determined not to burn these eggs.

"Yeah, starving," he says. "I got some stuff, too."

"Great! Put it down and come taste these."

"Uh, yeah. Can you turn around for a minute?"

"No, babe, you know I can't stop scrambling these,

or they'll burn."

"Lower the heat, honey."

"No, then they won't be fluffy."

"Actually, it's better to lower the heat and stir fast—never mind, Nori, turn around. Now. Please."

"Ethan…"

"Nori."

I lower the heat. Then think twice about it and turn off the gas burner and quickly do one more stir. "Hold on—" I open the oven and pop them in.

I turn around, and he's holding a bakery box. "What did you get?" I ask.

"You'll see." He pulls out one of the stools at the island. "Come sit down."

I walk to him slowly and eye him suspiciously. He puts the box on the island. I open it.

A pile of brownies. "That's a lot of brownies."

Is this some kind of late anniversary celebration?

I sit on the stool and inhale through my nose. "Mmmmm. They do smell good."

"Take one." He's behind me now.

I peer at the pile and as I reach for one, I see—

A box.

A. Small. Black. Box.

"What's this?"

"Take it, open it."

Oh God. I do and—oh God—it sparkles. It shines. Ohgodohgodohgod.

"Turn around."

I do. Ethan is down on one knee, and he takes the box from me, his fingertips brushing mine. I'm welling up as he opens the box, which makes a little creak noise that I probably will remember fifty years from now.

"Nori," he begins, and I put my hands over my eyes. He pries my hands away and gets back down on one knee.

"Nori—" He stops. "Take your hands away, Nori. Come on."

"But, but, this is, this is." I drop my hands, which have begun to shake, and my heart is pounding hard and fast.

"Nori Mytowsky, will you be my wife?" And he takes the ring and starts to put it on my finger.

I can't talk, so I start shaking my head back and forth so violently that I think I might have heard my neck crack, but he's not understanding or noticing because he's pushing the ring down my finger.

I find my voice. "No." Fingers shaking, I pull the ring off and set it on the counter.

He stands up, arms dangling by his side.

My heart thunders. I search for something to say and can only think of, "But I'm going to India."

"I know."

Silence.

I take a deep breath. "Before I told you about India, before all of it, our plan was to move in together. Not get married."

"This doesn't mean getting married right now. It means *engaged*." He says the word slowly. Then he adds, his blue eyes holding their gaze steady at me, "I saw this ring in Peru and thought it was perfect."

"It is."

A rush of love flows through me. I hate that I'm hurting him. "I'm sorry."

He doesn't say anything, those blue eyes rim with water. He doesn't even rub the tears away.

With my thumb, I rub them, and he lets me. I believe he saw the ring and thought of me. I believe he was ready to ask me to get engaged. But I also believe that asking me took on a whole new reason and purpose once he found out about India. I don't say this; I just keep rubbing his tears. He could have tucked that ring away for a little while longer, but if he proposes now, then I have to possibly give India a second thought. I know how he feels. I felt desperate when he told me about Peru. I thought of a million ways to get him to stay. Fake a pregnancy. Fake an illness. Cancel his flight.

I reach down for one of his hands, ready to tell him this and reassure him that I'm his, and he doesn't need to put a ring on it to prove it to anyone. He lets me take it, but it's limp, dead. I pull him closer. My arms wind around his waist but instead of hugging me back, he reaches behind me and finds the small black box. He plucks the ring off the counter. I feel him pull away and watch him put the ring in the box; the slapping sound of it shutting sends a long bolt of sadness through me. There's nothing I can say right now to him. Ethan rubs at his eyes and says, "I'm not hungry."

Neither am I.

Chapter 14

ANDY

The plane ride is quick because we both sleep the entire time and when we touch down, my mom is waiting outside the gate bundled up in her favorite long bright blue winter squall coat that, because she is so short, reaches her ankles. She waves a red-mittened hand at us. Next to her is—

—my father.

What the hell?

One might think, gee, I'm dating a girl. A girl my father happens to adore. A girl my father has said is perfect for me, so you might think that I'm all good. That *it's* all good.

It's not.

Because my father has a way of reducing me to a pile of sticks no matter if I've done something that I know will please him or something to piss him off and drive him further away.

Gwen leans in and whispers, "What the holy hell is going on?"

"I don't know," I say between gritted teeth. "Smile." I make all my mouth muscles move together into a grin. "Hey, Dad." We walk a few more steps, our rolling carry-ons and backpacks in tow. We stop inches from them. I reach down and hug my mom.

"What's going on?" I keep my voice light.

"Hello, Gwenie." My mom reaches out to hug and kiss her. My father smiles at her but doesn't make a move. Smart man, because if Gwen's expression is any hint, she'd probably haul back and kick him in the shins.

"I actually—funny story—I actually ran into your father about—" She turns to him.

He smiles, but the way his eyes are scrunching up—I know better. "About twenty minutes ago. I'm heading out to Baltimore for work."

"Oh."

"I was thinking, maybe, since my flight isn't for another hour and a half, if your mother and Gwen don't mind, maybe you and I could get a cup of coffee or bite to eat and catch up?"

"I don't know…"

Gwen pokes my side. I'm not sure what that means. Probably that I should talk to him but not to be a nice and good son. One of our previous, constant arguments before Florida and before the blackout was that I needed to sit that m-effer down, to use Gwen's words, and tell him what's what.

"Actually," Gwen blurts, "there's a sandal shop outside the gate. I know how much we both adore sandals, Cindy. We could definitely burn a half hour or so in there."

"Absolutely!" They beam.

Red creeps up his neck. Like father like son.

My mother takes Gwen's backpack and slings it over her shoulder, and Gwen starts to roll away with her bag. "See you two soon! Shoot me a text, and we'll meet you."

I nod and watch them go, adjust my backpack,

which is strapped to my back, and although I'm about an inch taller than my father, I feel about eight years old.

"There's a coffee shop over there." My father points toward the other end of the gate.

"Sure," I say. He reaches for my rolling carry-on, but I stop him. "I'm good."

He nods, and I intentionally walk a little in front of him.

We get to the coffee shop, which has a long line. We stand there side by side, making small talk about turbulence, the weather pattern lately, the irony of Nori's little sister joining my brother at Harvard next year, isn't that fantastic and then—

"Are you dating anyone special?"

The words sound like Mandarin coming out of his mouth, and I almost choke on my own spit except my mouth is too dry.

"Kind of." We move forward.

I omit the crucial parts that are: a.) it's a girl and b.) it is Gwen. My new pact with myself is to be honest with people I love. So screw those I couldn't give a steaming shit about.

My dad runs a hand over his perfect salt-and-pepper hair.

The gaggle of girls in front of us turns around and gives us an angsty stare. I want to stick my tongue out at them.

My dad looks around, maybe for an escape. He says distractedly, "That bag must be heavy. Let me take it."

"No, I'm good." I want to add that I'm in better shape than he is. Poor guy has to be twenty pounds thinner than the last time I saw him, and we Kirschner men are not that big and brawny to begin with.

The teenage girls place their order, which involves a lot of half-caf, decaf, skinny, grande crap.

We step forward.

"Two coffees."

"I'll take mine iced," I say. The sweat from our impending conversation makes me commit the ultimate betrayal of myself and order an iced beverage.

"Really?" He raises his brows. Weird what he does remember about me and what he doesn't.

I shrug. "I'm hot."

My father nods and pulls his wallet out to pay. I almost slap his hand away and pay for the damned drinks myself. To prove something.

I guess I do have some "repressed" anger as George has said when we've broached the subject of dear old dad. I let him pay, more to prove to George, who, okay, is not here, that I am NOT mad.

We take our drinks, and I don't use a straw but slurp mine loudly like the petulant, moody teenage girls that had been in front of us. We scan the crowd for a spot. I'm acutely aware of my backpack and how it sticks out like a middle school kid. At this point I've reduced my age by over a decade, and we haven't even begun the conversation.

"Over here," he says, and I follow him, pushing the cover back down over my drink and delicately maneuvering and squishing by other tables stuffed with families and couples.

He sits at the end of the long coffee bar, and I sit in the empty seat next to him. Awkward.

He sips noiselessly, and I open the cover of mine

and slurp, casting a glance at him and catching him doing the same at me. He smiles, but it's more like he smelled something bad. Which he could've. I'm definitely sweating heavily in my long-sleeve tee shirt. It's the one that Gwen bought me for my birthday last year. *Big Boys Don't Cry*. Hmmmm...

Dad doesn't notice my shirt or any smells. He is now, with full obviousness, staring right at me.

"So," I say and put my drink down, which is now almost drained dry.

"Tell me about things."

The crusted-over speck of jam on the table sure is interesting right now.

He tries again. "School's almost over. Law school on the horizon?"

I look past him at the even longer line of coffee hopefuls. I'll bite this time. "Maybe," I say, even though I've long since taken the LSATs and my applications are just waiting for me to hit Submit.

"Is this person you're dating someone special?"

I can't control this one because I want to confuse the shit out of him, and then I want to get up and leave. "Yes. Yes. *She, she* is very nice."

His eyes widen and red creeps up his chin. He leans forward. "She?"

I nod and sip my now empty, save for ice cubes, drink. I get a few drops of sugary water.

"I'm not sure how to respond to that." He says it the same way a defendant would claim to plead the fifth. Dad on the other side of the courtroom. I like the discomfort of that.

I put my empty cup down. "How about 'good job, son'?"

"I-I—"

"I'm going to let you off the hook here. Even though I really shouldn't. I really, really shouldn't because, let's be honest, *Dad*, you've been a shitty father for a long time." I shake my empty cup and the ice cubes clink together.

My father inhales through his nose and holds it in.

"Here's what's going on and then we can end this torture because I'm sweating and getting disgusting and because I will be seeing my girlfriend, yes, hear it and weep, my girlfriend, in a few, and I don't want to get too gross." I tap the cup on the table.

"Andrew—"

"Nah, there's nothing you can really say right now, Dad. You know, to right any of the crap that's happened. Please let me say my piece, and we can move on from there."

"Son…" His hands wrap around his cup, but he doesn't take a drink.

I laugh. "But actually, no, you don't get to call me that right now." I guess it's time to stop being polite and start getting real, as they say.

The hurt that flashes over him is not as satisfying as I had hoped it would be, but I keep going.

"I'm bisexual, Dad. Right now, I'm with a woman. I may be with her forever. Or not. I may be with a guy in my next relationship. But right now, you can rest easy because I'm with a woman." Relief washes me. Said it. Bisexual. It wasn't even that difficult and it didn't sound weird.

I keep going. Cats are marching out of the bag. "Actually, you know her."

"I do?"

My phone buzzes, and I pull it out and glance at the screen:

—*U OK?*—

I thumb type.

—*No come to strbcks now*—

"It's not Nori, is it?"

"No, Dad. But you're close."

"Hey, Mr. Kirschner!"

I turn and see Gwen flushed. My mother is behind her, both smiling eagerly, maybe too eagerly. They really are hopelessly similar sometimes.

"Yes, that's her. Right there."

"Where?"

Gwen bounds over and smiles at both of us, and I say to my father, whose confusion is, I hate to admit, quite lovely in the moment. "Gwen."

****

GWEN

Mr. Kirschner. Red-faced. Sweaty. Uncomfortable. Good.

"You guys need some more time?" Cindy asks, but really it's because I think she isn't sure what to say or what's happening.

Andy stands up and almost knocks me over with his over-stuffed backpack.

"No, I think we're done."

Mr. Kirschner grabs Andy's arm, and Andy actually growls. "Let me go, Dad. I'm all set. Enough father-son bonding."

"Hold on there, Andrew. I have something I would like to say."

Andy rolls his eyes like a teenage girl, and I repress a nervous giggle.

"Sit down." Mr. Kirschner still has a way of talking that can scare the shit out of you even if you can barely hear him.

Andy sits and we hover next to him.

Mr. Kirschner looks at me with a stiff smile. "You are a lovely, smart young woman. My son tells me you two are dating?"

"What?" Cindy wobbles backward, and I grab her, and then she grabs me back. "You two are dating?"

Andy holds up his hand, annoyed. "Mom, I was going to tell you, and you came here with an unexpected—I'm going to say it—*unwanted* guest."

"Andy!" I say to him, suddenly not enjoying this moment.

"No, no. Come on. You want honesty, Gwen, right? That's what you're pissed at me about, not being totally honest about who I date and about not telling you the whole truth, so let's all be honest." His parents are confused. "The *honest* truth here is that *Dad* is going to want to hang out with me now and do whatever pitiful, stupid things he thinks we should do together as father and *straight* son. The same things you and Jake do together, right? Lifting weights in the basement or shooting hoops outside? The things that I was always left out of growing up because I wasn't the good son."

Mr. Kirschner is stricken, his face long and his eyes sad, like he's remembering Andy and Jake as kids, Jake, bigger and stronger, outside shooting baskets with him on the driveway, and Andy standing to the side, trying to join in and just failing.

The sounds around us, conversations and dishes clanking, suddenly get louder. Mr. Kirschner straightens up. "Excuse me." He clears his throat. "You have no idea how I feel right now. But I will tell you. I feel like you are misleading this young lady who has done nothing but stand by your side for many years, and I think that if you are confused about what your sexuality is, then you should figure it out with someone else."

Grrr. If I could growl right now at that man, I would. I open my mouth to speak but glance at Andy first and stop. His face has never before revealed the kind of anger that I see right now. His jaw is set so tight it will snap and unhinge right here.

Although it is louder than a high school cafeteria at the moment, there is a stillness and silence that overcomes all of us. It's a bit like being in the dog park and seeing two really big alpha dogs bump into each other. It's like that moment right before one attacks the other.

That's when Andy punches his father right in the jaw.

Not a total surprise, but I still jump and gasp.

Another debilitating, awful silence with lots of background noise. Andy's father, wide-eyed and clutching his jaw, stands all the way up. Mrs. Kirschner goes to him, and it's like they're married again. She fusses over him and reprimands Andy. But it doesn't matter because two cops have shown up and are about to cuff Andy. Feels like they were watching the whole time, ready to pounce when the inevitable happened.

I think I'm screaming now, and it's all very tragic.

"Officers, it's fine, he is my son."

"Are you sure, sir?" They eye Andy up and down, which is funny but also kind of sexy. Andy pushes them off him. Total badass. Man, I'm learning many new things about my Andy.

"Yes, yes."

Cindy steps away from Mr. Kirschner and grabs Andy's hand, inspecting it.

He rolls his eyes, but I watch him nurse the hand.

The officers aren't leaving. "Are you sure you don't want to—"

"No, no. We're fine." All around, pairs of eyes are on us.

"Let's get out of here," Mr. Kirschner says, and we thread through the totally silent crowded coffee bar and finally make it out to the gate. Andy sweats visibly, as does Mr. Kirschner. Once we are far enough away from any swarms of people, he grabs Andy's arm. "Andy, you will talk to me. I'm your father."

Andy violently shakes the hand off and glares at his father. "Nope. I'm done. Goodbye." He begins to roll his suitcase and walk. My hands drop to my sides in defeat. Cindy does the same.

"Why do you always have to have the last word, Craig?" And then she takes my rolling bag in one hand and my hand in the other. "Let's go."

And we run to catch up with Andy.

"Gwen," Mr. Kirschner calls, and I glance back at him.

We hold each other's gaze for a moment before I turn and run to Andy.

Chapter 15

ETHAN
Nori and I sit across from each other, the plate of cold eggs and the pile of sickeningly sweet-smelling brownies between us. She reaches for my hand. I trace her long, thin fingers and then the veins, visible and winding, like confused roads. I can hear the sound of her breathing, shallow and short.

I stand up. "I'm going outside."

"To smoke?"

It's not an accusing tone, but I take it that way and shift my jaw, trying to hold in a scream. Because that's what I want to do. Scream and yell like a broken little boy.

On my way out, I dip my hand into that tiny closet by the laundry room and grab my lighter and a cigarette before I slam out the slider door.

Our entire relationship plays in snapshots in my memory. The soundtrack is every sappy tune featured in rom-coms. When we dated in high school, we loved to watch all that shit together. My main motivation was seeing one of those heartthrobs finally kiss the nerdy, good girl because it would make Nori pretty horny and guarantee me getting to second base.

I broke her heart, and I really only knew how bad when she drove us home from college that first semester. She didn't speak to me the entire time, but I saw her eyes water, and it was all that silence until the end that made me really get it. I decided there and then I would never hurt this girl again.

It's not cold out here, but I shiver and smoke and shiver some more. I don't walk down the steps to the beach to try and hide the smoking. I want her to see me feeling all fucked up.

The waves have started to roll all the way up the beach. The sky is overcast as the wind picks up. I want it to rain on me while I smoke. I want something to distract me from this pain, because for the first time in a long time, I want to punch a hole through something. I smoke quickly and wish for Nori to chase me, to come out here and put her arms around me. Even if I pull away, I don't want her to let go.

Shit.

I walk to the railing, suck on my cigarette, and watch the ocean roll.

When I hear her light footsteps, my heart lifts a little. I feel her next to me as it starts to mist. She takes the cigarette from me and puffs on it almost expertly, except at the end, she coughs. I start to laugh, and she smiles, grabs me, and pulls my face to hers.

"I love you, and I do want to marry you, Ethan. Just not right now."

I try to stay still and stoic, but she kisses me. I can't help it. I cave in and kiss her back, holding the cigarette away from us and lingering on her lips after and then pressing my forehead into hers when we finish.

I smoke the cigarette with Nori wrapped around me. The lull of the waves rolling makes me relaxed. "Do you remember when I found out about my mother?"

She squeezes me. "What made you think of that?"

"This." I blow the smoke up and away from the top of her head. "Proposal. Rejection."

"Jesus Christ," she says softly. "My rejection feels like when you found out your mother committed suicide?"

I nod. "I know that's fucked up. That it doesn't make sense." I kiss the top of her head, the pain of the memory, me at my computer, clicking on "East Bay woman falls to death from Mt. Hope Bridge."

"I'm not leaving you," Nori whispers into my neck. "Just like you went to Peru and came back, I'll be back."

But I'm steeped in the memory, remembering how I threw the mouse at the wall, and it shattered. Slammed out of my room and ran to where my father was in the garage, working on one of his old cars he used to have. Screaming at him and then crying until he grabbed me and wrestled me to the cold floor, both of us screaming and crying. Him saying, "I didn't know how to tell you," and me screaming back, "Were you ever going to tell me?" And him shaking his head over and over.

"Baby, I'm not leaving you." She takes my cigarette from me and rests it on the ledge of the railing. Then she puts her hands on either side of my face. "I'm not leaving you. I want to marry you. I want to spend the rest of my life with you."

We press foreheads again. Then I release her and take one more puff of the cigarette. We are quiet for a few more minutes and the memory of finding out about my mother fades as the waves roll in front of us.

"I want to take you somewhere tomorrow," she

says after I toss the butt over the railing.

I kiss her warm lips, slide my tongue all the way into her mouth, and she pulls me closer, if it's possible, and moves her hands under my shirt.

"I want to take you to this class at the yoga center tomorrow. It's a partner yoga class."

I almost laugh. "*Naked* partner yoga?"

She smirks. "No. Come on. We need it. I know that you're mad."

"I'm not mad," I say. Hurt more than mad.

"I think this will help," she offers.

I look into her brown eyes without saying anything for a minute. She goes to kiss me, and I move my head back. "So, if not now, when?"

Her eyes scan my face. "That's what Swami Nick says in class."

"What?"

"He says that when we are in an impossible hold, 'If not now, when.' "

"What the hell does he mean?"

"Don't wait to get there, be there."

"What?"

"It means that we are so afraid of the pain, of the hold, that we tell ourselves 'oh next time' but this is next time."

"That dude is a smart man, even though I think he has the hots for you. But he's right, and you should take his advice: If not now, when?"

She kisses me again on the jaw and whispers, "Soon, soon."

"You're breaking my heart," I tell her.

"I know all about that, Ethan," she whispers. "You have to trust me."

I've been in love with Nori since that moment when I walked into the cafeteria, a dorky freshman trying to be skater-punk cool—even though I didn't know anything about actually skateboarding. I saw her before she saw me. Long hair to her waist that she kept tucking behind her ear. Laughing and taking sips of Gwen's soda. When I walked over to the three of them, sweating from balls to neck, she said, "Hey, I know you. Social studies last year. You brought in a GI Joe doll for the Vietnam project." For some reason that made me laugh, and then I sat down and soon the four-headed monster was born.

We had this cool teacher for World History that year, and Nori and I happened to be in that class together. When we had our first partner project, I told Mr. Pontey that I had a crush on Nori and could he help a guy out. He winked at me and said, "I got this."

I went to her house, and she said we should bake brownies while we worked. Nori, man, she was hot in tight jeans and a tee shirt that said Girls Rule with little diamonds on the letters. She had really small breasts and was super skinny with her hair all over the place. She had everything for the project laid out and even some extra poster board and markers. Her parents were at work.

I had showered three times and played with myself so much the poor thing was hurting. I wanted to be calm and cool because my plan was to make a move.

She wanted to make the brownies right away. I followed her into the pantry and when she reached up on the shelf to get the box, a sliver of her creamy skin peeked out from her shirt. Then she turned and handed the box to me, and our fingers brushed. God, I remember the electric bolt that went straight to my pants, but I watched her as she moved a piece of that wild hair out of her face. Her lips were pink and soft, and she smiled slyly. Then, she furrowed her brow and leaned toward me. I swear my eyes and the poor guy in my pants bugged out at the same time because I thought, *This is it*. She's going to kiss me! But instead, she gently brushed my cheek under my eye.

"Eyelash," she said softly and brushed again.

I stood still, sure that my boner was out of my pants at this point.

"Hmmm." Then she leaned closer, her breath like cherries. She gently blew on my check. "There," she said and took a step back, but it was too late because my hand was already around the small of her back and the other was clutching that box of brownies.

We didn't leave the pantry for quite a while that night.

****

NORI

The yoga studio is small, with bamboo floors and smells of lavender and peppermint. All of the blocks and cushions are purple, and the walls are a soft green. Soft Indian music plays in the background. There are four other couples, and the teacher is Guru Shanti (real name Sheryl; she told me that over a cup of coffee one time after I taught a class last winter when we were visiting). The other couples are older than us. One could be our grandparents. Another is two women who could be friends or could be partners. This partner class is geared for any kind of coupleship. The other two couples are around my parents' age, and they sit far from each other not talking.

We all sit on our mats in silence.

Guru Shanti smiles serenely at all of us and says nothing. This used to unnerve me, and when I glance at Ethan, I can see what he's thinking, but I nudge him and give him a smile.

"Welcome to partner yoga. Tonight, because you're all couples, I want you to set an intention and that is to remember why you're together, why you're here in this studio tonight."

As she leads us into chanting *om*, I close my eyes, and it's hard for me to go inside myself. I'm far too concerned if Ethan is hating this and maybe even still hating me a little.

As we sit with our eyes closed and the *om* ends, Guru says, "Reach out and brush fingertips with your partner and hold there for a few moments and conjure up that memory of when you first knew that this person was important to you."

And the memory that comes to me isn't quite that because we have had part one and part two of our relationship. Part one was mainly me just thinking he was hot, a more lust-fueled moment—in my pantry, freshman year. And part two, I can't remember the exact moment that I knew that this was it. I do remember the torture of knowing I wanted to be with him, the years in between part one and two, and he wanted to be with me, but we could not get there yet.

****

I don't remember how I found out that Ethan was going to Clark, but I remember the knowing and the terrifying but thrilling sensation in my body that I would have another four years with him. Four years away from our town and all the gossip and rumors.

Four years away from the Terrible Moment that we had when we broke up.

He asked for a ride home that first week of college to get his car, which he conveniently had left at home, even though freshmen were allowed to have cars on campus. I agreed. It was funny how we really hadn't had a full conversation in over a year and a half but once we were on campus, it was like we knew each other from home and all of the baggage of what had happened in the past didn't matter as much.

The details of what we talked about are fuzzy. In fact, that we actually spoke at all, that's debatable. He says we didn't. I'm not sure. I know what I wore. A pair of pale yellow cropped cargo pants and a black tank top, my arms brown with sun. My hair was newly cut short, and the slight natural wave was curlier. The music we listened to was a playlist from his phone that had songs that we definitely made out to or played while doing homework together back in high school. I know details, like snapshots, close-ups of things. His hand resting on his knee. His nails and cuticles smooth, a patch of hair on his hand, a detail I noticed because it was new, and I remember thinking, *Everything has changed since we dated.* He's taller, his hair is shorter, and now he has hair in places he didn't before. It was a dirty thought that made me smile internally. Every so often, Ethan would tap a finger in time to whatever music was on. An awareness, like the sensation of heat, was between us as I drove, one hand on the wheel, the other resting on the gearshift.

But the pivotal moment was when we arrived at his house.

I pulled up to his house, not turning into the

driveway. The sky was still cloudless blue, the sun high, and the air warm and thick with humidity. We had to drive with the windows down because my air-conditioning was broken. Beads of sweat collected on my forehead and even the back of my knees felt damp.

I let the car idle, and finally, for the first time in the hour and a half that we had been in the car, I turned and looked at him. He was already eyeing me up and down.

"You look hot."

I flushed and laughed nervously, and then he rubbed his head and laughed. "I mean that you look hot, like literally, you look like you are hot—temperature-wise. Do you want to come in and get some water?"

I nodded because right then I felt it, the heat and the humidity assaulting my body. The car no longer moving and the window no longer blowing air. And then we lingered, this small linger, and our eyes clung to a mutual gaze. This overwhelming relief filled me, and I said, "Yes," but it was more of "Yes" to both wanting the water and to "I forgive you. I mean it. I really forgive you."

And then the next moment, inside his house, the air-conditioning was giving me goosebumps and his hand was rubbing my arms, and then in his kitchen, he searched for a bottle of water. I know he said something, and then he was right in front of me, holding a glass of water, and I reached for it, took a sip, and said, "Good water" because I couldn't find any other words at that moment. He was close to me, the closest he had been since sophomore year when we broke up. Dizzying, that moment was. Even thinking about it now, the hesitation and the vibrations between us, the raw, unfiltered desire to be that close.

He said, "Mind if I have a sip?" and I nodded and watched his mouth open and close on the glass. He tipped it back and drank with his eyes closed.

He put the bottle down and kissed me.

"Years. For years I've waited to have the opportunity to kiss you again," he whispered to me after.

****

At the end of the class, we sit in lotus and chant *om* with our eyes closed. As the sound fills me, I remember something else. Something not so long ago as the memories of Ethan and me. I think of my dad. Of wanting to make things right before I leave for India.

A year away is a long time.

Chapter 16

ANDY

When we get home, Mom begs us to come to the house for a few days, *together*. She doesn't ask about the new status of Gwen and me. She makes a lot of small talk in the car while Gwen and I are pretty quiet.

We pull into the driveway and the air smells cold. When we get out of the car, the ground is solid with ice. We carefully make our way up the driveway. I see my breath and Gwen's and Mom's puffing out into the gray overcast. I have a sick feeling in my stomach, and all I want to do is take a nap.

We get inside the house, which is almost as cold as outside. I go to the thermostat and press it until it hits seventy. More small talk with Mom and Gwen, and they tell me to go to bed.

"What are you guys gonna do?" I yawn.

"Girl stuff." Mom starts to unzip my bag, which is on the kitchen table. "Laundry? Make dinner?"

"I'll do the laundry. No one wants me near a stove." Gwen laughs.

I give a faint laugh. My eyes are heavy. They practically close before I can hit the steps up to my room. The house smells of cinnamon and pine, but as I hit the upstairs hallway, I smell gardenia from my mother's room. I haven't been home in a while, not even for the summers, since I've been working through each one and taking extra classes.

I open the door to my room, and it's still decorated like I had it in high school, including the Bradley Cooper and Beyoncé posters. I don't bother to shut the shades and tumble onto my bed.

I fall into a twilight-like state, reminding me of when I had my wisdom teeth taken out. Images and scenes of Gwen and me play out a movie in my mind.

When we all first started hanging out, Nori would say that Gwen had the biggest crush on me, and I never knew what to do with that. Gwen was funny and flirty with me sometimes but never aggressive. I was shy, and the idea of making a move on anyone was terrifying.

****

I realized I wanted to kiss her one day in biology freshman year, about two months into school. She and I weren't in the same bio class as Ethan and Nori—we were in the GT program, Gifted and Talented. Gwen was my lab partner. We used to have to take copious notes from the overhead while Mr. Crowman lectured in this monotonous voice. Gwen was neurotic in her quest for straight As, and I spent a lot of time staring at her, but she didn't seem to ever notice. I never tried to distract her, mainly because it was fun to watch her without her knowing I was. How focused she was, unmoving except to write the notes, whereas all the rest of us shifted around, bit the ends of our pencils, sighed, and counted the minutes until the end.

One day I was staring at her, and I thought, *Wow, she is beautiful*. She wore long braids down her back or sometimes it was brushed shiny, the color of grapefruit skin, and long with a single barrette. One day she wore a white jean skirt and when she shifted her knee to re-cross her legs, I saw it. Her underwear. A pink swatch of fabric, and it was like, let there be light! This is a girl and she's pretty and what does that mean? I was a little late to the puberty party. This was one of the first times I really noticed girls—as in, they have underwear, and they are like a swatch of heaven. Not too long after this, I caught a quick glance of Ethan in his underwear and had the same exact reaction. One that I tucked away (along with the boner) for another year or so.

Sitting there in bio, I popped a boner and had to squirm around in my seat a little bit.

A few weeks later, as usual, the four of us were spending a Friday night at Gwen's house—her parents were the most relaxed about everything. We spent a lot of time watching movies, playing air hockey or video games. The dynamic between the four of us had started to shift a little. Some of these nights we had split up to take "walks," and on other nights, during a movie, I would notice that Gwen was cuddled right up to me. One time she even put my arm around her, and I suddenly thought of that day in science when I saw that swatch of pink. Ethan and Nori had graduated from tickling and teasing to tonsil hockey at this point, which bummed me out a little; making out in the corner wasn't fun for anybody but them.

Then came that night we decided to give in to our collective curiosity about getting wasted. Gwen found an unopened bottle of vodka in the freezer when she was looking for ice cream, and I knew enough about alcohol that we should put it in something. Voilà! Orange juice in the fridge. She thumped it out onto the counter. It's a blur what exactly happened next.

I know that we wound up in her parents' Jacuzzi

really meant for two. I know that the sight of Ethan, black boxer briefs clinging to his ass, and Gwen, white see-through bra suctioned to her breasts, nipples erect, confused the hell out of me. But more importantly, it excited me in the scariest way. Nori was like a sister to me and although she had the most incredible long legs, smooth and shiny, she didn't do for me what Ethan and Gwen did. I wanted to kiss them both. Preferably at the same time.

And then we were. All in the tub, lights out, candles lit, laughing and sitting in each other's laps and licking soap bubbles off each other's shoulders, Ethan's smooth but rippled with muscles against my tongue and Gwen's body soft and slick. As the bubbles popped and the vodka bottle was drained, we all dried off and collapsed on her parents' huge bed.

Gwen had a little twinkle in her eye as we lay facing each other while on the edge of the bed, Ethan and Nori curled up and fell asleep.

The joke is that we don't remember anything specific from the night and that for all we know we all made out with each other, maybe even Ethan and me. Ethan has joked that my lips are as soft and full as Nori's, meaning he wouldn't know the difference.

With only a towel around me and one around Gwen, she didn't break eye contact.

"We should make out," she said in a whisper, and I remember how the moon or the stars, whatever the light was that came through the skylight above us, made her face glowy.

I blinked as the red crawled up my neck.

"Go for it, dude!" Ethan mumbled from the corner where I had thought he and Nori were busy with each other.

Gwen was inches from me. I turned to her, and she was grinning big. I started to overthink. Should I touch her cheek? Cup her chin? Then I thought, screw it, and leaned all the way over and kissed her softly on the lips. She didn't kiss me back the same way. She opened her mouth, and I remember thinking, *Oh, wow! We're doing this and we're doing this right here.*

"Oh shit!" I remember hearing Ethan say. Nori made a low whistle.

We broke apart, and I grinned too. Ethan leaned over and grabbed my hand for a high five.

The last thing I remember about that night is, once dressed and waiting for our parents to come get us, teeth brushed and chewing a whole pack of cinnamon gum to avoid getting caught drunk, Gwen whispered to me, "I've wanted you to do that since we met in the cafeteria."

****

As I relive that moment, I turn to my side, wanting to sleep but these deep, long-ago memories keep pushing their way through.

Occasionally Gwen and I would hook up. Here and there. Mainly secret make out sessions. But it got weird for me pretty quickly. See, she would be kissing me and sometimes I would wish it was Ethan—but not necessarily Ethan, just someone who wasn't a girl. I thought a lot about the night in the hot tub, all of our bodies wet and slick and how I wanted to kiss Gwen, but I really liked the way Ethan looked without his clothes. I wasn't sure any more what I wanted. I started to notice when guys were getting changed for gym in the locker room, and I even had a few dreams about kissing guys. Kissing Ethan.

Things were a mess in my head.

And after that summer everything for me was kind of a mess anyway. Nori and Ethan broke up, and Ethan started hanging out with his football friends and Nori got me in the breakup. Soon, things with Gwen officially ended, and it was weird between us. Especially when she found out I was gay through that tool Heyward. Nori and I clung together. Her, broken, and me, confused. The truth about me and Gwen was that I ended it before anything could happen because I knew, deep down, that I might be gay (never even considered bisexual at that point), and I didn't want to drag her into my confusion, didn't want to be some closeted gay dude with a girlfriend as a cover.

I roll back over and open my eyes, stare at the ceiling. That time period was ripe with confusion and Gwen was tangled up in it. So I understand why she has been hesitant. I blink away the past and wish Gwen was with me now, curled up on my chest with the ends of her hair tickling my face.

****

GWEN

Cindy and I are in the basement sorting all the laundry. I do Andy's laundry all the time. Having a pair of his boxers in my hand isn't something I really pay much attention to. Cindy giggles as I retell her some of the events over the past few months.

"I'm sorry. It's hard to focus on what you're saying as you stand there, sorting my son's underpants like it's nothing. No wonder he keeps you around." She winks at me.

I laugh and finish stuffing the dark clothes into the

washer.

"Let me ask you something." Cindy reaches for the soap and pours some in the dispenser of the washer. "Forget Andrew for a moment. I mean, we do need to get to him—believe me—but let's talk about you." She closes the lid.

I nod, leaning against the dryer as it rumbles.

"Do you think this is going to work out?" She leans over and presses the buttons of the washer.

I breathe in deep. The question of the hour.

Over the hiss of the washing machine starting up, I answer her. "I don't know."

She grabs another basket of what must be clean towels and balances it on her hip for a moment and says, "Do you think this would have happened if, say, you hadn't moved in with him?"

"What do you mean?" I take the basket from her and put it on the floor between us. I know exactly what she means, and I think of the outburst with Nori at the condo, but I'm stalling because I don't know how to answer her.

She bends down and takes a towel. "Do you believe that you and Andrew would have gotten together if you weren't sleeping in his bed?"

I blush, something I don't do. Then I take a towel and fold it. "How did you know?"

"Gwen." She takes the folded towel from me and puts it with hers and holds them both. "There is one bed and that couch of his is barely big enough for two people to sit on! Come on." She stares at me, like *come on, 'fess up.*

I grab another towel and fold it, feeling her eyes on me before she sighs. With her foot, she pushes another empty basket between us and plops the folded towels in there.

"Maybe not. No. I guess it wouldn't have happened," I say, putting the towel I folded on top of the others. "But that doesn't really matter now."

She doesn't respond or make eye contact. I worry she's angry with me, with us. I watch her fold another towel, and I say, "I think that I've always loved Andy."

She stops folding and looks me right in the eye with complete concern. "And I believe the same from him to you, even though I have to admit, I'm confused. My son dates boys? My son dates girls? My son dates both?"

"He's bisexual." I need to get more comfortable saying that.

She nods, but there is a hesitation from her. "I don't know. I'm worried; maybe it's the mother thing, but I'm worried. Worried because I'm not sure I understand what's happening with you two. Worried because I'm very fond of you, dear, you know that and you're like a daughter to me." She touches my hand.

The dryer dings.

She hands me the basket of folded towels.

I take it from her.

"I'll get the rest," she says.

"So?" I hold the basket against my stomach and wait for her to finish.

She sighs. "If this doesn't work out, I don't know how you two could go back to being friends."

"It's too late either way at this point."

Tears brim her eyes. "That's really what I wanted to say to you. That you need to think about yourself right now and not only Andrew because chances are, this is going to end up breaking both of your hearts."

I nod, then take the basket upstairs, trying not to let what she said make me cry.

I set the basket down in the kitchen on the table and then call back down to Cindy. "Want me to start dinner?" Though I have no idea what that even means since the last time I cooked was when I lived on campus at Columbia—Ramen Noodles.

She comes to the bottom of the stairs. "No. Let's do Chinese food. It's Friday night, after all; that's what we do, right?"

I smile; that's what we did in high school. Chinese food, Friday nights, Andy's house.

"Go check on him," she says.

****

I walk up the stairs, pausing at the pictures of Andy from infancy to high school graduation. They are in a similar display that the Mytowskys have of Jeni and Nori. In my house, my parents have a whole room dedicated to me, a shrine of award certificates, and pictures. That's the only child syndrome for sure; maybe that's why it's always been important to me that we stay friends. Nori has Jeni, and Andy has Jake, but they aren't close with their siblings. Maybe that's the reason for our loyalty.

I get to Andy's room, where the sun has sunk low and the light that comes into the room is shadowy. Andy is curled up on one side of the bed, the covers on the other side still tucked into the top of the mattress. I walk to him and watch him sleeping, his eyes closed and mouth in a little frown. I run a finger over his stubble. This is one complicated guy. I lift the covers and sit on the edge of the bed. One of his eyes opens.

"Sorry," I whisper. "You've been sleeping for a while. We're going to get takeout." I brush his shaggy hair out of his eyes.

Without opening the other eye, he says, "Wasn't sleeping. Thinking."

I slide into bed, and he pulls me onto his chest, stroking my hair.

"I don't want to hurt you," he says.

"I know," I whisper, and tears are already sliding down because I think of what Cindy said.

He wraps his arms around me tight, and we stay like that for a while.

Chapter 17

ETHAN

We finally stop the oming and chanting stuff and sit back-to-back.

"Breathe into each other. Support and nurture one another with breath and love," the teacher instructs us, her voice all whispery and Zen.

I like this. Nori's warm back and the bones of her spine pressing into mine. I breathe in the smell of lavender and peppermint.

"Leaning into one another as we breathe slow and deep."

The leaf that bobs and weaves down the river of my memory is that day, the first day of sophomore year, at Nori's locker, waiting for her. It was almost our one-year anniversary—a lifetime in high school—we had even survived the summer with her away at camp.

Or so we thought.

****

It was a cold day for early September. I remember I forgot a jacket and my sneakers were untied. Reaching down to tie my sneakers and almost falling over. Nervous. Terrified. Looking up and seeing her power walking down the hall, her big backpack bulging with fresh notebooks for the new year. I freaked out and darted into the doorway of one of the classrooms, peeking out once she got to her locker. No one else was there yet. I watched her. The locker banging open. Unloading her backpack to the top shelf of her locker. The rustling of her coat as she shrugged it off. Hanging up her bag. Then—

I stepped out of the doorway, and as she reached back into her locker, I was right next to her.

"Hey!" she said, her eyes big and happy; the memory of that "hi" still makes my throat close. Innocent, that's what I kept thinking. *This girl is pure innocence, and I am about to destroy her.*

"What's wrong?" Her eyes dropped and worry replaced happy.

"I have to tell you something."

She bit her lip. "What is it?"

And I, the genius jackass I was, blurted out, "I cheated on you." And then because I was smooth, I moved toward her like I was going to give her a hug.

The next thing I knew, my Nori pushed me away. I fell backward, ass over head.

And that's when the side doors to the school, just a few feet from her locker, busted open and the entire school flooded in. I called out to her, but she was gone.

What a dickhead I was.

My gram, who lived with Dad and me at the time, adored Nori and when I got home that day and told her we broke up and even why—mainly because I couldn't stop crying, tough guy that I was—I got the longest and loudest lecture that included "That girl is the best you will ever have." And Dad, who was home between tours, chimed in, "You screwed up big-time, buddy. A girl like that Nori is irreplaceable." And then my gram went into this whole thing about how her ex-husband, my father's dad, had been a cheating bastard and I was going to wind up just like him and *you think there is always another girl, something better and something different but there isn't...*My gram was a wise, wise woman.

I remember my gram and Dad told me that I had to go and apologize to Nori. I didn't want to. I was embarrassed and mad at myself. Not to mention the girl I had hooked up with was a senior and the whole school knew about what I did—Nori was the last to know because she had been away at camp. By the time I had gotten home and confessed to my gram and Dad, text messages and Facebook posts had gone viral, detailing my indiscretion. Even though it sucked to tell Nori, I was glad she heard it from me and not the internet.

So, I did what any dickhead teenage boy does; I showed up at Nori's house, uninvited.

I stood at the edge of the driveway. Rain was starting to dot the asphalt as I stared down, terrified to look up and make the long walk down to her door. I didn't have to because she came outside wearing a hoodie sweatshirt and hugging her arms to her chest. She stared at me with red eyes and no expression on her mouth.

I checked behind her for her parents, who I was sure would clobber me if they saw me out there with her, especially Mr. Mytowsky, who always let me know with his eyes how much he hated me. At that point, I was pretty sure, since the whole town knew about my mishap, her parents knew as well.

I jammed my hands in my pockets and walked to Nori.

Her eyes filled with tears and her face was set in total anger.

I Love That Girl

I started to move toward her, but I stopped. "Don't cry," I said. "I'm a dickhead. I fucked up." I gave her a small smile. The waterworks started for her, and I felt lower and lower as she kept wiping away her tears.

"Don't cry, Nori."

I reached out to wipe some tears with my thumb and pulled her to me, and she let me hold her for the longest half a second of my life.

But then she made this awful sound and shoved me away.

"No!"

I couldn't stand it, and I grabbed her and hugged her to me, but she stepped on my foot and pushed away again.

"Nori!"

She clenched her fists to her side. "Please do not, do not give me an explanation or details because frankly, I got all the information I need from the entire fucking school. You, you, Ethan Ledger, are the shittiest, most disgusting person I know. You couldn't make it a few more days till I got home! You go to a party without your girlfriend, and within minutes, you're doing shots and have your hand in some slut's jeans and then she's blowing you on a pool table—"

Years later, before we drove back home from college but after we had been there a week, we finally talked about the whole thing. The funny part is there was no blowjob and there was no hand in a girl's pants. There was a thirty-second in-and-out that was not memorable, and yes, there were shots—too many, and yes, there was a slutty senior, well, just as slutty as I was, frankly. The truth was, I was immature. I was drunk. I was a virgin.

I spent the next two and a half years after that moment on her driveway every so often, usually drunk, trying to show her how sorry I was, and though she dated other people and I tried to, I knew deep inside the part of myself I don't completely understand still, that she was mine and I was hers.

****

"Come back into the present moment," the yoga lady says, bringing me back to now, when I have Nori. "I want you to slowly move from sitting back-to-back to knees-to-knees in easy pose."

I open my eyes slowly and let them adjust for a minute. Nori mouths, "You okay?"

I nod. Our knees bump together, and the teacher says, "Now touch, palm to palm, and come to standing together, this requires communication and slow synchronicity. You must listen with your bodies."

Nori and I may be far apart in weight and height, but she is incredibly strong with all the yoga. We press into each other's palms and move with our eyes right on each other. I let myself follow her, but I also, as we press and start to move our legs to stand up, I try to listen to her with my body. There is this little current between us that seems to let us easily move to standing.

"Drop your palms. And bring them to prayer."

I glance at Nori while she stands in prayer.

We're going to be together, forever. I know it.

****

NORI

My eyes won't close.

Lying on my back next to Ethan, who's dead asleep, I stare up at the ceiling in my bedroom, faint marks from the tape I used years ago to hang up my beloved smiling Buddha poster are translucent reminders of my nightly prayers throughout high school. *Dear Buddha, please help me pass algebra. Dear Buddha, please give Ethan crabs for cheating on me. Dear Buddha, please get my parents to leave me the fuck alone about college.*

God, do I wish Buddha was here right now.

Those last two weeks in Florida were so perfect but since we've been back home to my parents' house, sleeping has not been my friend.

Also, little sis, Jeni, is with us, but my parents have come and gone—my dad has a trip to North Carolina for a conference and he never goes anywhere without Mom so she's there, too. They are due back tomorrow, and I'm kind of dreading seeing my father and hearing more lectures about Throwing My Life Away on Some Woo-Woo Bullshit.

Staring at the Buddha poster that isn't there, eyes burning, I blow a long breath out.

In just a few more days, I leave for India, and Ethan goes back to school. I turn on my side. Tonight's dinner of pizza is not sitting well in my stomach. I flip to my other side. Not any better. I inch out of bed and when I stand, I'm kind of woozy. Shit, this isn't what I need. I've had PMS for the last day or so, glorious sore boobs and all. God, being a girl is swell.

I have to admit to being glad about the hormone overload, though. I'd gotten a little bit of a freak-out going when I realized I was a couple of days late, but Gwen had reassured me that Plan B usually messes up your cycle, and clearly, she was right.

I go to the bathroom and sit on the toilet, tired but awake and trying to count the days since my last period.

I give up. Who knows? But I must be getting it. I do get a craving for grease around that time. Hence, the godawful non-vegan so-called pizza I'm now paying for.

I touch my forehead. Cool. Good. In order to get on that plane, I need to be fever free and not throwing up.

I go downstairs and through the kitchen, stopping to grab a cup of ice because somehow chewing ice sounds like a good idea—maybe it's good for nausea?—and then head toward the basement door on the other side of the house. I'll watch Lifetime. Nothing like a really good chick-in-crisis-movie to help me sleep.

But when I get to the top of the basement stairs, I see the door is open and hear the TV.

I skip down the steps but slow to more of a drag as my stomach sloshes around in my abdomen.

"Jeni?" I see the back of her head, where she sits on the couch in the dim light of the TV.

"Hey," she says without turning around.

I tip the cup of crushed ice and chew. This is weird. The whole time I've been back, I've barely seen her. She's either at the gym or holed up in her room, doing godknowswhat, probably writing a novel or inventing the cure for cancer for all I know. She's come out to dinner with us a few times—she does like Ethan. She went to South America for a semester her junior year of high school, so they talked about sandboarding in Lima and climbing the Inca trail of Machu Picchu throughout the entire meal, which was a relief to me because that meant I didn't have to hunt for things to say to her.

She clicks the remote in the dim light. I walk over and slump into the couch beside her and even take part of the blanket she has. I chew, and she clicks. I go back up twice for ice. She doesn't ask me about the ice, and I don't ask her about the fact that she hates Lifetime movies.

And my whole body feels sore. Jesus Christ, period, hurry up.

"I might be pregnant."

I choke on my ice.

"I slept with Jake. Andy's brother Jake. We've been hooking up since he came home from school." Typical Jeni drops major bombs with no inflection of her voice, no gestures with her body. If she wasn't a carbon physical copy of my father, I'd say she was adopted.

After the second bomb, I'm full-on having a coughing attack. She doesn't flinch but simply and robotically slaps me on the back twice and like the enchantress she is, she cures me of my fit, and I stop.

She clicks the TV off and drops her head down. Still reeling from her bombs, I awkwardly pat her shoulder. I skip the obvious yet rhetorical-ish questions like *didn't you use protection,* and *haven't you heard about the ever awesome saved my own life Plan B*? "Why don't we find out for sure?" Then the slightly wrong yet very appealing idea occurs to me: if she is pregnant with Jake's baby that means Andy and I would finally be real family, linking us for life, no matter what happens with Gwen.

There I go, not thinking like a yogi as usual. How many hours till India?

My little sister, who has never behaved like a little sister should, including never annoying me by wanting to play with my toys or stealing my clothes because she skipped that phase of childhood, looks up at me with her big eyes and her perfectly straight bangs, and as one single, fat tear spills, she nods, and whispers, "Let's do it."

****

Mother-fucking shit, it's cold. I glance at my sister as she buckles her seat belt. Other than her red eyes, she is completely unruffled by both her potential problem and this ass-bitingly cold weather. But I managed to get a little sly smile out of her when she and I did the forbidden and grabbed the keys to my father's BMW SUV, which was nestled comfortably in our heated two-car garage. Not only would I have a warmer ride, but then I wouldn't have to wake up Ethan—who still remains ignorantly and blissfully asleep—to help me scrape the ice off mine and dig it out of the four feet of snow that covers it. I love how my parents have "people" to plow our driveway, but those people chose to dump all the snow onto my car.

I turn the wheel with ease while Jeni cranks up the seat warmers. We idle down the street slowly, and I flip the radio on because I don't know what one says to one's sister, who she barely talks to, when they are on their way to get a pregnancy test. We sing along, together, to a pop song all about wanting to dance with somebody. Another thing Jeni hates—pop songs…or so I thought. Then again I thought she hated boys, sex, and bangs, and apparently, she's very familiar with all three.

****

The lights in the store make me squint when I step through the automatic doors as they swish open. Not Jeni though, she walks like a dancer or an equestrian, spine super erect and chin in a slightly tilted up fashion. How are those bangs so straight? I pull out my shades from the pocket of my heavy winter coat and slide them on. Migraine is imminent. My feet are cement blocks as I lift them in my heavy snow boots, with each step further inside, my whole body gets heavier and colder, despite the long winter duster and fur-lined boots I'm wearing. *Please do not let me be getting sick.*

The only place open is the supermarket, so we have to scan up and down the signs of the aisles to find the one that says Feminine Products. We pause before walking down, and, of course, I flash to a month ago, the pharmacy with Ethan, the numb feeling that overtook my body and the expression on the checkout guy's face. In my memory, he's straight out of a rom-com where he speaks into his microphone and says, "PRICE CHECK ON PLAN B BIRTH CONTROL." I almost laugh, but tears prick my eyes. *Fuck. Fuck. Fuck.* Need to focus on Jeni. Again, India is very much needed in my life.

I feel her slide her mitten hand in mine, and suddenly, we are eight and four, walking to our neighbor's house across the street for the first time, alone, sans parents. Her enormous brown eyes, looking up at mine, no trace of fear anywhere except the widening of her eyes. But I clutched her hand in mine and looked left and right and then escorted her safely across.

Kind of like what I have to do now.

We walk together, dually lead-footed, or maybe hers is due to fear—who knows? My boots make loud thud noises while hers are soundless. We stop in front of the section of condoms, fertility tests, HIV tests, and then the pregnancy tests.

"How late are you?" I whisper, wondering if we need one of those early detection ones. I've had quite a few college roommates need late-night runs to the campus pharmacy. I know way more than I really need to about the various flavors of pregnancy tests.

"Three weeks."

"You waited three weeks!" I resist the overwhelming urge to shake her senseless.

Her eyes fill with tears.

"I'm sorry. Doesn't matter."

I grab four different tests, one of the early detection variety. "Just to be sure," I say.

She nods, the tears rolling down, and with the bangs, she looks like she did as a four-year-old. That's when my heart starts to pound. What is that I'm feeling? Fear. And love. And protection. And sadness. There is so much I don't know about my little sis. I throw my arm around her and kiss her silky head. "Don't worry. It's all going to be fine."

We pay for the tests, throwing in a bag of peanut and chocolate candies because suddenly that sounds really appealing. We also stop on the way out at the soda fountain. "Just need a little more ice," I say apologetically while filling up a paper cup.

But she isn't paying attention to me or my ice. "We can't take it at home," she says grabbing the bag from me.

"We can't?" I say between crunches of the best-tasting ice ever.

"No! Mom and Dad are coming back tomorrow morning…pretty early, and they will find it in the recycle bin and…"

"Who the hell recycles a pregnancy test?"

"Right." Her eyes scan my face but not because she's looking for me to say anything. It's her manic-I-gotta-figure-this-out problem-solving face. Same expression she has when she sits at the kitchen table and does her four hours of summer homework.

Her face switches to an I've-got-it look. "I guess we can put it in the trash and bury it way down." I nod and start to pull her toward the exit, but she stops and screeches, "No, they'll know! I know they'll know."

"Shhhh!" My grip on her arm tightens.

But panic-strength trumps my hold on her, and she breaks free. "I gotta find a bathroom."

I give up. Too tired.

Suddenly, my lead legs become lighter, and we fly down the aisle that has a sign for the restrooms. I push her into the swinging door, and she yelps, but I ignore her and push her into the handicap stall so we can both fit.

I slam it shut and lock it. "Take your pants down."

"I have to make a seat first!"

I watch her pull bits of toilet paper off the roll and make a seat while I sigh and roll my eyes.

"Public toilet seats are filled with—"

"Right now, that is the least of your problems. Pull your pants down."

We say nothing as I rip open the box, quickly read the directions, and instruct her to hold the stick in her urine stream for five seconds.

We look away from each other while she pees.

"Here." She hands me the stick, and I use toilet paper to take it from her and put the little cover back on.

She doesn't stand up. "Now what?"

"It says wait five minutes for a full result."

She wipes and flushes and pulls her pants up. I stand with the stick in my hand. We stare at each other, her face pale to the point of translucent, and then I glance down. One strong line. Pink and proud. I have enough experience with this to know she is not pregnant, and the relief that fills me is better than savasana.

"So?" she asks.

"Not pregnant."

"Really?" The color returns to her face, and she smiles in a way I haven't seen since she was little. Then she grabs me into a hug, even though I'm still holding her pee stick and neither one of us has washed our hands.

"Thank you," she whispers into my ear.

****

When we get through the automatic doors, she lets out a yelp and high-fives me as I click the automatic start button on the remote for the car. Once we're in the car and buckled in, the heat blasting, I feel a rush of something unfamiliar, at least whenever I'm around her, and that's a rush of connection. Or maybe understanding.

I don't put the car in drive. Instead I turn to her, her face so smooth and young, those goddamn bangs making her look younger than almost eighteen.

"Did you guys use condoms? Don't you know about Plan B?" I hear the anger in my voice, mom-anger, chastising anger, and it both shocks and pleases me. "How could you have waited three weeks? What would you have done if you were pregnant? Are you just running around having unprotected sex? Do you even know where Jake has been? I know he appears to be this nice, perfect little Harvard-boy, but you don't know how people can be when they are at college—"

Her face regains its original composure and stillness. She inhales but doesn't let it out. "It will never happen again."

A million other questions and thoughts flood my brain but instead I just put the car in reverse and drive us back home.

Jeni hugs me before going back to bed and adds, "Thanks, big sis," before disappearing down the dark hallway to her room. The words sound like Swahili coming out of her mouth.

Finally, fatigue sets in and I almost just put myself on the couch to sleep, but then I realize I have a whole bag of pregnancy tests still in my hand.

What to do?

****

When I open my eyes, I'm sideways, lying with my cheek pressed into a throw pillow on the couch. I try to lift myself up, but sleepiness makes it feel like I'm lifting myself with bricks on my back. The scene before me comes into full view as my eyes adjust to the sunlight coming in. I'm in the living room, on the white sofa, and as my eyes travel around and blink to wake up, I see on the floor…

The pregnancy tests. And then it all floods back to me.

After Jeni went to bed, I had to pee and somehow wound up taking a test. I squint and see that, no, I took all three of the remaining tests.

I reach down like I'm on a lifeboat and the ground

is the sea, and I'm searching for some sort of lost object or maybe the hand of a lost love. Grasping one of the tests but hesitating to look at it because cold fear sends the realization up my body…I already know. I knew last night. I knew from the minute I sat in the bathroom staring at the smiling face of the woman on the box of the first test, wondering was she smiling because she knew the line was one or two. Was she smiling because she found out she was pregnant or that she wasn't? Why the fuck was she smiling? I peed and counted to five and then put the stick on the counter and counted to sixty (turns out one of the tests showed results in as little as one minute). When I picked the test up and saw that it had two lines, I got confused. So that means *yes* or does it mean *no*, and then I had to reread the instructions and then I got even more confused, so I took the next test and then the next and…guess the fuck what?

Turns out. I'm fucking pregnant.

****

I must have dozed again because the next time my eyes open, Jeni and Ethan stare down at me.

"You scared the crap out of me." Ethan knits his brows in concern.

I sit up, wipe my cheek, and moan. Shit. Shit. Shit.

"What's the matter?" Ethan sits next to me.

Jeni shoots me a panicked look and then glances down at the ground. The tests are gone.

But she knows.

"I don't feel so great," I admit. Maybe those were false positives. It can happen.

But not usually three times from three different tests.

"Let's get her upstairs," my sister says.

They help me stand. My stomach makes a faint growling noise, although I'm not hungry. We get me all the way up to my room. I feel like I'm floating outside my body. This is not happening.

"Rest," Jeni says, covering me up with the bedspread.

"Can I have some ice?" I rub the satin of the blanket beneath the bedspread. Maybe if I just go back to sleep this whole nightmare will end.

Panic flicks across Jeni's face.

And I give her a *don't say a word* look. Her smile is tight as she scurries off to retrieve the ice.

After they leave, Ethan sits at the edge of my bed. He rubs my hair and then leans down to kiss my forehead.

I start manically rubbing the satin on my chin. "PMS. You know how it is. It sucks."

"So you're always telling me. If that's it. You're not getting on that plane if you're actually sick. You can get there a few days late." He strokes my cheek.

"I'm probably fine." I close my eyes. Sleep, sleep, sleep it away. "I have a few days. I'm sorry, Ethan. I don't think I can make good on that promise anymore." I open my eyes and smile.

Ethan knits his brows again. "I guess I'll have to fly to India for spring break."

"Wait, are you serious?"

He grabs his phone and taps a few times. Shows me the screen, which is a boarding pass.

"That is amazing! You are the best ever!"

"Easy, killer. You need to lay down, and I'll rub your feet if you want."

I lay back, and he reaches under the covers and starts to rub my feet. I close my eyes.

My sister comes back in with a glass of ice.

My eyes fly open.

NO!

She has all three tests in her hand.

"I'm sorry, Nori. You have to—"

"Helllooo?" The word echoes and bellows across the entire house thanks to the high ceilings.

Mom and Dad!

I look from a perplexed Ethan to a concerned Jeni, and then—

"Girls?" Footsteps coming up the stairs and then…

"Surprise!" Mom, gleaming smile, tan and sparkling in her rhinestone-studded black sweat suit she only wears when traveling by plane. "We came home a little early to make sure we had some time to—" Her face drops. "What's that?"

My dad is behind her, equally as tan and in his travel attire, black tracksuit. "Why are you in bed?"

Jeni stands with the bouquet of pregnancy tests, ballet pink lines on all three.

My mother and father, side by side.

"Sweetie?" Mom cocks her head and directs this to Jeni. Panic floods her face, and she says, "Are you…? Are those…?"

My father makes a disgusted sigh. That man wears annoyance like he wears his custom-made suits and ties, which is what I'm sure he will change into now that they are off the plane. Guarantee that he has to go into work even though he just got home from a business trip.

Jeni looks from me, to Ethan, and back to my

parents. "Yes. Yes. I'm…pregnant."

I have never loved my sister's lack of emotional expression more than right now.

"That's ridiculous!" my father says and laughs. "You're going to Harvard." Like Harvard is equivalent to…I don't know…Plan B or an abortion or a magic wand?

"Yes. Yes, I am. I will do both."

"Do both? Do both? Having a child isn't like working and going to school. You don't 'do both.' " This is from my father who clearly has forgotten that my mother did, in fact, do both with us.

But my poor mother is shaking now, and my father is so mad that the red in his face is bursting through his deep bronze from being on a tropical island and then down south over the last few weeks.

The whole time this dialogue is going on, Ethan's gaze is boring a hole into me, causing all emotion to start to seep out. Unlike my little sis, I don't hold a thing in, at least *well*.

I grab Ethan's hand and say, "Those are mine. I'm the one who's—" I stop and swallow the burst of tears welling up inside. "Pregnant."

Everyone sucks in a breath, and then Ethan says, "So you're not PMS-ing?"

No one says anything else. My father eyes Ethan with a predatory stare, and Mom wraps her arm around Dad's, as if she's restraining him.

"This is really, really awkward." Ethan rubs his forehead.

I struggle to sit all the way up and then say to him, "I'm sorry."

Jeni puts her hand on my shoulder. "I'll go get you

that ice." And she slips out of the room.

"Ice?" my mother says.

I nod, distracted by the absolutely pained look on Ethan's face.

I hear my father sigh, and then he says, "I've got to go make a call." And disappears through the door.

My mother starts to follow him but pauses and turns back to me, her jaw tense and her eyes wide. "Just give us a minute," she says quietly.

As Mom leaves, Jeni returns, holding an oversized coffee mug that says HARVARD. It's brimming with ice. She comes to the bed and hands it to me.

No one says anything else while I crunch on my ice.

****

A half hour passes while I eat ice, Jeni sits by the window in my reading chair, and Ethan sits on the bed. Silence. They spend the time exchanging looks with each other, at least when my eyes are open. Sleepiness washes over me, but not enough to knock me out. I doze in and out, all the while chewing and slurping ice, which has now numbed my entire body and brain so that the only sensation throughout is cold.

I shiver and suck up the remaining water in the mug that covers my entire face when I drink from it. Sloshing and gurgling sounds erupt loudly from my belly, and Ethan and Jeni both jump up expectantly.

"Pancakes," I say.

Jeni nods and pulls the covers down my shivering body, and Ethan hands me my robe.

"Pancakes," Jeni repeats smoothing down her bangs that don't need smoothing.

Ethan helps me put the robe on. "Let's do this."

Mytowsky family history, of which Ethan knows all too well, includes countless Dad-fail moments saved by his famous, mouth-meltingly yummy cinnamon chocolate chip pancakes. I finally land a lead role in a school play my senior year and Dad schedules a golf weekend with colleagues he can't get out of. Dad doesn't remember to show up to Jeni's nationals a few years ago because he put the wrong day in his agenda and missed her winning first place. Both incidents resulted in us waking up to stacks of pancakes and apologies. Even small, countless moments of Dad flipping out on us (me, mainly because Jeni never messed up) over everything from bringing home straight B's on a report card to me declaring I was going to Clark over Brandeis, result in stacks of pancakes the next morning. No apology. Just food.

Right now, Dad doesn't know it, but he owes me some fucking pancakes.

We walk out of the bedroom and down to the kitchen where they flank me on either side. My parents, no longer in their traveling attire, sit at the kitchen table with coffee. They don't say anything when we walk in. The sound of the clock above the stove ticks and tocks agonizing seconds. Standing here, a warm wash of anger and sadness, like two waves coming from either side of the bay crash over me. Ethan's hand is sweaty in mine.

I want to grab my father by this fucking silk necktie and scream, "I'm going to be fine!" But the problem is, up until this morning, I would have been able to say that with conviction and now I can't.

Instead, I burst into tears. Bury my face in my hands, letting the reality crash in on me. "I'm sorry," I sob and hate myself as I say it.

Ethan pulls me into his side and murmurs, "This isn't anyone's fault."

Jeni says something, but Dad shouts over her, "Oh, yes, it is, mister!" Somehow Dad is up and brandishing a wooden spoon like a sword. "You are responsible for this, young man!" The wooden spoon is now hovering over Ethan's head, while Jeni pulls me out of the way, indicating that you can be both smart, beautiful, and idiotically strong.

"Stop!" my mother screams.

"Dad!" I try to step between them, but Jeni's hold is herculean.

"Mr. Mytowsky, I—"

"You what?" Dad sneers. "You what? Forgot to put on a condom? Forgot that this young woman had all the promise in the world, and now you've ruined that?"

Really? Dad thinks that about me?

"No! I—" Ethan begins.

"You listen to me, young man. My daughters are not going to be shackled with children and husbands, sitting at home, wasting their talent." He turns to me. "Yes, I was not thrilled with India, but I had to accept it because you are passionate about it, and you want to do something with it, with your life. But now, now that hot pants there knocked you up—"

"Roger!" That's from my mom.

"Dad!" From Jeni, who has lost all of her normal composure, her bangs wildly sticking up in all directions.

"Mr. Mytowsky!" Ethan steps away from me and toward my father so they are almost nose-to-nose. "With all due respect, though I'm not sure you deserve it right now."

Gasp from my mother. A whispery "Yes!" from my sister. I cover my mouth because I feel a smile creep in.

"Mr. Mytowsky, I love your daughter more than anything, anyone in this world. I bought her a ring. I proposed to her—before I knew she was pregnant. So the one thing you need to get straight is that she has me by her side, and there will be no 'shackled to a husband;' we're partners. And second, we used protection, but obviously, it didn't work. For that, I apologize."

They stare at each other, two dogs baring fangs, breathing hard.

I know what I should do. I should pipe in that it really is my fault. That we used double protection, only I sabotaged the double part.

Instead, slowly, my dad steps back, his eyes still on Ethan, but they drift to me and my sister. He puts the wooden spoon down on the counter, sighs, and walks out.

"I really thought there would be pancakes," Jeni says, patting down her bangs.

I tear up again and look over at the stove, noticing the griddle is out and a silver mixing bowl is next to it.

Mom doesn't say anything.

"I can make them, Nori." Ethan sounds sad.

I shake my head and close my eyes. Then I feel arms wrap around me. Mom, Ethan, Jeni. Their different perfume and soap smells mixing together.

My whole body pounds, like my heart has swollen up to fill me from head to toes. Thoughts flood my body. I flash to me shoving my hand into my jeans pocket for the pill. Images of me putting it into my mouth and spitting it out and putting it back in again a whole day later. I question myself. Did I even really take it? Did I take a Tylenol instead that I left in my pocket? Shit. Why didn't I take it right away?

I close my eyes. Arms squeeze harder around me. Everyone breaks off except Mom, who whispers, "I chewed ice through both of my pregnancies. Only thing that cured nausea."

If only I knew that before.

Chapter 18

ANDY

We've been home for about three weeks. The routine has fallen back to where we were before Florida, those few weeks we had of living together and the seamless flow of the day to day and then the nights.

It's perfect.

We never went to see George because neither of us think we need to…except one thing. When Gwen and I are out, we hold hands and people—waiters and waitresses, movie ticket sellers—refer to us as girlfriend and boyfriend, and we are. But we've avoided some pretty important realities coming up, namely what's going to happen after May. She doesn't know about med school yet, which is a big factor, I think, in the future. I saw her list of schools on a sticky note on her laptop. When I saw Georgetown and Tufts, I applied to BU because it's close to Tufts, and I also applied to Georgetown. I'm hesitant to bring it up because that means a talk about the future…and what if she doesn't see one? We're living in the moment, each moment, avoiding any talk of what comes after graduation.

A few days before school is set to start back up for me, we sit in a little café on Thayer, sharing a croissant egg sandwich and *The New York Times*. It's crowded, but the kind of crowded that's comforting. I catch her eye. She smiles. I want to kiss her. I always want to kiss her.

And then out of the corner of my eye I see *him*.

Oh, no. God. Shit. No.

"Gwen," I whisper, barely moving my lips and holding the paper up so that I can't see *him*.

"Huh?" She doesn't move. I nudge her under the table.

"Gwen, three o'clock. It's Shane."

"Shane?" Confusion. Then, recognition.

Not that Gwen would recognize him in the flesh because he was such a shitty person I never let her meet him. Our dating, or whatever the hell it was, lasted a few months, but he was the one who told me I had to pick a team and that I was a fake gay guy using my gay thing to piss off my father.

"We should start making out right now." She starts to stand up.

But my heart is hammering. I really, *really* don't want him to come over here.

"No!" My tone is sharp.

"Why?"

"Because I don't want a whole drama. He made such a scene the last time I saw him."

She sits back down. I see him out of the corner of my eye throw his head back and laugh, touch the arm of the guy he is with. I shudder. He was very aggressive in all kinds of ways.

"Andy, what does it matter?" She takes the paper and starts to fold it up.

I'm distracted by the memory of one of the last things that asshole said to me: "*You know what you are? A self-hating, straight guy. You, my friend, are one fucked up brother who is only going to hurt whatever guy or girl you wind up with."*

A total dick. And he really didn't have much of one anyway. Not that I was ever a size guy anyway.

"Actually. I'd like to meet this fellow." She stands straight up and snatches the paper away.

"Gwen—"

"Andrew Kirschner!" That effing nasal growl.

He and his friend are standing right at our table, and miraculously, the table next to us has cleared.

I stand up because I'm polite. He grabs me into a light hug, the kind that feels like being wrapped in overcooked spaghetti. "Hi, Shane," I say.

Shane steps back, flings his scarf over his shoulder, and smiles—first at me and then at Gwen.

"Hello, Andrew! Now who is this? Is this the famous Gwendolyn?" He flashes his bleached teeth at her. This is a guy who also waxes his beard instead of shaving. Who goes to tanning booths in the winter and loves Fire Island. A few of the many reasons why we didn't work out.

Gwen stands up and offers her hand first to Shane and then to his friend. "Yes, I am she! But it's actually just Gwen. And you are Shane, and this is…?"

"Yes, this is my boyfriend. Actually, fiancé! Christopher." He holds up Christopher's hand, which has a tiny diamond ring on it.

Christopher obviously hasn't graduated from high school. Or he waxes everything on his face, too. He gives me a firm handshake and shaky smile.

"This is a lovely reunion of sorts." Shane promptly pulls out a chair from the table next to us and pushes poor Christopher to sit and grabs another.

"What are you up to, Andrew? Breaking the hearts of those Brown boys, or maybe girls?" He perches on his chair.

I try to control my eyes from rolling and the red from creeping onto my cheeks and also there's that newfound ability to punch people in the face. I guess that's what all the straight sex is doing to me. I feel homophobic for even thinking that. My face burns with shame of all kinds.

"No." I surprise myself with the response and then I add, "Actually, I'm dating one person."

"Who?"

"She's right here."

"Gwendolyn? *The* Gwendolyn? The *best friend* Gwendolyn?"

"It's Gwen," she says cheerily and ignores Shane's shock as well as what I've proclaimed. She seems to have another agenda because she sits back and crosses her arms. "So, *Shane,* how long did you and *Andy* date, because he tells me about everything, but I don't remember hearing much about you."

Poor Christopher. He wants out and now.

"We dated a month or so, and I caught this little sneak one night at a bar hitting on a girl!" He puts his hand to his chest like oh my. "But you know, it all makes sense now."

That is not what happened, but I don't bother to correct him. I ran into a girl from the one class I TA-ed.

Christopher starts to laugh, but in the end, helplessness and confusion abounds.

Gwen leans in. "Really?"

"Truthfully, *Andy* and I were not a match. Right?"

I nod vigorously and down the rest of my coffee.

"I mean, I'm—I'm into"—he drops his voice—"everything in the bedroom, but *Andy*, certain things, or should I say, areas were off base." Then he smiles broad. "I once tried to put my—"

Christopher grows balls suddenly and puts his hand over Shane's mouth. But Shane shrugs it off and holds Chris's hand down at his side and says in a scary sweet way, "It all makes perfect sense now. Anyway, what happened was we were at a bar, and Andrew was actually hitting on a lesbian."

"I was not hitting on her, Shane. She was a student in a class I was the TA in." I talk to him exactly the same way I did when we were what you would call dating, but it was more like dueling.

"Oh, yes. You were touching her arm and her knee? Come on, you know, Gwen. Andy is not a touchy-feely guy."

Gwen nods.

"I'm watching this from across the bar where I had run into my most recent ex, a total bear, you know. Not my type at all, but I stay friends with all of my exes." He stops and eyes me.

I think I want to punch him more than I wanted to punch my father.

"The girl was really not into it, obviously, and when I came over, I threw my arm around Andy and gave him a big old kiss and, boy, did he get red. Guess I ruined your plan." Another dagger stare. "Anyway, the girl started laughing, and she said oh, thank God! I thought you were straight and trying to hit on me!"

I swear today is a constant state of opposite day.

Gwen tries to hide the huge grin. She finds this all amusing while I'm humiliated.

As I open my mouth to tell Shane what a douchebag I think he is, he wallops us with, "So what's the future hold for you two lovebirds? I bet Andrew here is hellbent on law school to try and please Daddy. Maybe you'll follow him, Gwendolyn? You'll get married and have babies?"

That's it. I stand up, abruptly brushing my hand over Christopher's cup of coffee, splashing it all over his lap.

"Shit!" He stands up too and starts wiping the coffee from his pants with a napkin from the table. Gwen hands him the pile of used napkins we had from our breakfast.

I stand there watching everyone.

Shane eyes me, beady and small. "I feel sorry for you, Gwen. *You* are a hot mess, Andy Kirschner." He turns to Gwen. "Thank you, sweetie. Christopher, baby, are you all right?" Christopher nods miserably, and then they both say goodbye to Gwen but say nothing to me.

As they leave, I yell, "And it's Andrew to you, you asshole. Andrew and Gwen!"

I continue to stand there. Gwen watches them go, and then she turns to me and grabs my arm.

"What a dick." I shake my head.

We both stare at the mess on the table, and then silently clean it up, bringing our dishes to the counter. After we go back outside, the sun warming us in the cold air, I take her mittened hand and say, "So what are we going to do?"

Gwen is up under my nose. "I don't know what you mean." She kisses my lips softly and then steps back. I hold her close, her eyes flicker with anxiety.

"About us."

She stands up on her toes and kisses my neck. "Go home and make hot monkey love."

"Gwen, you know what I'm talking about," I say, feeling tingles from her kisses and fighting the urge to just make out with her and stop talking.

"I don't want to talk about it right now," she mumbles into my neck.

"Why?"

"Because—" She moves to the other side of my neck and kisses it. Tingles dart all over the place, making my head foggy. "—I'd rather do this. Actually, I'd rather do this…naked."

My body caves and I circle my arms around her and make out with her like we're in high school…only better. When we break the kiss, I say into her ear, "This conversation is happening. You can't keep distracting me with your feminine wiles."

"Oh, yes I can, Andy. Haven't I proven that?"

Touché!

****

GWEN

Hot, crazy love. *Check.* Showered. *Check.* Surprise Andy with Beyoncé tickets, seats so close to the Queen B that her sweat will rain down on us. *Uncheck.*

Andy's still in the shower, and I'm in the bedroom, towel wrapped around me, staring into my closet. I can't get dressed until he gets out and sees the tickets, which are casually laying right on his bureau by his deodorant. My outfit is already put together on a hanger—crushed velvet black mini dress, patent leather thigh-high boots, and my ripped jean jacket. If I put that on before he sees the tickets—deadest giveaway ever.

I pick up my brush from the nightstand on my side

of the bed and start to brush out my hair when my phone *omms*.

Shit. I glance at the tickets. Andy will be out any minute and missing his classic surprise-face—a cross between pain and pleasure much like another face he makes—is not an option. I hit Decline.

But the phone starts in again. *Grrr*. The shower is still running, so I grab the phone, hit Accept, and say quickly, "Can I call you back in a few?"

"Hi, Gwen, it's Jeni."

Weird. But I'm still staring at those tickets. Too distracted to try and figure out why Jeni is calling me from Nori's phone. Though, a small tremor of panic flutters in my chest. "What's up?"

"Nori's pregnant."

My heart seizes. My brain blinks.

OhMyFuckingShit.

"She was afraid to call you. I think she's just in shock. I'm going to put her on now." Jeni's monotone somehow emphasizes the ohmyfuckingshitness of this news.

I sink into Andy's bed and hear muffling through the phone.

"So the pill didn't work." Nori's voice is nasal like she's been crying.

"Shit," I say, glancing over at the picture of us from spring break. Smiles and kisses. "I guess you're part of the two percent."

"Two percent?" She blows her nose. I wait before continuing.

"Yeah, the two percent that the morning after pill fails." I tear my eyes from the picture and let them fall on the bulletin board filled with tacks and nothing else.

"You don't think it's because I took it too late?" she whispers.

"No. It wasn't that late."

"But it could be, right?"

"I guess." I pull on a thread from the gray comforter, wishing I had perfect words to say but then notice the shower has stopped. Shit. Shit. Shit. But Nori is talking again. Something about *bringing Jen to the pharmacy last night*. Something else about *did I know Jake and Jen were hooking up*. Something else about *chewing ice* and then pancakes and her dad. My brain is on overload. I say *uh, huh*. Knowing that this is a really scary moment for her and that a good friend would stop being so preoccupied by Beyoncé tickets and focus on that fact that the girl is fucking pregnant, but then the bathroom door swings open. Andy, naked and glorious, grins at me. When I shake my head back at him, his face falls. "Who's that?" he mouths.

"Nori," I mouth back and try to focus on what she's saying, which now is something about waking up this morning to pregnancy tests all over her body. What the hell is she talking about?

Andy sits down next to me. I can't explain anything, so I just hit the speaker button, and we listen together as Ethan, in the background, says, "…doctor on Monday to confirm the results."

"Results?" Andy whispers to me, but Nori is saying something…

"…India has to be postponed. I guess." Then she bursts into tears.

"That depends on whatever you decide to do." I puff my chest out a little, confident that I now have the perfect words for Nori: "You know, this is your body.

This is your decision, and thank God, we have a choice in this country and, thank God, you have the resources."

"And thank you, Planned Parenthood," Andy mumbles, taking the phone from me and turning the speaker button off. He presses it to his ear and states what I guess he just figured out. "So you're pregnant." Then he nods his head and says *uh, huh* a few times and *I know,* and *we love you* and *we'll be there* and all that stuff you're supposed to say.

I take the phone from him.

"I'm not getting an abortion." Nori blows her nose and adds, "I don't need to."

Then Andy stands up and walks over to his bureau. SHIT! I leap up and rush to it before he can get there, all the while babbling to Nori, "The idea is that it is a choice and the word *need* sort of implies that it's not." Andy reaches around me for his deodorant, but I beat him and hand it over. Meanwhile, Nori is silent. Andy is practically wrestling me away from his bureau so he can get into one of the drawers, and the whole thing feels futile, so I just step to the side and turn away.

"I'm sorry," I tell Nori. "I have no idea what I'm saying. I love you. I love you both, and if you want to have the baby, then I'm there, I'm your coach. I'm your, whatsitcalled, *doula*. I'm your—"

"OH MY SASHA FIERCE!"

Andy's arms circle my waist, and he squeezes me so hard I gasp.

And Nori is laughing, crying, asking if I would be in the delivery room.

Andy is also laughing and crying for such very different reasons.

I choke out into the phone, "Can we come see you

guys? Sunday?"

We set a time and say goodbye.

Andy picks me up and swings me around. My towel is on the floor. We fall back onto the bed, laugh-crying and holding hands.

"I feel bad being so happy right now." He rubs his eyes with his free hand.

I roll to my side and kiss him. He kisses me back and then kisses the tickets. Then his face knits into worry. "Poor Nori. How did it even happen?"

I shake my head. Not my place to tell him about the morning after pill fail. Not to mention this could lead into discussions about *what would happen if*, with us, which could turn into an intense conversation about the future, and I'm not really ready for that.

"No time for bumming out tonight." I stand up and shimmy my naked ass. "You gotta help me pick out my most Sasha Fiercest outfit."

He smacks my ass and says, "Crushed velvet mini dress."

I sigh. Great minds think alike.

****

"Oh, my Sasha Fierce!" I say, leaning into an equally sweaty Andy. The back of my bare thighs stick to the seat of the T. I'm too tired to take out an antibacterial wipe and clean them. *Whatever.*

He kisses my damp forehead. The train lurches and pulls us forward. The only other passenger is a guy asleep on the other side of the car.

"Your dance moves are far better than Lady B," I say, my head on his shoulder. "The benefits of dating a gay guy."

The whishing and bumping sounds of the train

rolling through the tunnel fill the air between us. Darkness.

We get through the tunnel. I pull away from him and put my hands on either side of his cool, damp face. "That was supposed to be funny."

He keeps his face forward and doesn't say anything.

"Are you mad?" I say to his unmoving profile.

Dark shadows mixed with flashes of light splatter over his cheek.

"I'm sorry," I offer.

He still says nothing. The train car slows and stops. The door slides open, and the sleeping guy wakes up and tumbles out.

After the door closes again, I say, "Are you mad because I use the word *gay* to describe you?"

He doesn't say anything again.

I look out the window at the inky blackness.

"No," he says.

I nod, still looking out the window.

Goose bumps from the cool air jetting out of the vent above us dot my arms.

We're enveloped in darkness again. Reminding me of the first night we slept together.

I turn to him and slide one leg over his lap, and he pulls me on top of him. I straddle his body. In the darkness, unable to see him, we kiss and kiss. He pulls my dress up and slides his hands under my underwear. I feel the vibration of him making a noise in the back of his throat, but the bumping over the tracks is louder and fills my ears. I grind against him, and he grips my hips, and we move and move.

I bury my face into his neck and smell the concert

on his skin. Sweat and alcohol and pot and body. We continue to move against each other, and his hands grip harder. I move until I breathe hard into his neck, grip the back of the seat and feel myself let go.

Andy rubs my back and kisses my neck, making his way to my face and then my mouth.

The lights flicker and I move off his lap. He puts his arm around me.

"Not bad for a gay guy, huh?"

"Not at all," I reply, closing my eyes.

Chapter 19

ETHAN

Nori and I sit wrapped up in each other in front of the fireplace in the Mytowskys' living room. The last *Twilight* movie is showing at the dollar movie theater in the town next to us. She never got to see it when it came out, and I've avoided watching it on HBO with her. But Bella has a baby in this one, and she's married to her vampire high school sweetheart. It all works out. Good timing to see it.

Nori hasn't spoken a lot since yesterday. No one has. Jeni took off to spend the night at a friend's (a.k.a Jake's a.k.a. Andy's dad's house). Mr. Mytowsky suddenly had to go to his office and is coming back tonight in time for a party they have to go to. Even though I know she and her father need to talk, that's not a priority for me right now.

I squeeze her to me and kiss the top of her head.

"After the doctor's appointment on Monday, no matter what the outcome is, it's going to work out. Right?" She turns her face up to me.

I make sure my voice is calm and my face relaxed. "Yeah. We'll figure it all out."

"Right." Her eyes search mine. "I'm not due until September. We can graduate and then…you can get a teaching job and then—"

I rub her shoulder. She wants to make plans for

something that I don't think we can really make any for, but I know it makes her feel better.

"Sure."

"And…I guess, we should, you know…" Is she going to say *get married*? "We should move in together."

I nod and let her go on, but it does sort of bother me that she hasn't brought up getting engaged, at least. I have to remember this is probably ten times scarier for her than me, so I have to reel it in and simmer down a little.

Mrs. Mytowsky walks into the living room, hair coiffed, clothes shiny. "I wanted to check and see if you guys are still going to the movies tonight."

Nori nods.

"How are you feeling?" She steps over to us.

"I'm fine as long as I have my ice." Nori picks up her cup from the coffee table.

Mrs. Mytowsky smiles. "You know, Nori." Her smile fades, and tears fill her eyes, but she shakes her head quickly, and somehow, they disappear. "Your father needs to warm up to this." She pats Nori's hand. "You'll see. He will."

Nori takes a crunch of ice in response.

Mrs. Mytowsky doesn't leave yet. Instead, she perches on the chair across from us and lets Nori finish chewing.

Nori pauses before shoveling more ice into her mouth. "Mom, thank you."

"For what?" She smooths her skirt.

"Just. For not freaking out." Nori crunches her ice and smiles.

She leans over and kisses Nori—and then she, to

my surprise, kisses me too. She smells like expensive perfume.

"Now you, young man, you take excellent care of my Nori."

"Yes, ma'am!" I say and take Nori's hand and kiss the back of it.

After she leaves, Nori puts the cup back on the table and says, "Are you sure you want to see the movie?"

"Vampires are cool."

She laughs. "I won't be offended if you fall asleep during the movie."

"Good." But that definitely won't be happening. I'm way too nervous about the black box in my pocket. I pat my leg inconspicuously to make sure it's still there.

All set.

****

"Oh my God, I think that was the best one! So perfect! The ending." Nori sighs and cuddles close to me as we walk out of the theater.

"Yeah." It was terrible. I mean, aside from the action scenes and the cinematography, it really was a terrible movie, but nonetheless it is the perfect backdrop to what I am about to do. "I'm glad you liked it."

"It was a good distraction." She tilts the cup of ice she's been carrying and takes a huge crunch.

I laugh. "If this is your biggest craving, I guess it's fine. Pretty easy for me to get in the middle of the night."

"True. Craving. Ugh. This is really happening."

We stop walking when we get to the car, but I turn

to her and say, "Let's go get some dessert at that little place in Bristol."

"Sure. Hmmm. Maybe I do have another craving. A piece of apple cake sounds good."

So far my plan is working well. She's in a good mood. She didn't say what I was hoping she would: something like, *They can make it work. The vampire and the human. Why can't we?* Or, *Hey, they had a kid, and it all worked out.* But romance and happily ever after is in the air.

We drive back through Barrington, Warren, and finally to Bristol. The holiday lights are still up in the downtown area, making everything even more perfect for this moment. I pull up to the front of the Beehive Café and park.

We enter through the creaky old door and wait for a table. No brownies tonight. That didn't work out so well last time. Not to mention I have no idea what the sight or smell of them will do to her, considering her condition.

The hostess brings us to a cozy spot in the corner. I pull the chair out for her, and she sits, smiles, and then suddenly her mouth curls, like she's going to throw up.

"I smell chocolate and coffee, and it's making me want to hurl." She puts her hand over her nose.

"Do you want to leave?" Please don't want to leave.

"I don't know. Gosh, it's strong. Is it strong?"

My Nori is so pregnant.

"No," I say and grin at her. This is sort of funny.

"Sorry, you really want dessert, and you put up with that movie. Don't worry. I'll be fine. Let's order. I think." She scans the menu. "Can I get a sandwich?"

We both laugh. "Whatever you want, honey."

The waitress comes and takes our order. Nori asks for a cup of crushed ice and adds, "Make it a pitcher." She follows that up with, "And a hamburger, no bun, cooked well done."

My mouth drops open. "When was the last time you ate hamburger?" The waitress returns in a flash with the pitcher of ice and two glasses. One already filled with ice.

"High school," she says, tilting her cup of ice into her mouth.

This is going to be a very interesting nine months.

We sit in the silence, except for the sound of people talking at their tables around us and the sound of Nori's loud crunching.

Fuck it. I'm ready.

"Nori—" I take her hand. "—I need to tell you something."

She kisses my hand and says, "Actually, there's something I have to tell you."

****

NORI

I rub my finger over Ethan's strong, big hands. Hands that I missed so much when we were apart in the fall. Hands that I will have on me as I go through this pregnancy.

But before I fall into and accept this new reality, I have to come clean to Ethan who, surprisingly, in all this, hasn't mentioned or asked about the Plan B pill. He probably figures it didn't work, or his super sperm defied it.

But I need to tell him that I didn't take it right away, and when I did finally dig it out of my pocket and take it, many hours had passed, reducing the efficacy to probably nothing.

I begin to open my mouth, but the waitress returns with a large beef patty and the smell is heavenly and supersedes the other smells of sickeningly sweet chocolate that has permeated the air of the restaurant. I start to cut into my food. I see that Ethan's mouth is dropped open. He hasn't touched his giant piece of apple cake.

I pop a forkful of beef into my mouth, and the taste is perfection.

Ethan laughs. "I need to take a picture of this and send it to Gwen and Andy."

"NO!" I say and hide my face with my hand.

"It's adorable."

"No, it's not. I'm like some kind of carnivorous dinosaur." I stop and notice the amount I have consumed already. "Jesus!"

After a few minutes of mutual chewing, my craving is satisfied. I put my fork down and say, "Before you say what you have to, I have to get this off my chest."

Ethan wipes his mouth with his napkin. "Wait. You're not going to tell me that the baby is Andy's, are you?"

I laugh. "Funny. But that would be a story." My smile fades, and I play with the fork for a minute and then say, "Here it goes. You know how I took that pill?"

"Yeah."

I start to say more, but he interrupts, "Nori, you know that none of that stuff is one hundred percent."

I watch him take the last bite of cake into his

mouth and wait for him to chew and swallow. Then I say, "I know, but it might have worked if I had actually taken it."

"What?" He grips the fork.

"I mean, I did take it." I sigh, stare down at my plate, which has one more forkful of meat.

"What do you mean?" he asks. "Did you take it or not?"

"Ethan, I wanted to. I tried to. But I had all these crazy thoughts. I felt like I was murdering our baby. I know it's nuts, and I'm not some pro-life maniac, but I had a moment and it sort of lasted another day and a half."

Ethan's eyes widen.

"But I did dig it out of my jeans pocket, and I *did* take it."

He sighs.

The noises from the restaurant seem to increase a little and then a loud crash. We both turn, and it gives me a minute to stuff that last piece in my mouth. He turns around, and I swallow quickly.

We listen for the crash and the yelling in the kitchen to quiet. Other patrons stop talking and give each other looks.

"Let me understand this. You didn't take the pill until the next day?"

I nod.

"And you decided to wait until now, right now, to tell me?"

"Yes." My voice is small. God, this is bad.

He shakes his head slowly, from side to side, and I cannot read his expression.

"I never thought I'd have to tell you, Ethan, and

then when we found out I was pregnant, I was so overwhelmed with that. So there really hasn't been a good time—"

He throws his fork down.

Here it is. I've pushed him to the limit with my insanity.

"Nori." He's standing up. Shit, this is not what I expected. I mean, I thought he might be a little mad but—

"Nori Louise Mytowsky." He's holding a box, that same black box, and his green eyes penetrate me. He's bending down on one knee. "There's no way that you can *not* want to be my wife, not after what you just told me." He beams at me, and I exhale long and deep, beaming right back at him.

"Will you—"

"Yes!" I leap up, but he pushes me gently back down. "Can you let me finish?"

I nod.

"Will you be my wife and baby mama for life?"

I laugh as tears fall. "Yes, yes!"

****

ANDY

Gwen runs a finger over the tiny diamond. "Engaged. Like real grownups!"

I lift my mug of tea. "*Mazel*!"

Ethan kisses Nori's hand.

Nori leans forward and grabs her cup of ice. She's been chewing on it since we sat down.

"What's with the ice?" I ask, putting my mug down.

Ethan laughs, and Nori says, "It's my first official craving."

"There's been a second official craving too," Ethan says. "Guess who's eating meat? *Overcooked* meat?"

"No!" Gwen says.

Nori shrugs, chomping on her ice.

"Sooooo. When's the wedding?" Gwen asks, dipping her biscotti into her tea.

Nori watches her and then reaches for a biscotti. She smells it and then puts it back. This pregnancy thing is pretty funny.

"I'd marry Nori tomorrow," Ethan says, taking the biscotti that she put back.

Nori wrinkles her nose while Ethan takes a bite.

Ethan stops mid-chew and then puts it back on the plate. "But we don't want to put any stress on Nori. She's growing life in there." They gaze at each other.

Nori wipes crumbs off his lips with her thumb and adds, "I can't even think about planning anything right now."

"All right, you hippy-psychos. Seriously? Women give birth in rice paddies in China. They drop it like it's hot, swaddle the baby in a blanket, stick it under a Baobab tree, and go back to work." Gwen points to herself. "You should listen to me. I'm practically an OB-GYN."

"That's right! She's delivered babies!" I chime in.

"And speaking of Baobab trees," Gwen begins fishing a piece of biscotti out of her tea and slurping it off her fingers. Adorable, probably only to me. Gwen continues, "You totally could bring a baby to an *ashram*. It's all peaceful there. And babies don't do much for the first five months or so."

Not until I notice the lingering silence that follows Gwen's comment do I realize she is talking about what

I can only assume is a very sore, oozingly sore subject. India.

I cut Gwen off before she can continue.

I point to Nori's empty glass. "Need a refill?"

"Actually, my mouth is kind of numb." She forces a smile. "So, what's going on with you guys?"

"I'm sorry, Nori, but I have to say just one more thing—"

"No, you don't." I glare at her.

"Yes, I do!"

"No, you don't!"

"Yes. I. Do."

Ethan rubs his forehead. Nori holds her empty cup, which I really want to fill just to give her something to do other than look very uncomfortable.

Gwen puts her mug on the table and leans all the way forward. "I know how much you wanted to go to India. I'm just trying to point out that women always think they have to give up all their dreams when they have a child or get married, but they don't have to. *You* shouldn't have to."

The silence that follows is florescent and electric and awful.

Nori's eyes are red and watery. "Don't you think I know that? Don't you think that's all I've thought about since I saw all those pink lines on all those fucking sticks? Don't you think I know how unfair all of this is?"

"Babe, I'm in this with you—" Ethan puts his hand on her knee.

"I know! I know, Ethan. But no matter what we've been saying about all this, that I can just defer India for a year and that, hell, you and the baby could come with me, that you're going to be a hands-on dad, that we will be equal partners in this…that the reality is we have no idea. *I* have no idea."

Gwen's face is streaming with tears, and she leaps up and kneels in front of Nori, puts her head in her lap and sobs. "I'm such a bitch. I'm so sorry. What the fuck do I know?"

Nori hesitates. Ethan and I exchange worried looks, but then Nori starts to stroke Gwen's head. The corners of her mouth turn up into a smile. "You don't know shit, my friend. You don't know shit."

****

In the car, Gwen and I click our seat belts in. I turn the engine on, and she cranks the heat. Cold air blasts through, so I lower it while the car warms up. I put my arm on the back of her seat and pull out of the driveway.

"So, you think they're going to be okay?" she says to me.

"Totally," I say and mean it.

"Me, too," she says softly. "I hope we can be the baby's godparents—"

"Jews don't do godparents, Gwen."

"I know. But I'm not Jewish."

I glance at her, and we both laugh. "If you want to be the godmother, I'm sure they would take you up on that."

Silence envelops the car ride as I turn out of Nori's neighborhood and head down to the main road. The same thought I can't stop obsessing over rises up in my brain. I try to push it down, but it doesn't budge. *Us, what about us?* God, I don't know how to bring this up.

"Let's go to the beach." She slides a hand over my

knee and squeezes.

"Really? It's kind of cold." I reach over and put my hand on her thigh. "Unless what you want to do is warm each other up…we haven't done it in a car." Maybe a big talk can wait some more. We do have five months.

She slaps me playfully on the arm. "Oh and get caught by the ever-present Barrington police, trolling for drunk high school students? Believe it or not, it's not sex on the brain that I have right now."

I let my hand rest on her thigh, but my stomach knots up a little. So I'm not the only one who wants to talk. Which should be a good thing, except now I'm nervous about what she might say and thinking maybe it's a better conversation to have after sex.

"What's up?" I say lightly.

"Let's park at the beach and look at the moon. It's full tonight."

I make a left and follow the road to the beach and when the parking lot comes into view, I see the moon, high, a perfect circle, shining white in the sky. Glimmers of white ripple over the water, which is still. I can't even hear the sound of waves. As beautiful as the night is, I know that's not why we are parked here at the beach. The beach is where you go to talk.

I keep the car on but cut the lights and push the gear into park. She increases the heat and keeps her profile straight ahead. Her forehead is smooth, and her hair is in a messy bun, tendrils falling against her cheek.

"I got into the University of Rochester." She plays with her silver bracelet we bought together the day we ran into Shane; I'd needed retail therapy afterward. "I found out this morning. My mom got the letter at home and called me."

My heart surges. Part of me wants to scream, *Don't go there! It's too far! What about us? Can I come too?* I push that part of me back and try to focus on my hammering heart. I turn to her and see that she's still not looking at me.

"I wasn't going to tell you. I figured why should we even deal with it now when it's far away." She finally turns her face to me, and I see her eyes are wet. "But that's not true. I have to decide. More envelopes are at the house. I just didn't let my mom open them. I have to go pick them up tomorrow."

"Where else did you apply to?" I ask her because, though I did glance at her list once when she had it posted on our desktop computer, I only remember BU and Georgetown. When I went to check the list again, it had been taken down.

"University of Massachusetts, Cornell, Brown, Dartmouth, Georgetown, and Tufts." She stops. "I know you applied to BU and to Georgetown."

But there is no hint of an expression of happiness about that.

"Please tell me what you're thinking right now, Gwen."

She closes her eyes. "I'm afraid."

"To tell me what you think?"

"To decide about our future right this minute. To tell you, I'm probably going to go with University of Rochester."

My whole body is held in my heart, which continues to hammer away. Why so far away, is what I want to say but instead I croak out, "I can go with you." My voice is so shaky.

"I don't know if that's the right thing."

"Why?"

"Because it's asking you to follow me, to follow what I want."

"What if what I want is you?"

"You want more than me, Andy."

"What if I told you I don't even care about law school?"

She gives me a half smile. "I would believe you."

We look at each other, her blue eyes watery and red. My throat is tight with a growing clump of tears.

She touches my cheek, and a tear falls, and she rubs it away with her thumb. "I love you," she whispers and presses her forehead to mine. I whisper it back and kiss her softly.

"What do we do?" I ask her.

"I don't know," she says.

"Let me come with you. Wherever you go."

"I don't know if I could live with myself if you do that."

"Let me worry about me."

"What if we don't work out?"

"I'm willing to take the chance, Gwen."

She doesn't say anything. We have our noses practically pressed into each other and she says very faintly, "Me too."

My heart bursts, and I press my mouth to hers firmly and say, "Thank you."

We hold each other for a while in the moonlight in silence.

Epilogue
NORI—A little over a year later

Ruby and I are in front of the long vanity mirror in my mom's bedroom, me in a velvet cushioned seat and her standing behind me. Her electric eggplant purple hair sticks up perfectly all over and matches her equally electric eggplant cocktail dress. I adore her *fuck you* to traditional blue for mother of the groom.

Yes, she is officially mother of the groom. She and Dan tied the knot over the summer when they were up visiting us. On the beach, officiated by my Swami Nick.

Ruby lifts a lock of my long dark hair and looks hard at me in the mirror.

"Please don't lecture me about how I need to take better care of my hair. I've been a little busy, you know."

"I wasn't going to do that, Nori." Her face softens. "I was going to say how proud of you and Ethan I am."

"Aww. You've gotten so mushy since becoming a wife," I tease her.

"Maybe." She picks up the curling iron but pauses before taking it to my hair. "I also feel like I need to apologize."

"What for?"

"For telling you to screw being tied down and to go do you."

I watch her hold the lock of hair and then wind it around the curling iron. "To be fair," I say, "you said that at a time when none of us knew I was pregnant."

She cocks her head and rests a hand on my shoulder; her touch is warm. "Doesn't matter. You and Ethan have real love. Pregnant or not, you were on the right path to forever."

"Ruby! Such poetry coming out of your mouth!"

She smiles shyly as she holds the curling iron and lets the heat sink into the lock of hair. "And I know that you won't give up your dreams. You, my dear, will be part of the few percent of us gals who can have it all."

"Just not at the same time," we say together.

We linger at each other another minute in the mirror. And she picks up more hair to curl.

"India was just postponed," I say, hoping I sound more convincing than I feel.

"You have time, and you have a man who will help you make it happen. Don't worry about it," she says.

She pauses mid-curling and crinkles her eyes like she's trying to figure something out.

"So what are you going to do with it?" I ask, pointing to my hair.

"I think we should curl it and let it cascade down your shoulders. We need to hide those mams a little. You're busting out everywhere!"

I laugh and tug at the straps of my gown, straps Mom had to sew into the dress because the original ones were not supportive enough for my "mams." Soon I close my eyes while Ruby continues to use the curling iron, the smell of heat filling the room. I'm in a kind of meditation when we hear a knock on my bedroom door.

I watch through the mirror to see who comes in.

Jeni. She grins and walks, actually drags herself, into the room. "Hey, Ruby. Hi, big sis."

Ruby smiles but continues her work, now in the fluffing and spraying stage.

"Hi," I say, not moving my head. "How are you feeling?"

"Like shit on toast," she cracks. We all laugh.

Little sis's personality emerged after what we now refer to as Pregnancy-Gate.

"You shouldn't have offered to drink for me last night," I offer, referring to the quasi-bachelorette party we had last night at home. Us girls and a few bottles of prosecco, which I couldn't participate in because I'm nursing.

"Save it, Dolly." She gestures to my boobs, which continue to spill out over the bodice of the dress.

"I know." I sigh and try to rearrange them again.

"Didn't you have a fitting last week? You didn't look like that."

"That's because I wasn't filled with milk." I sigh again. "Jeni, how much time do I have?"

"I just need another fifteen minutes," Ruby says.

"You have approximately forty-five minutes." Jeni reaches down and puts her hand on my boobs, which I barely notice. Once you have a team of doctors between your legs and your parents are in the room while you're getting stitched up, you don't even notice if someone feels your boob.

"I think you need to pump. Those are like rocks."

I glance at the digital clock on my bed stand. "Where's the baby?" I ask her.

"Mom still has her."

"I think I might as well nurse. Molly's due for a feeding."

Ruby stops working and looks at me and Jeni in the mirror. "Just give me ten minutes."

****

Less than ten minutes later, my hair is perfect curls arranged in a half up half down fashion. "Perfect for nursing and easy to take down after."

Ruby is gone along with Jeni to go deal with any guests who may be arriving. Some of whom I'm particularly nervous about. Namely, Andy and Gwen.

Mom and Dad come in, and I'm sitting in the rocker that Mom moved into her room to help with night feedings. I have a large blue blanket over me.

"Here she is!" Mom leans down and hands Molly to me. I take her soft and warm body into my arms.

Dad grins. "I'll let you two ladies take over for now."

"Thanks," I say to him, and he leans down and kisses Molly on the top of her head.

"I'll be waiting downstairs, my girls!"

We watch him go and turn to each other, tears filling both of our eyes.

"He's really come around," she says, searching around for a tissue.

"On the bureau," I tell her and open the blanket to adjust Molly onto the support pillow. I cradle her head and—ahhh—relief. She is suckling happily, eyes already closed. It is the best feeling. Hard to believe that when I first started, my nipples bled, and I thought I was dying.

Mom blows her nose and then grabs one of my blush brushes and reapplies some to hers and then turns to me and sighs. "I'm such a mess!" She sits on the edge of my bed and arranges the skirt of her turquoise dress. She smiles at me, and little tears dot the corner of her eyes again, which makes me tear up.

"Stop," I tell her.

She reaches for the box of tissues and takes one to my eyes and dabs. "You take your time. Our guests can wait. It's your day, and baby Molly's and Ethan's."

She smiles at me, and we sit in the silence, save for the tiny suckling sounds and murmurs from the baby.

I rock some more and gaze down at the back of Molly's head filled with black hair. Like her daddy.

Suddenly the door opens, and it's Jeni again. "Ruby needs to do your make-up. She'll be back here in five. Can you be finished then?"

"Yep."

"I'll get back out there." Mom stands up and leans over and kisses the top of my head.

Once they're both gone, I finish up with Molly, who is now passed out, and I lay her in her bassinet; we have one in this room and one in my room. We've moved back with my parents while Ethan substitute teaches and tries to find a permanent teaching job. And Mom and Dad like to help out, even letting the baby sleep in their room once in a while.

Ruby hustles in and silently finishes my make-up. She doesn't say a word, which is a first. Jeni comes in as Ruby hustles back out.

"Hey, you can let Molly sleep," Jeni whispers. "I'll give Jake the monitor, and if she wakes up, he can come get her."

"That's probably a good idea," I whisper back. Jake and Jeni have been home to babysit so frequently that Jake's mastered both diaper changes and bottle feedings. A pang of sadness hits me when I think about Andy and how much he's missed out on Molly so far.

We slowly and soundlessly put me back together. Jeni stands behind me to fix the train of the dress and the veil. I catch her in the mirror, her face serious and her hands gently moving around me. My throat closes a little.

She catches my eye.

Jeni sighs and reaches for a tissue from the box on the bureau in front of us. "I wish I had some kind of profound thing to say to you." She grabs a tissue and blots her eyes then takes a few breaths.

We look at each other again in the mirror and say nothing. She takes another tissue and blots my eyes. I reach out and touch her hand touching my face. "I'm just glad we've gotten closer. I feel like I should have been a better big sister to you all this time. I think I was just jealous of you." I kiss her hand and close my eyes. "I'm sorry."

"We gotta stop crying!" She takes her hand away and hurriedly redoes my eyes and her own. "We need to get you married. Gotta get things legitimate for my niece."

"Right," I say, opening my mouth as she reapplies lipstick.

Then we hear a little murmur and freeze.

Silence.

"We better hurry up!" I whisper.

I apply a little more blush and fluff my hair, and we both lean over the bassinet and see Molly, sleeping, with her face to the side and her hand brushing the silky swatch of a satin blanket. The cure-all for when she cries.

I start to tear up again.

****

ANDY

"Oh, shit," I mutter.

The wedding starts in ten minutes.

"I'm sorry, Andrew. This is all my fault." My mother clutches the wheel with both hands and is sitting so that her nose is practically pressed right up against the windshield.

"It's fine, Mom."

Even though it is a balmy fifty degrees with sunshine, practically a heat wave for early March, Mom's driving like there's ice all over the winding roads that lead to Nori's house. My mother finally sold my childhood home and now lives outside of Barrington, closer to where she works in East Providence. It's only twenty minutes away, but it's feeling like hours with her driving.

"Gwen is coming, you know," she says nonchalantly, and I'm surprised she's waited this long to bring it up.

My body increases in heat, but I reply lightly, "I assumed she was."

"She almost couldn't. It's exam time for her."

"Oh?"

"This is why you should have a Facebook," my mother says.

"Mom, I'm too busy to have a Facebook."

"Andrew, no one is too busy to have a Facebook. If you did, you would know as I do that Gwen took her exams early so she could come to the wedding."

"Really?"

"Yes. She and I are 'friends,' although she's rarely on it."

Silence. Trees whiz past and the road begins to twist more. About ten minutes away, I calculate. It's not that I haven't thought about Gwen coming to the wedding. It's more that every time her name comes up, I think about other things. I try hard not to think about how things were left between us.

"I know you don't want to tell me about what happened with you two."

"It ended. You know, it happens." Out the window, I stare at the cloudless sky and the bare trees.

Mom clicks the turn signal. We're on the street. My heart hammers, and in the passenger mirror, I check that my hair is perfectly tousled. It's shorter than it's ever been, and I finally shaved my post-break-up beard.

"You're so handsome." Mom leans over and cups my chin. I let her but roll my eyes.

"And by the way, I've been to see the baby several times, and Nori says she's been calling you and asking you to come over."

"Law school is hard," I say. "And I'm not a twenty-minute car ride away anymore." We pull into the neighborhood and park in the first empty space. Cars line the street all the way down toward the Mytowskys' house.

I open the door. And then help my mother out. She's wearing a pair of heels, and the ground is a little wet.

My phone vibrates in my pocket. I glance at it and laugh.

—*Where r u? want you to c me be 4. In my room.*—

"Who's that? Gwen?" Mom sounds hopeful.

"No."

I text Nori back.

—*b there in 5.*—

"It's Nori. Mom, I gotta sprint. You okay to walk?"

"Sure, baby." Then adds, "Remember to look for Jake. He and I plan on sitting together." I nod. It's still new—both my reconnection with my little brother and his new relationship with Nori's little sister. Apparently, we will never get away from each other now.

I kiss Mom's cheek and sprint all the way down the block. I cut through backyards like we used to when we were in high school. That's when this guilty, sad feeling washes over me. I haven't been the best friend I used to be to Nori since she had the baby. Too busy nursing my broken heart.

As I scale a low-hung fence and dart between some pine trees and then almost sink into the muddy patchy lawn of Old Man Berger, I tell myself this is the end of mourning Gwen and me. If I have to double my sessions with my new therapist, so be it.

Nori's backyard is ahead, and I see that a huge tent with sides has been set up. Kathryn has outdone herself. Through the windows of the tent, guests mill around, eating shrimp and crudités and drinking champagne. I check my phone for the time and dart around the fence through the back of the house. Smiles and nods to the guests while I search for someone familiar but only see people from town and high school who I vaguely remember.

I weave through and make my way to the stairs and am texting her on the way and then I get to the top and—

Oh.

"Nori," I say. "You look…"

She grins and grabs her boobs. "I know! Can you believe how big they got?"

I laugh. "I wasn't…"

"Aw, come on, Andy, aren't you ever going to be tempted by my boobs?"

I run to her and hug her tight. Tears prick my eyes and I swallow and hug her closer. "Beautiful," I manage to say in her ear.

"Don't you make me cry, Andy. You have no idea what a postpartum breast-feeding woman is like. I cannot cry any more today!"

I step back and can't stop smiling as I wipe my eyes.

"I've missed you, Andy."

"I know, Nori. I've been a shitty friend."

"No, you're a hurting friend, and I know how you operate. It's okay, but now it's time to rejoin humanity."

"I'm here."

"Besides, if our siblings continue on the way they have been, we may be related soon!"

"I know! Can't believe the princess and prince have found love with each other."

We look at each other and then laugh. "Actually, it makes perfect sense."

"How's school?" she asks.

"Great," I say. "How's motherhood?"

"Exhausting." She motions to her mother's room. "She's sleeping though. Shhhhh. Come see her and then you can walk me down. It's almost time for me to become Mrs. Nori Ledger. Mytowsky-Ledger."

I follow her in and there's a white noise machine going, making the room very peaceful. I smell lavender, too.

"Look," she says.

We peer into the bassinet together and the most beautiful creature with perfectly formed hands, one clutching the satin part of a blanket, and her skin pink and creamy. "Do they all turn out like this?" I ask her.

"No. My Molly is the most beautiful baby in the world."

We stand, watching her in the sound of the white noise. Peace for the first time in a while.

"Time to go." She hands me a small white machine with a speaker and a tiny screen. "You hold this. We'll leave her here, and if she wakes up, can you come get her? Jeni forgot to grab it."

"Uh...sure." It's time to step up big-time to make up for all these past months of abandoning my best friend.

She glances in the mirror, readjusts her breasts, runs her hands down the bodice, and then adjusts her veil. She's stunning.

"Let's go," she says and takes my arm. I clip the baby monitor to my suit waistband, and we walk out.

****

GWEN

"Med school. Yeah, I was thinking about med school myself, you know. Do you remember in bio I was always that kid with my hand in the air?" Arnold Manchester, class asshat and unfortunately a new employee of Mr. Mytowsky's, has bum-rushed me. "You know we were in bio together freshman year? Yeah, I was awesome at bio. Nori wasn't in our class, though. God, I had the biggest crush on her, but she was all about Ethan even though he was such a dick. Isn't life weird, and now here we are. At their wedding."

He chews shrimp with big fake teeth. His skin is tanned so intensely that at first I actually thought he was a burn victim. But he's too orange.

I nod and nurse my glass of wine. Why they

decided cocktail hour, then ceremony, and then reception, I do not know. God, where is anyone? One of Nori's college friends? Ruby? Shoot me, someone. Earth, open up and swallow me—

"Gwen!" Ah, my savior.

"Nice chatting with you, Arnold."

"Hey, let's hook up on Facebook. I'll send you a friend request." He flashes his enormous rabbit teeth at me. I try not to cringe and instead give him the thumbs-up. I'm swallowed up by the crowd for a moment, and when I'm spit out, I see Andy's mom.

"Cindy!"

We embrace and hug, rocking from side to side. Jake stands next to her, a bigger and taller version of Andy, which makes my heart hurt a little.

"Hello, Gwen," he says and leans down for a hug. We embrace and then Cindy grins at me.

"Sweetie, you look amazing!" She steps back but keeps her hands on my shoulders. "I love your hair. Gosh, it's like a fairy princess!"

"Thank the med school gods for that one because this girl barely has time to shave her pits, let alone cut her hair."

We laugh. And after a moment of shock, Jake does too.

She says seriously, "Andy's here."

"I figured. You know, almost a decade of friendship will do that."

"Gwen, listen to me. You both really should talk."

I take a deep breath.

"Gwen?"

I turn around to face Andy. The voices of the guests, their laughter and clinking of glasses, fill the space between us, but beneath that I faintly make out the song that the harpist and cellist play in the corner. It's from an old war movie, which Andy and I watched when he was taking History of American Wars. He was trying to finish his thesis and had to take this one requirement that he somehow forgot. One of the assignments was to watch this old movie and critique it based on his knowledge of war and the role America played in that war. We bawled through the entire movie, holding onto each other.

Why in the hell would someone play this at a wedding? All around me I expect to see people horrified or crying. But no. Everyone is having a grand time.

Fuck.

I smile—or try to—at Andy, but there is this enormous lump in my throat. As I walk closer and closer, I hear Cindy behind me, who says, "I need to go to the ladies' room, you two catch up."

We walk all the way to each other. Andy's eyes are red, too.

"Jesus, why the hell would someone play that at a wedding?" is the first thing that pops out of my mouth.

"I know." He glances over at the musicians. "Maybe we should go over there and tell her to stop."

"Yeah, we should tell her she is breaking people's hearts out here." He gazes right at me when I say that.

I sigh. "It's so beautiful, though, isn't it?"

"Yeah."

We stand and stare at each other, listening to the sad melody, and then I say, "I hate this song."

"Me too."

I marvel at his shorter hair and then we are

hugging, and he strokes my hair. "It's so long. What, they don't even let you get a haircut in med school? Or are you too far out in the boonies up there in Rochester to find a place that can cut your hair?"

I laugh into his shoulder and tears fall. I wipe them before I step back. *Get it together, sister*, I tell myself. This is Nori's wedding, not the place to lose it.

"I've missed you," he says. "Miss hugging you."

"Andy, stop trying to smooth talk me. It's a wedding, of course we're going to hook up." I try to be funny.

He pulls away. "Gwen, I don't want to hook up with you."

"Be that way, then." I step back, trying to keep it all light and funny, about to crack a joke about switching back to guys, but he stops me with the look he's giving me.

"Listen," he says. "We need to talk. Obviously not now, but—"

Suddenly the tinkle sound of silverware on glasses interrupts us, and we turn and there's the harpist on the microphone. "The Mytowskys and Ledgers would like you all to gather under the tent outside. It's time for the bride and groom to say their vows!"

We're caught up in the swarm. I grab Andy's hand and we walk together. That lump in my throat grows bigger as I anticipate what I'm about to see, witness years and years of love. It's almost too much for me and tears cloud my vision. I let Andy lead me out to the tent.

"Gwen. Andy." Ethan is scrubbed and shaved, beaming.

Dan is next to Ethan as best man, wiping his eyes,

and Lady Delilah by his side on a leash. I reach down and rub her ears and see how she resists jumping up to kiss me. They stand inside the house while everyone else is filtering out to the tent.

"You guys are walking down together," Ethan says.

I look at Andy and then Ethan.

"I thought you weren't having a wedding party?" I say and realize I'm shaking at this point.

"Nori sent me a text, and she wants you two to walk down before Jeni." Ethan reaches out and hugs me and then shakes hands and slaps backs with Andy. Dan does the same and then turns to me.

"Hello, Gwen." Dan reaches out and takes both of my hands in his. "You and Andy here make a fine-looking pair."

Andy blushes.

"I want you both to be part of the wedding, too," Ethan says. "It wasn't just Nori's idea."

My dress! I look down at the long skirt. Nori and Ethan planned this all along. My dress is the same shade as Jeni's and Mrs. Mytowsky's. That's why she insisted on coming with me to pick it out when I was home over Thanksgiving.

"Did you know about this?" Andy whispers to me.

"No, but notice my dress matches Jeni's and Mrs. Mytowsky's. Nori tricked us."

"We can't say no to the bride."

"Or the groom," Ethan adds and then pulls us back with the rest of what is clearly the wedding party. "She didn't think you guys would do it."

"I have to admit, I was surprised she didn't ask me or anything," Gwen says.

The music changes, and now Pachelbel's *Canon* plays.

"You guys are after me and Dan and Ruby." He thrusts a bouquet of flowers at me and hurriedly pins a small matching flower to Andy's lapel.

We both lock eyes and then watch Ethan, Dan, and Delilah join Ruby, who waves to me.

Andy says, "Here we go." I loop my hand through his arm, and we begin to walk.

Mrs. Mytowsky squeezes my arm, and Mr. Mytowsky says, "Good luck."

My parents are there too; flew in from Arizona where they now live for half the year. They wave from the aisle. I scan the audience. I see Cindy, who is already streaming with tears. Andy and I continue until we reach the end. Nori still hasn't come out yet, and I stand on the other side of Ethan, separated from Andy, waiting. I look over at him out of the corner of my eye. I see Jeni come. My heart is pounding like it's me getting married, and then the music changes.

The entire tent of people stands up, and I scan the crowd again, but I can't stop stealing glances at Andy. I watch him wipe one eye and then the other. Both of my eyes fill to the point of spillage, and I wipe and wipe. Thank the gods for waterproof make-up. Part of me wants to run out of the tent, through the yard, and back to my parents' house on the other side of the neighborhood. But they have tenants there now. Could I run all the way back to Rochester? I would rather be cutting up a cadaver than standing here and watching this.

No, I wouldn't.

I see Nori. She is a fairy tale. White princess-cut

dress that billows out in a circle. The bodice has these designs that are etched in diamond and pearl. Her hair is curled, the veil fastened with a tiara. She hadn't wanted me to see the whole get-up until the wedding. She said it was the first and last she tried on.

I want to lean over and say to Andy, "Get a load of her tatas." The thought makes me almost laugh, but I worry if I move my face at all, I will start to bawl and not be able to stop.

Nori walks with her parents on either side of her, and in her hand is a bouquet of red and white flowers. She catches my eye and says thank you, and I mouth, "You're welcome."

She reaches the chuppah, where some guy who is not a rabbi but still looks holy and is clearly the officiate stands. The rest of us stand, her parents stop, and her father lifts her veil and—

A cry comes out, but it sounds like it's coming from a video or voice recorder. Everyone squirms in their folding chairs, craning necks, and turning to find the source of the noise. Delilah actually barks, making everyone turn. Nori bristles with alarm, and Ethan does, too. The yoga-looking officiate coughs and looks around.

Andy says quietly, "Oh, God," and then produces a baby monitor from his suit pocket.

The crowd titters with laughter and a few *awwws*. Nori smiles stiffly at everyone and takes the monitor. Ethan leans over her shoulder and then Mrs. Mytowsky and me. All staring at the small speaker box.

Molly makes another short high-pitched cry. Delilah makes a whimper.

The crowd giggles and *aww-poor babys* more.

The officiate whispers to Nori and Ethan, "Maybe one of the grandmothers could get the baby?"

Nori starts to lift her dress, like she's going to take off down the aisle and get baby Molly.

But then Andy puts his hand on her arm and stops her. He says, "I'll go get her."

"We'll both go," I say without hesitation.

"Thank you," Nori whispers to us.

"Thanks, guys," Ethan says.

Andy puts the monitor in his pocket, forgetting to switch it off so that when we run down the aisle, the crowd clapping for us, everyone can hear, though a little muffled, baby Molly squeal almost like she's laughing.

We laugh and continue, hand in hand, toward the back door of the house.

Baby Molly squeals some more.

I yank open the door and push past the catering crew, pulling Andy along. Getting that baby feels like the most important thing I've done in a long time. More important than stitching people up at the clinic I intern at and more important than any test I've taken recently. More important than the pain in my heart as I hold Andy's warm hand in mine. We wind down the hallway, and I hear baby Molly full-on giggle. Andy stops me before we open the door; he wants to say something, but I put my fingers on his lips and say, "Don't."

But he grabs my finger and holds it. His eyes are intense and focused on mine. "Why didn't you ever text me back or return my calls?"

"Because...you were right." I don't move my finger.

"I didn't want to be right."

A loud cry rings out, no longer a squeal or a laugh, vibrating through the hallway because of the baby monitor.

"Andy, we have to get the baby!" I'm shaking now.

He squeezes my finger tighter. "Sometimes I wonder if I should've gone with you."

My eyes brim with tears. I shake my head. "No, you shouldn't have. I wanted to bail, too, Andy. I think you knew that."

We look at each other, and silence fills the air between us. The baby monitor is just white noise. Then, a faint sigh.

"She's back asleep," I say, my eyes never leaving his.

He takes one step and closes the small space between us. "I have tried to tell myself I'm over it, over you. Driving in the car with my mom, I kept telling myself, it's fine. I'm fine. But the minute I saw you, I wasn't fine." His breath is on my cheek, and he grazes it with his lips.

I close my eyes. Wait for that fear to creep in. He loosens his grip on my finger, sliding his hand all the way around mine.

Just then, the baby squeals loud.

We both jump and then laugh. I squeeze his hand and say, "I've missed you so much."

He kisses the back of my hand and says, "Let's go get the baby. Together."

A word about the author…

Psychotherapist by day and writer by night, Hannah R. Goodman prefers tea over coffee, cats over dogs, and staying in over going out (especially if that means watching reality dating shows!) Her accomplishments include earning extra letters after her name—MFA, MEd, CGS, LMHC. Additionally, she's been published by several online publications, including MindBodyGreen, OC87 Recovery Diaries, Zencare.co, The Mighty, and Scary Mommy. In 2018, Black Rose Writing published her contemporary YA novel *Till It Stops Beating*, which was praised by reviewers for its realistic and hilarious depiction of first love, first loss, and first mental breakdown. Her publishing history goes back almost twenty years when she published *My Sister's Wedding*, which won first place in the 2004 Writer's Digest Self-Published Books Awards Children's/Teen Division.

Thank you for purchasing
this publication of The Wild Rose Press, Inc.

For questions or more information
contact us at
info@thewildrosepress.com.

The Wild Rose Press, Inc.
www.thewildrosepress.com

www.ingramcontent.com/pod-product-compliance
Ingram Content Group UK Ltd.
Pitfield, Milton Keynes, MK11 3LW, UK
UKHW022338301224
452994UK00011B/529